accepted FATE

CHARISSE SPIERS

Copyright © 2014 by Charisse Spiers

All rights reserved.

No part of this book may be reproduced in any form or by any electronic or mechanical means, including information storage and retrieval systems, without written permission from the author, except for the use of brief quotations in a book review.

This is a work of fiction. Names, characters, places, brands, media, and incidents are either the product of the author's imagination or are used fictitiously. The author acknowledges the trademarked status and trademark owners of various products referenced in this work of fiction, which have been used without permission. The publication/use of these trademarks is not authorized, associated with, or sponsored by the trademark owners.

Cover Art © Clarise Tan
Formatted by Nancy Henderson

2nd Edition 2018

Love isn't something you find.
Love is something that finds you.

—Loretta Young

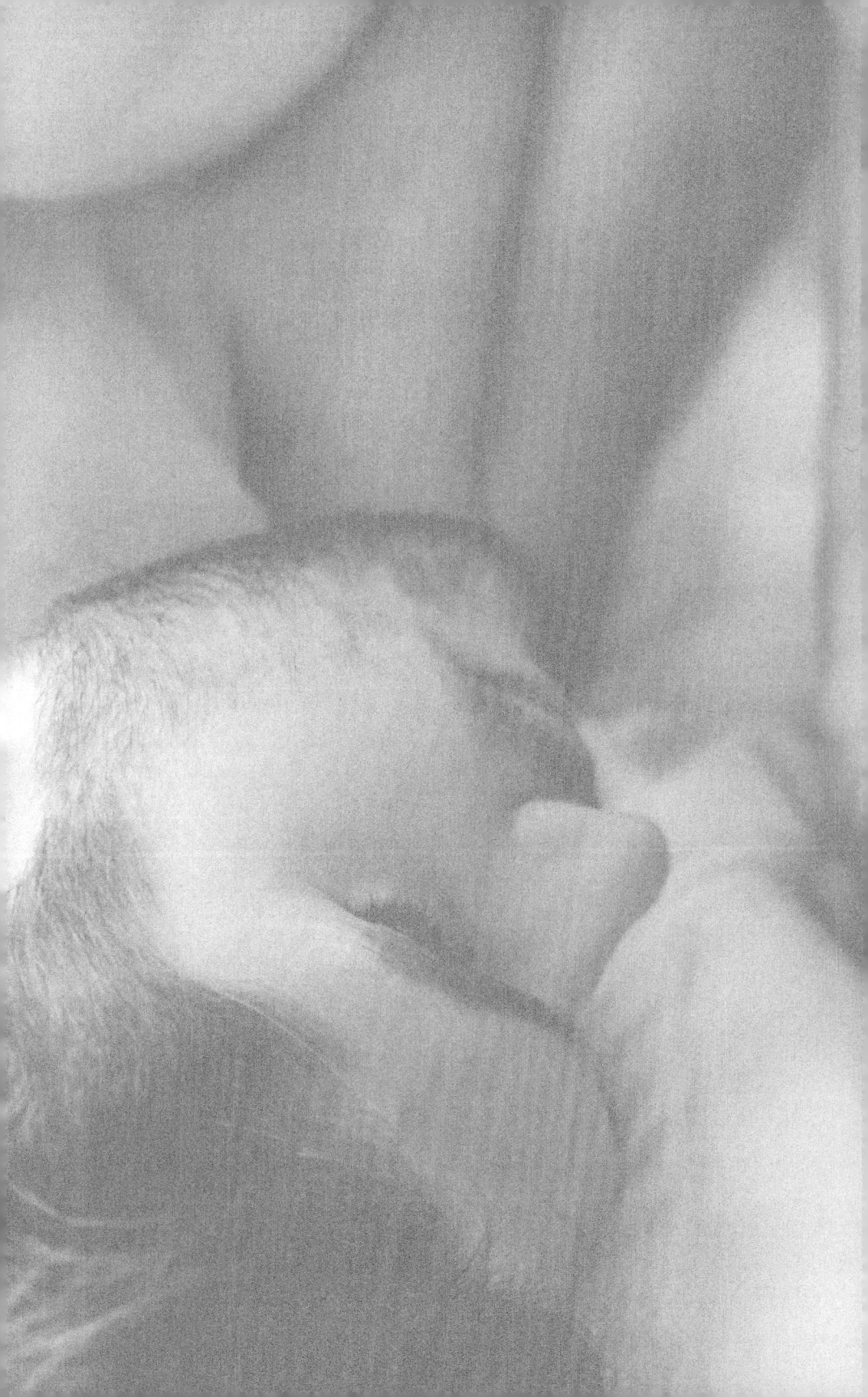

ONE

Kinzleigh

It's Friday, the week following junior year and the start to a perfect summer. I can't wait for two whole months of shopping, no schedule, and lying on the beach. Everything in my life is going the way I want it to. Making squad captain was just the cherry on top.

Mom left a couple hours ago since she's due in court on some big case, Dad is always gone before sunup, and I haven't seen my brother, Konnor, since his high school graduation last Saturday. I have the house to myself again. I'm starting to sense this is going to become a normal thing this summer.

I put my arms above my head to stretch. I look over at the clock on my bedside table—eight thirty—the perfect time to get up and head to the gym. And I do mean *cheer* gym not fitness.

I need to be practicing, so I can keep my body limber. We already cut down on squad practice over the summer months, so it's up to me to make my own schedule. I need to call my coach before someone else books his schedule solid.

Sitting up and getting ready to get out of bed, my phone starts ringing. Looking at the screen all lit up, I see Presley's name and her photo. Touching the green answer button, I wait for it to connect. "Hello?"

Still somewhat half asleep, a noise comes through the phone. *Is that a treadmill? What on earth is she doing?*

"Please tell me you're not still in bed, Kinzleigh Baker. We only have a couple short months of fun before we're back to being slaves in high school and you're not going to waste it away sleeping. I will form an intervention if I need to," she says sarcastically, with a smile in her tone.

I smile to myself and roll my eyes, because Presley knows me a little too well. *She cannot possibly be running while she's talking on the phone, can she?* She doesn't even sound out of breath. "Presley, I get up early ten months of the year, so why would I get up early during my summer vacation? How do you expect me to enjoy freedom from school if I can't sleep in? What are you doing anyway? Did you call me while you're exercising?"

She sighs playfully. "Okay for one, what's with the twenty questions? Two, you're a lost cause, Kinzleigh. How many times do I have to tell you, if it's Monday through Friday, the hot guys work out early or late at the gym and not midday? Most people actually have a life to get to. Don't you want some of that amazing muscle for yourself? Don't you want to watch the sweat bead up on the skin of a hot guy standing mere steps away? So close that you can smell it . . ." *Eww.* "You don't want to go with the old and ugly people, do you?"

Presley has always been a little too crazy about the male population if you ask me, but what do I know? I'm single and intend to stay that way. I have seen the recurring cycle of love and loss. Heartbreak is something I intend to avoid at all costs. I'd rather take precautions up front and steer clear than to deal with the consequences after the fact. "No thanks, I'll leave that for you. I'm fine having my precious sleep time . . . *alone*."

My brother, Konnor, is only a year older than me, and my only sibling, so we have always been close. He was with the same girl for three years, and a month before graduation he walked in on her at a senior party with his best friend buried between her legs. The bitch didn't even have the decency to act upset.

Instead, she blamed it on the fact they were about to head off to colleges on opposite ends of our great big state—California—when she should have been the adult she's supposed to be at eighteen and broke things off if she wanted to fool around. He beat the crap out of his best friend, Logan, putting him in the hospital for almost a week.

The month following, Konnor went off the deep end, started experimenting with drugs, and stayed drunk. If it hadn't been so close to the end of the year and his GPA not already high, he might not have graduated. He almost lost his football scholarship to the University of California at Los Angeles—UCLA. My parents freaked out, of course, and made him start talking to a therapist.

Since my dad is alumnus and donates a lot of money to the football program, the coach gave him until startup of summer training to deal with his issues. He was the best quarterback at our school and was offered scholarships from several schools across the country, but is barely holding onto a good thing because of love. He is one of so many people that end up hurt.

No, thank you, I'll pass.

"Oh, right, I forgot I'm dealing with a prude." She laughs back at me, before becoming serious again. "You need to venture out and meet a guy. It's unhealthy to completely cut guys out of your life. We're going to be seniors in the fall. One day you're going to regret missing out on things like dating. It's fun. Don't you want to go to prom and homecoming at least once? You shouldn't miss out on everything in high school just because you're afraid of getting hurt. No one said you have to fall in love, but please, let me set you up one time."

"How many times do I have to tell you dating is your thing, Presley? This conversation is pointless; you know this. We've had it like a thousand times already," I whine through the phone, falling back down onto my pillow. "I don't have to date to enjoy my life. Besides, I have too much to do to work toward my future without having some guy requiring more of my time than I have to give. A career, and even school, is more important to me. Now, you know that I love you, but what do you want?"

She sighs. "Fine, have it your way, but don't think we won't revisit this conversation later. I'm not giving up. For now, get your skinny butt out of bed and meet me down at the beach in an hour. We have to work on your pale skin before Cabo. You know we leave in a week. Don't make me come get you, Kinzleigh, you know I will."

She's so bossy when she wants to be, but that's one of the things I love about her. Presley has been my best friend since I can even remember. It's a typical story from growing up in Laguna Beach, California, but second generation. Our moms were best friends growing up and still are. They went to law school together and even made partners at the same law firm, not to mention we're the same age. You know they're close when they planned pregnancies together. We were destined to be with each other from the beginning.

Presley and I are completely different; although, maybe that's what has kept us together since we were in diapers. We seem to balance each other out. Where she's outgoing, I'm shy. She is tall and slender with long, cascading brown hair and sapphire blue

accepted FATE

eyes, whereas I'm short and petite with platinum blonde curls and bright green eyes.

I twirl my hair around my finger and sit quietly, just to make her wait a little. She's a very impatient person. I can already tell she is becoming irritated by the huffs coming from her mouth. "I was going to call Andy and set up a practice. What about after?"

"Getting my keys ready, babe. What's it going to be?" I laugh, imagining her really driving over here just so she can prove a point.

"Okay, fine, but you owe me a practice and I'm going to work you hard, so you better get those muscles ready. I'll see you in an hour." I disconnect the call and head for the shower.

Standing in the shower, my hands covered in a thick layer of coconut-scented suds from washing my hair with my favorite shampoo, I start thinking about our trip to Cabo San Lucas next week. There is no telling what Presley is going to try dragging me into. I'm not sure if I should be excited or scared.

My parents take us, and one friend each, on a weeklong vacation every summer. Usually, Presley and Logan tag along, but I'm not sure who Konnor is bringing now that Logan is out of the equation. That's one thing that makes me nervous—the unknown.

Presley has always had a thing for my brother, but she can't seem to get him to look past the *little sister's best friend* issue. Plus, he has always had the Sophia blinders on until now, so I'm not sure if or what she will try now that he's a single man. That probably means a shopping trip this week, knowing Presley. Not that I'm complaining. Retail therapy is a girl's best friend.

Twenty minutes later, now washed and shaved, I'm running around my room in a towel, throwing various items into my pink beach bag sitting on my bed. Digging through my drawer I finally find what I'm looking for; my new turquoise and peach swirled bandeau bikini top and matching bottoms. I fell in love with it the moment I laid eyes on it last week and had to have it.

Since my parents work long hours, Dad gave me my own Amex when I got my driver's license. As long as I stay out of trouble and keep my grades at A's, I'm able to spend as I please—using good judgment, of course.

I pull on my swimsuit and black, lace cover-up, before I walk to my closet in search of my flip-flops. Combing my fingers through my wet hair on the way out, I then throw my head forward and tousle the blonde strands to rid of extra water until they curl up. It should be dry by the time I reach the beach.

Standing back up, I dab on my gloss and throw it in my small makeup bag along with my hair tie. Finally, I perform my routine mental checklist before I go.

Towel, check, sunscreen, check, tanning oil, check, shades, check.

I grab my purse from my desk and slide it on my shoulder, shoving my beach bag on the other, and head for my bedroom door. Having almost everything I need for a day in the sun, I turn off my light and close the door.

Running downstairs into the large kitchen, I grab some supplies for the day. I take a few granola bars from the food pantry and a couple bottles of water from the refrigerator, tossing them in my tote to reside with the rest of my stuff. I walk through the house, making sure everything is off before I leave for the day.

Once finished, I set the alarm and close the front door. Digging my keys from my purse, I turn to my beautiful, black, Range Rover sitting in the drive and unlock the doors with the remote. It's normally kept in the garage, but the detailer came by and cleaned it this morning.

Mom and Dad surprised me with it on the morning of my

accepted FATE

sixteenth birthday. Mom kept telling me I wouldn't be getting a car until later, since Konnor and I are so close in age; however, I was depressed, because Grams had died earlier that year. Grams was my dad's mom and was as close to me as Mom. My parents were gone a lot with work; therefore, I was with Grams almost daily for fifteen years. She fought a three-year battle with cancer before it defeated her.

I felt shattered and lost, losing all hope for happiness. I stayed in my room for months after she died, with the exception of being at school. Right then, I learned, never allow yourself to love anyone other than family, no exceptions.

The pain of losing someone you love hurts too much to risk it when it's avoidable. The day I felt that kind of pain, I knew then, I would never allow myself to feel it again if I could control it. Loving a man is controllable; family is not.

Friends became a distant memory that year. Needless to say, I guess Mom and Dad felt badly for me.

The morning of my sixteenth birthday, I stepped out of the front door, ready for school, and headed for Konnor's silver BMW parked out front. That's when I saw it sitting in the driveway, glistening, with a big, red bow. That car is my baby. It marks a turning point for me. One chapter closed and on to new beginnings.

I shake off my thoughts and pull down my aviator shades, walking toward my car. Time to hit the beach . . .

Pulling into the beach, I recognize Presley's White Mercedes almost instantly. It takes me a while to find a place to park, because apparently, everyone else had the same idea today. The beach is packed, and I consider turning around and going home.

Contemplating what I'm going to do, I glance over and see Presley making her way toward my car. How does she even know I'm here? The girl has to have ESP—so much for making a run for it . . .

I grab my cell phone from my purse with one hand and stow my purse beneath my seat with the other. As she moves in closer, I remove my keys from the ignition. Lifting my bag off the seat, I toss my cell and keys inside and then open the door and step out.

"I was starting to wonder if I was going to have to come and pick you up," she says. A smile begins, along with a mischievous look in her eyes that tells me she's up to something. Nothing good ever follows that look. I place my bag on my shoulder and hold onto my door in case I need to make a dash for it.

"What are you up to, Presley?" I ask nervously, fidgeting with my cover up. She moves faster, as if I'm about to take off running, and then grabs my hand and shuts the door.

"What makes you think I'm up to something?" She loops her arm through mine and continues. "Don't you trust me?"

The tone in her voice alone says it all. *No, I shouldn't, and I should get back in my car right now before I go any farther.*

She must see the hesitation on my face, because she pulls me down the sidewalk, toward the beach. I concentrate on the rays from the sun bearing down on my skin, the heat enveloping me. The seagulls are screaming overhead, drowning out the sounds of the beachgoers. The salty sea air calms me, but only for a moment.

As the water comes into view, I begin to understand that look on Presley's face. Some of the girls from the cheerleading squad have plastered themselves right in front of a group of guys playing volleyball. I recognize some of them from the football team at school, but the rest of the boys don't look familiar.

Great, this is going to be awkward.

I've never been one of the flirty girls at school, because I really don't see the point. I get a front row seat to Presley's show every day and that is enough for both of us. Flirting serves one of two purposes—looking for love or trying to get laid—and I do not want either.

Love stands in the way of dreams and aspirations, cripples you, and makes you dependent on someone else. It sets you up for failure, because you're always going to get hurt. If you don't get cheated on, you get left behind. I have worked too hard for my dreams to get shattered over something completely preventable. Since you can't control who you fall for, I just avoid it all together.

Look at my brother, wallowing in pity, because he let someone else take priority over everything else in his life. He gave away his heart and mapped his whole life out according to the wants of another with the expectation it would last forever. Now, here he is, brokenhearted and settling for his second-choice school, as well as the possibility of losing his dream to play college football if he doesn't get his crap together before season. What did he do all that for? Absolutely nothing.

I look over to Presley standing behind her towel, adjusting her perky C-cups, as if her breasts aren't hanging out enough already. Shaking my head, I pull my towel from my bag and spread it flat beside hers.

In a way, Presley doesn't date either; at least not one person. After her breakup with Corey last fall, she swore off men, in the emotional sense anyway. Her heart will and always be made of ice because of him, or so she says. I think it's because secretly she's keeping her options open in hopes of attaining Konnor.

Her and Corey were similar to throwing fire to gasoline, his jealousy leading to constant fights, so for now she enjoys being an upper-class slut. I only call her that in love and because she's my best friend, no judgment. She would agree if you asked her. She's always careful, and it works for her.

"Do you have to do that? Adjust that top any more and they're going to fall out." Taking a seat on my towel, I pull my hair back in a loose bun on top of my head and grab for my bag. Digging through its contents, I pull out my iPhone and earbuds, along with my water and tanning essentials. Pulling off my cover-up and flip-flops, I toss them in the bag and set it to the side.

The waves crashing against the shoreline makes for a peaceful day. The sound could take anyone's stress away. There is a reason it's used for white noise. It's calming. Even with the high-pitched squeals and laughter that accompany it from the kids screaming in the distance, running back and forth as the water rolls onto the sand.

There's a slight breeze out, making the heat welcome. The gritty specks of sand are already covering my feet. I begin spreading the sunscreen on my face and shoulders, before applying the tanning oil to the remainder of my body.

Presley sits beside me on her towel and begins coating her legs with tanning oil as well. "Hey, just because you're celibate and hate male attention doesn't mean the rest of us do. Maybe you should try something new. You're becoming a bit of a grump these days. All of that built-up sexual frustration is starting to show." She laughs, swirling her finger in front of my face. "You never know, you might like having the girls played with." She winks as her eyes trail down to my chest.

Rolling my eyes, I turn to acknowledge some of the other girls from the squad. "Hey, you guys. What's up? It's nice out today, right?"

Lexi and Madison are sprawled out in their beach loungers on rental. I still haven't figured out what they have against the sand. What's the point in coming to the beach if you aren't going to enjoy it to its fullest? They always were the prissy two of the group.

I'm starting to think they can't hear me, when finally, Lexi pulls her eyes from the volleyball game and slides her shades down her nose, lifting a brow. "You really have to ask with all of that man-candy right in front of your face?" She smirks, as if I just asked her what two plus two is.

I scrunch my nose, causing my eyebrows to wrinkle. "You too? All of you are hopeless," I say, and lay down to work on my tan. At least one of us is going to leave with some dignity intact. It looks like that person is going to be me, since I'm the only one that's not practically drooling over the shirtless guys in front of us.

I plug my earbuds into my iPhone and start my music. The softness of the voice mixed with the heat blanketing my bare skin, my breathing evens out and I grow tired.

Almost asleep from listening to the sweet voice of Colbie Caillat—adding an island vibe—something smacks me right in the center of my face. Startled, I scream—more like an elevated squeak—and jump to my feet. "What the heck?!"

I look down at the sand and see a volleyball lying beside my towel. I bend over and reach down to pick it up, so I can toss it back to the guys playing. "You could be a little more careful!" I yell, grabbing the ball in my hands as I stand up.

When I turn around I'm staring right at a chest—a sweaty, smooth, tan, and muscular chest. My face is so close I can feel the heat radiating off his body. My eyes widen and trail upward to see who is standing in front of me. They lock with a pair of dark blue eyes, deep and rich, like staring into the midnight sky. For a second, I forgot where I am and what I was doing, at a loss for words.

As my eyes scan his face, Mister Beautiful Blue Eyes swallows, his Adam's apple bobbing up and down, and then his mouth opens. "I'm really sorry about that. I guess I got caught up in the game and stopped paying attention. Are you okay?"

Dang, that voice; it's so deep and raspy. Is that an accent? Southern, maybe? Great, I'm still staring at him. I probably look like an idiot. What is wrong with me?

Now would be a great time to speak, Kinzleigh.

"Yes, I'm fine. Here is your ball back." I extend my arm, palm side up, supporting the ball.

He takes the ball with one hand, pulling it against his hip. Wow, his hands are big, and clearly controlled to be able to do it one-handed without dropping it. He extends the other hand out, a wide smile spreading across the bottom half of his face, revealing straight white teeth. "Forgive my manners. I'm Breyson, and you are?"

I look down at his hand, staring like he's grown an extra limb. My eyes wander. First, to his navy and orange swim trunks, covering a nice set of tanned, muscular legs. He must play some type of sport to have a body like that. His abs are defined, tightening each time he breathes. He has a V of muscle that disappears into the waistband of his shorts. His hips are narrow, widening into a pronounced chest, defined and smooth.

My eyes won't stop the embarrassing stroll up his body.

His arms are built, slightly flexed before me from his stance, and I wonder how they would feel wrapped around me. His jaw is long, his lips perfect and pouty, barely open. His eyes are thickly lined with dark lashes, despite his hair being lighter—the shade of dirty blond, and short mostly, but long enough on the top it could hold gel. It looks shiny and thick, perfect for running fingers through, grabbing ahold of, and holding on for dear life. Wow. In my entire seventeen years, I've never witnessed something so beautiful.

Suddenly, he looks unsure of what to say, and that's when I realize what's going on. I'm standing here as if it's my first encounter with a human after being locked up in a room my entire life.

Good job, Kinzleigh. Now, not only will he think you're a stuck-up brat, but also ignorant and weird.

Presley clears her throat. "Are you just going to stand there or are you going to introduce yourself sometime today?" she asks, removing her shades as she looks up from where she's lying on her towel. "Not that I mind the view from down here, but you're going to give California girls a bad rep."

Judging by the look on her face, she is pleased with the sight before her as well. She stands and glances over at me, a smile forming on her face, and then looks back at him. "Please excuse my friend. She must have gotten hit a little too hard. I'm Presley." She knows I was staring. I'm never going to hear the end of this. She's always trying to set me up with people. Now that she's seen a break in my armor, she's never going to stop. She closes in and elbows me in the ribs.

I pull my sunglasses up to rest on my head. Placing my hands on my hips, I try to clear my mind. "My name is Kinzleigh. Sorry for being rude, you caught me off guard."

He's staring at me with a smirk on his face, as if he's really amused by me. *Awesome!* Based on the cocky grin, he knows I find him attractive.

"Well, Kinzleigh, it's nice to meet you. Y'all wanna play? There's room for a few more. As an apology, you can be on my team. It's a guaranteed win," he says playfully, winking at me. His smile comes back full force and my stomach flutters like I've just started down the drop of a rollercoaster.

All of a sudden, I'm hot and I feel dizzy. Maybe I'm hungry. It's been a while since I've eaten, and I never usually skip breakfast. That has to be the explanation for this weird feeling I have. Where in the world is this guy from? I wonder if all guys there look like this. "Y'all? Come again. You're not from around here, are you?"

Please say no.

I really don't need this right now. I've got too much going for me to be interested in some boy. It's the heat. Has to be the sun frying my brain.

He shrugs, bouncing the ball from hand to hand. "Nah, just visiting some family. You going to play or what?"

I've got to do something to make up for my weird behavior earlier. "Yeah, okay, sure."

The girls quickly jump in and volunteer to play, as if they've been waiting for the opportunity. I guess if you put ten attractive, half-naked men in front of them, they have the motivation for anything. Thank goodness I don't have to do this alone.

Breyson hands me the ball back, appearing happy with my answer. "Ladies first."

He needs to stop smiling at me like that. Every time he does, I start to shake, and my breathing becomes heavier. He's sexy, and I don't think I have ever looked at a guy like this.

Why, oh why, didn't I stay home today?

This is the last thing I need right now. I haven't worked twenty hours a week in the gym for the last twelve years—cheering and stunting and perfecting routines—to suddenly get distracted by some guy. I don't care how sexy that accent is.

I take the ball and smile. "As long as you don't get in my way." Growing up close to the beach, everyone knows how to play volleyball, and well. He smirks, as if that is exactly the opposite of what he is going to do, and backs up to give me some space.

About an hour later, we're up three points. I'm waiting for Lexi to serve, and suddenly, I feel like he's watching me. Now feeling paranoid, I glance at him underneath my shades, from the corner of my eye. He's looking right at me, as if there is something he wants to say.

Maybe there is something on me. I start discretely doing a self-check to make sure my swimsuit is still in place, when I hear him chuckle.

I glance back across the net and see the ball sailing through the air. Not even thinking, I take off running to hit it back. Before I can stop myself, I collide with Breyson midair and land flat on my back in the sand beneath him. Electricity shoots through my body and I feel like I can't breathe. His body is lying perfectly aligned with mine, pressed against me. "Oh my gosh, I'm so sorry." My voice comes out strained.

His eyes are staring straight into mine, as if he's trying to read into my soul, to discover all of the secrets that lie inside. He puts his weight on his forearm in the sand, next to my head, while his other brushes up my leg, stopping on my hip.

A moan slips from my lips at the contact, causing me to close my eyes. When I open them, he bites his lip as his eyes move down to mine. My face starts to flush.

He's so close his breath tickles my face, and I find myself wishing he'd kiss me. Everything else has faded away, except him. We could have been here, staring at each other, for five minutes or five hours. I don't have a clue. It seems I can't think looking into those deep blue pools. Presley clears her throat, breaking me from my somewhat frozen state. "Guys, are we going to play or just stand here and watch you two all but hump each other on the beach?"

Embarrassed, I place my hands on his muscular chest and try to push him back, not having any effect at all. "Can you please get off me?" I say, irritated I act so stupid around him.

This is not like me at all. I should know better. How could I allow myself to be sidetracked by some guy? I don't even know him! How can someone I just met put me in a state of bliss in front of all my friends? I've never acted like this. I'm humiliated.

He stands and offers out his hand to help me up. I take it and stand to my feet, quickly brushing the sand from my body, and trying to gain control of the emotions that are obviously in a state of panic. I'm in uncharted waters, a foreign state of mind.

Knocking the remaining sand off, I realize, I have to get out of here. "Thanks, I just remembered my parents needed me home early. I have to go. It was nice to meet you." He looks as if there's something he wants to say or do, but doesn't, and I find myself slightly disappointed, though I don't know why. I'm the one leaving. I rush over to my towel, shove everything in my bag in a hurry and take off toward my car.

Hands shaking, I unlock my door and climb inside. In the past, I would always change in the bathhouse, because I take really good care of my car and would never allow sand inside. This time, though, I'm going to have to make an exception.

I don't know what has come over me suddenly, but I never get stupid around a guy. Frankly, I just don't care. I'm not that kind of girl; never have been. I can admire a hot guy and then move on without acting. To this point it's never been an issue. I've seen too many girls put their dreams on hold to chase after a boy and I will not be one of them. When he's gone, there may not be any chances left.

Pulling into my driveway, I notice Mom and Dad's vehicle parked in the open garage. That's strange. It's still reasonably early and they are never home before seven during the week, at least never together. I'm not sure if I should be excited to spend some time with my parents or nervous something bad has happened.

The first thing running through my mind is that something bad has happened to Konnor. Ever since he walked in on Logan and Sophia, his ex, I'm terrified I'm going to come home to find he has done something stupid like take his life. I love my brother and he's never been a depressed guy, but when he loves something he gives it everything he has. He's passionate. That's what makes him a good athlete. Every time I think of what that witch did to him, I could kill her. I still may. No one messes with my family; especially not some stupid whore.

Trying to calm my nerves for what I'm about to walk into, I inhale deeply. I've been known to be a worrier over people I care about. After Grams died, I was on medication for anxiety, but have had it under control recently.

Come on, Kinzleigh, they would have called if something had happened to Konnor.

It could even be nothing. Maybe they just had a light day at work. Getting out of my car, I walk toward the front door and place my hand on the doorknob.

You can do this, calm down.

Opening the door, Dad is sitting in his recliner reading today's paper and Mom is flipping through a magazine on the couch. Nothing looks wrong, but maybe they are just trying to break it to me gently. Dad speaks first, lowering his newspaper. "Hi, sweetie, did you have fun at the beach?"

Now I'm really confused. They look like they are in a good mood. "Mom, Dad, the two of you are home early, and how did you know I was at the beach?"

Mom looks up from her magazine and smiles as if that was the silliest thing she's heard. "Your swimsuit would be the first clue." Then it dawns on me; I was in such a hurry to get away from *him*, that I forgot to even put my cover-up back on.

Suddenly, feeling very naked, I cradle my beach bag in front of my chest. Mom and Dad are more of the conservative type and they always instilled that in us. They wouldn't be too happy with me running around in only swimwear. "Oh, right, sorry. Why are you home so early? Is everything okay?"

She laughs as if I'm the one she should be worried about. "Of course, sweetie, everything is fine. You're not starting to get anxious again are you? I won that big case I've been working on, so your dad and I thought we would all go out and eat to celebrate. Plus, we have some news to discuss with you and your brother. Konnor should be getting home soon and then we'll go. I called him about an hour ago and he said he's been training and working out with Kyle."

I wonder what could be so important that they can't discuss now. My parents have never been able to hide anything, and something tells me I'm not going to like what they have to say. I let out a breath, trying to relieve some of this tension I've built up. "Okay then, I'll head upstairs and get ready."

TWO

Breyson

I remain standing here, watching her walk away, and though I know I should go after her, I can't. She's just a girl. I've never been one to chase after a girl—I've never had to.

But this may be one of the times I really want to say screw it and go. That girl is the most beautiful thing I've ever seen. There is no way she's single, or is she? Something about her stirs primal instincts that need to remain at bay. Going after her wouldn't be fair for several reasons.

First is the fact that I sort of have a girlfriend back home. Secondly, I'm only here for a week and then it's back to Mississippi for me. I know I could be selfish, enjoy a week with a gorgeous girl, then head home with no strings attached except for a great memory, but something about her says it wouldn't be enough. Her eyes tell me I would want more, but that's something I can't give myself.

We wrapped up the game shortly after Kinzleigh took off. As soon as she left, the girls with her went back to lying on the beach to 'tan' as they call it. I've never understood why any woman would want to sit in the sun and bake for fun. Maybe that's just the football player coming out in me. When you run outside five days a week, hours on end with shoulder pads strapped to you, cooking in the sun is not something I consider fun.

I usually come down for a week every summer to stay with my cousin Ryland. We're the same age and he was my next-door neighbor and best friend back home, until they moved here when he was fourteen. I flew in this morning for my annual week in the California sun. We usually just chill on my first day here, because I'm jetlagged, but he said today was supposed to be a pretty good day for surfing.

Since I'm from the south—where the only waves are from the tide rolling in and definitely not big enough to surf, thanks to the barrier islands—I usually just sit out and watch or find something to do. Ryland has attempted to teach me a few times, but he gave up my second summer here. Some of us are just designed for land sports.

I just now realize I'm still staring at the street where Kinzleigh left when I hear Ryland in the background. I turn around and he is talking to that Presley chick as if he knows her. I wonder if he knows the blonde. This girl has her breasts practically in his face.

It looks like someone is getting laid tonight. Wish it were me ... Wait, what am I saying? You have a girlfriend, dumbass. It's going to be a long week.

I shake off my thoughts. He grabs the swimsuit string between her breasts, pulling her closer.

"Where's the party at tonight?" he asks, grabbing her ass and pressing her against him. I have to admit, it's times like these I wonder what the hell I was thinking when I agreed to date Natalie.

It seemed like a good idea at the time, because we've been

friends since freshman year. She's always flirted with me, as most girls from school do at one point or another, but it was mostly platonic. I usually ignored it, until about four months ago.

She stepped up her game and practically raped me at a school party when I was drunk. I was hammered, and I don't even remember having that much to drink. I'm still not sure how she managed to get me so drunk that I slept with her. I couldn't have stopped it if I wanted to, though. I was horny as hell and she was practically naked, rubbing against me. Besides, what high school guy turns down offered sex with a hot girl?

None.

I felt bad, since we were friends, and realized there were some perks. Anytime I wanted sex, she gave it up freely. No work was required and that worked for me . . . or so I thought. Now, I'm not so sure.

I made sure she understood I could give her sex and the title she was looking for, but nothing more. I was game for fun, but that's about it. It works for us, because she's okay with not getting the emotional, romantic, and bubbly shit like letters between classes, date nights and talking on the phone for hours. Definitely no *I love you's*. I don't do it, ever. There are no exceptions.

Presley is running her finger down his arm, looking as if she can't wait to get him alone. "Logan's graduation party is tonight. You should come." As she says the word come, she places her lips to his ear, saying something only he can hear. His face takes on a look I understand, causing him to squeeze her ass. "I promise I'll make it worth your time," she says, running her finger underneath the band of his shorts.

Ah hell, I guess tonight I'm flying solo. This is too complicated. I don't like restrictions. Maybe I should just call Natalie and break if off, have a week of parties and sex with no commitments and deal with her when I get home. The more I think about it, the better it sounds. It's an asshole move, but she knows how I am. I do what I want, and I don't care what anyone else thinks.

They aren't anywhere close to finishing this up it seems, so I take it upon myself to get everything moving along. "Yo, Ry, what's the plan?"

I'm getting tired of watching them eye-fuck each other. I have other things I could be doing and watching someone else isn't one of them. Voyeurism isn't my thing. A pair of green eyes comes to mind, though. I rub my hand through my sweaty hair, waiting for him to answer.

He tosses me his keys. "We're hitting up Logan's tonight. Wait for me at the truck, yeah?"

Catching the key ring midair, I nod my head. "Aight, but hurry up. You can pick that up later."

I've been sitting in the truck for about twenty minutes now. I have no idea what's taking Ryland so long. What could he possibly be doing with a girl at a public beach, surrounded by hundreds of people? I get it, the bastard is horny, but I'm pretty sure he isn't lacking.

Ryland has always had a string of girls following him everywhere he goes. The guy has a tan and a set of dimples and he knows how to use them; not to mention that whole surfing thing he has going on.

He finally gets in the truck with a smile that was not present the last time I saw him—a post orgasmic smile. Well, shit. Kinky bastard. Didn't know the little freak had it in him.

Tapping at my wrist sarcastically, I look at him. "Would you care to explain what took you so long?" I can tell by the look on his face he won't be in such a hurry to get to that party now.

"Hey, if I get offered a pre-party surprise by a hot girl without doing any of the work to get it, I'm not turning it down. Besides, I've been trying to get with Presley for a while, and now that she doesn't have Corey following her around like a freaking puppy, I'm hittin' that. I just needed to give her a little motivation for what she'll have inside her later. A little oral representation . . ."

That's information I would have been perfectly fine without. "Do I even want to know where you had the guts to pull that off?" I can't imagine where on a public beach that's possible without him getting arrested for indecency.

He smirks at me and raises his brow. "Don't ask questions you don't want the answers to, because you know I won't spare any details. Modesty has never been my thing. I'm proud of what I got." I nod, understanding exactly what he means as he pulls out of the parking area.

We pull into Ryland's drive and he parks his truck. One thing I like about Ryland is that even though he moved across the country, he hasn't conformed to the ways of all the other rich kids here. When he got his license, his parents offered him a fancy little sports car. Instead, all he wanted was a lifted-up GMC Sierra with mud grip tires and rims. His reason—he had to have a place to haul his surfboard and his parents couldn't argue that valid point.

That's probably the only reason we've remained friends throughout the years. He's family, but distance complicates things. But he's down-to-earth and doesn't care what other people think. He was raised in the south, so, like me he has that deep southern drawl. Somehow, though, he makes it work for him here. I think it's part of his appeal.

Dinner took longer than usual. It often does on my visits here from the lengthy conversation that comes with catching up. His parents ask a lot of questions, and because I rarely see them, I happily answer. It always ends talking about football—a rehash of the last season. My uncle still keeps up with my games, even all these miles away. After Ryland and I finished dinner with his parents, we both slept through our food coma the twelve-ounce sirloins induced, and finally started getting ready for the party a couple hours later.

I stand in the shower underneath the rain of water, the steam swirling from the heat and fogging the glass. I let the hot water rain down my face and I blow out, before wiping it with my hands to remove the salt stuck to me. My fingers comb through my hair, standing it up on the top.

She pops in my head. *Kinzleigh.* I saw her coming from a mile away. I could tell before she got to the beach she was going to be attractive, but I didn't expect her to take my breath away. No other girl ever has.

Once my eyes caught sight of those bouncy, blonde curls and emerald green eyes, I could barely look away. I wanted to meet her then. It was all I could do to continue playing ball with the guys I'd met before Ryland went to surf.

I wasn't doing too good of a job, obviously, because instead of paying attention I sent the ball sailing in her direction. I couldn't help it, though. Every time I looked over at her, my eyes held, because she was doing something else that was turning me on.

When she was rubbing oil all over her firm little body, in my head, those hands rubbing down her inner thighs were mine. Every time she adjusted her bikini top, making sure she was covered, those perfect breasts bounced slightly, as if they were begging to be touched.

I probably looked like a total asshole when the ball hit her in the forehead. What I won't admit to anyone was the reason I wasn't paying attention was because I was adjusting myself to hide my arousal from watching her.

I place my hand on the shower wall, trying to clear the thoughts of her from my head, but it seems my mind has ideas of its own. All I can think about is how cute she was when she jumped up, startled. I tried hard not to laugh, so she wouldn't take it the wrong way.

Her hair was pulled in a bun of loose curls on top of her head, begging to be pulled free. She was trying not to scream, but failed, and what came out was more of a squeak. The sound was similar to a mouse. I wonder how she sounds when she's turned on instead of startled.

Great, now I have thoughts of that voice panting and moaning in my head.

I look down to my soldier standing tall. *Dammit.* I rub my hands up and down my face, trying to stop thinking about this girl, but instead my mind starts to reel some more. I'm going nowhere fast.

What the hell . . . No one will know.

I squirt some conditioner in my hand and start to stroke myself to the memory, spreading it around as my mind takes me back. I was standing at her towel with a legitimate reason to be talking to her, so I didn't look like a creep. She had no clue I was behind her. I had to clench my fists to keep my hands to myself. I bit my tongue to avoid verbal outbreaks.

She was bent over instead of squatting like most girls do, her plump, round ass staring me in the face. Her swimsuit had slightly shifted over her right cheek. It would take barely any effort to slide it over, grab her hips, and slip inside. And in my mind, it takes even less effort to picture it.

That's exactly what happened.

Small thighs that don't touch, a perky ass with enough grip, and height short enough that moving her would be so easy. *God, I bet she's tight.* And no straps on her top. Perfect for just pulling it down to take a peek and mouthful of her nipples. Pink, hard, appetizing little buds I could bite and lick.

I clench my shaft harder to indicate the grip I think her body would have on me if I were between her legs, and quicken my strokes, thrusting inside her from behind.

She turns her head, those bright green eyes hooded from the feel of me. Her cheeks are flushed with a light shade of pink. She likes what she sees. That's one look that remains the same, no matter the girl. My mouth pulls into a smirk on one side. I guess my dad's nutrition and exercise obsession really paid off.

Her neck glistens from sweat as the sun hammers down on her skin. Her lips open, her soft voice expelling with, *Breyson, make me come.*

Shit. This isn't going to take long.

Our eyes meet, the pleading of her request in them, and every time they locked before it was as if gravity was holding them together.

The hot water runs down my sensitized body. I want her muscular legs wrapped around me as I inch inside her. I want to look at her. I turn her around and shove her down on her towel, following until I'm holding myself off of her.

My breath catches in my throat and all I can see is a pool of green that shimmers in the sun, her head rolling back in ecstasy as I slide back inside. The conditioner adding a slick layer makes it easier to imagine what the inside of her feels like.

I study her face as I move, pushing in and pulling out. She has the cutest little button nose. Her sun-kissed skin is blemish free and she has the most beautiful full lips. Lips made to kiss, to suck, and to be sucked.

Damn.

Mentally exploring that beautiful little body, my movements pick up, stroking faster, clenching harder. I kiss her full breasts, her top now sitting around her flat and toned stomach.

She wraps her legs around me, her heels digging in. She had the cutest little feet, toenails painted pink and her ankle wrapped in a small, silver chain holding some kind of charm, a heart maybe. I can't be sure.

Her body feels warm, her breasts full. I pull her closer and kiss her, rubbing my hands along her body as I continuously dive into her. She moans against my lips, her back arching and pushing her chest into me. Her chin tips up until her neck is longer and her veins are more prominent, and she finally clenches around me.

That thought and I'm done, a growl tearing through my throat with my balls clenching, heat ripping through my dick as the hot, white cum releases into the shower, mixing with the water as it runs toward the drain. I watch it disappear, my dick jerking in my hand until I'm finished, my breathing labored as I press my forehead against the shower wall, letting the water soak my back.

I'm broken from my thoughts of her body pressed against mine with Ryland beating on the door. "Dude, are you going to stay in there all night? Girls don't even take this long. I still have to shower too, you know."

Crap, how long have I been in here? Standing slumped, hands against the wall, underneath the shower, I look down and realize I'm still aroused. *You've got to be kidding me.* How can I still have a boner? I've got to get this chick out of my head. I have a feeling it's not going to be that easy.

Jerking off. If it weren't so ludicrous it'd be laughable. I rarely have to anymore now that we're all driving. And here I am, strokin' it to a girl I just met—and not the one titled as my girlfriend—in my best friend's shower. This is a new low for me.

I have to come up with something quick—something believable between two guys. Ryland knows it doesn't take me this long to shower, and I sure as hell am not telling him I just busted a nut in the next room. "I'll be right out. I had to take a shit." I yell back, so maybe he will move away from the door.

"Make sure you spray, dick."

Relieved he bought it, I hurry through the rest of my shower and emerge from the bathroom, towel wrapped around my waist.

Ryland is laying across his bed, flipping through the channels on the television. He looks over, a smile forming on his face, as if he knows my dirty little secret. "If you needed some quality time with your little buddy, all you had to do was say so and I could've used the shower downstairs," he says, shaking his head at me as he laughs.

Well this is embarrassing, no matter how close we are. It makes me look like a loser that never gets laid. "Shut up, asshole! That's not what I was doing and there is nothing *little* about my 'buddy' as you call it. How do you know I wasn't taking a shit?"

"Because you always go in the guest bathroom to shit and I heard your grand finale in there. Must have been a good spank bank. Tell me, who was it starring? The hot little blonde at the beach you scared the shit out of by almost dry humping in the sand?"

I bite back a laugh, remembering the look on her face when she realized we were in the middle of everyone before she ran off like her house was on fire, my jaw flexing from the act.

"Go to hell. The shower is all yours." The laugh comes anyway.

Pleading the fifth may be equivalent to agreeing, but the words will never come out of my mouth. There is no way I'm admitting what just happened because of a chick I only saw one time.

"Enjoy her in your head, because you'll never touch her. Trust me, we've all tried," he says in passing, before disappearing into the bathroom. And then it replays.

The hot little blonde at the beach you scared the shit out of by almost dry humping in the sand? Experienced girls don't get scared. Shy. She's just shy. I head over to my suitcase to grab my clothes, shoving any other thoughts out of my mind before I get my ass in trouble.

I'm standing in front of the mirror, spraying some cologne, when I hear *Crazy Bitch* by Buckcherry playing on my phone. This is the last thing I need right now.

Waiting on Ryland still, I grab my phone and walk outside onto the balcony for some privacy. "Hey, Nat, what's up?" It's silent, as if the call has been disconnected. I look down to see if she hung up, but the timer is still clocking the call. Placing it back to my ear, I hear her sniffle like she's crying. "Natalie? What's wrong?"

She sighs. "Were you even going to call me while you were there?"

What?

When did she turn into the needy, emotional type? We rarely talk on the phone. Usually, it's just text messaging. Now, suddenly, I'm more confused than ever.

Scrunching my brows, I begin rubbing my forehead. "Was I supposed to call you, Natalie? Because I must have missed that message when I texted you from the airport. I'm visiting family."

Based on the silence you would think I slapped her.

Finally, she sighs again, sounding hurt this time, "All I'm saying, is it would have been nice to hear from you. We usually see each other at least every other day and now you're gone for a week. You are my boyfriend, you know. Is it so wrong to want to hear from you? We used to talk on the phone every day before we started dating and now you only text me."

Obviously, she rehearsed this before she called from the sound of it. This is exactly what I was afraid of when I agreed to date her. Girls can't handle emotionless relationships. At least if it's just hooking up there is a mutual understanding. No matter what they say, the second you say you're exclusive they get attached. Next, it's pledges of love and jealousy.

She's always been good with giving me my space. I don't know why she's suddenly being a pain, but it's not going to work out in her favor if she keeps it up. I never should have agreed to date her, because it's probably going to ruin a perfectly good friendship.

Starting to feel guilty, I sit down on one of the chairs. Closing my eyes, I try to think of the best way to handle this. Before I can even say anything, she blurts out, "Breyson, I love you."

My eyes go wide in shock. Surely, I didn't hear that right. "Natalie . . ."

I don't even get the chance to finish before she starts to panic. "I'm sorry. You don't have to say it back. I just thought you should know. I didn't mean for it to happen, it just did. It's true, though, Breyson. I love you and I miss you."

Yep, I heard that right. Damn. Damn. Damn. We've been friends for three years—good friends—and everything is about to turn to shit. This is my fault entirely.

I'm about to be the biggest dick in the universe to someone important to me. What else can I do, though? I don't love her. She knew this going in. I exhale the breath I didn't realize I was holding. "You know I can't give you that, Natalie. I told you this in the beginning. Look, maybe this wasn't the best idea. I care about you and I always will. You were my friend before my girlfriend. We crossed that line and now we have to deal with it. I thought you wanted the same things, to have a good time. I can't and won't do love, Natalie. I'm not interested in cuddles, kisses, and romantic gestures. I will never be a member of the sappy love society. The risks outweigh the benefits. This was supposed to be about two friends that like to hang out, but also like sex. I thought you needed the title so you didn't feel like a slut. I can be faithful to you physically. Sex with one is the same as sex with many, but emotionally, I have nothing to give. Ever."

I sit, waiting for a string of cursing or crying, but something other than silence. I hear a door close in the background. I hope she didn't say all that in front of a friend or have me on speaker.

I'm starting to wonder if she is going to speak, when she finally barks out, "Don't you dare break up with me, Breyson. You may not see it now, but we're good together. I can give you what you need. I only told you so you would know how I feel, but I'll never mention it again until you feel the same. I wasn't looking for anything in return. I'll let you go for now, but text me later."

She really doesn't get it. I will never feel that way about her. You can't force yourself to feel that way about someone. It's there or it's not. To be honest, the thought of loving someone freaks me out. With her it's just not there, but I'm mentally spent from this conversation and it just started. I'll have to deal with this when I get back home. For now, I need a drink. I need to forget—about this conversation, about Natalie, and about a certain someone with blonde hair and green eyes. "Bye, Natalie."

Feeling frustrated, I walk back inside in search of Ryland. He has to be ready by now. For him to have something to say about the time I spent in the shower is insane. The boy has changed clothes like ten times in the last thirty minutes. If I didn't know he had something swinging between his legs, I would think he was a girl. I don't even want to know what he does standing in the mirror that long.

I've looked in like three different places already with no Ryland in sight. "Ry, you ready?" I call out across the house.

I finally find him sitting on the couch, putting on his Puma shoes. Looking up at me, he must sense my sudden change in mood. "Are you all right? You look a little pissy," he says, leaning back against the couch, before throwing his arms up on the backing.

I lean against the doorframe, crossing my arms over my chest, because thinking about it again, I am a little pissed. "It's nothing, just dealing with some of Natalie's shit. I need to have some fun. You ready to go?"

He stands up and grabs his keys from the coffee table. "Yeah, let's go. I have just what you need."

A huge house on the beach comes into view. We park across the street, because of all the cars already here. The stone driveway leads to a four-car garage of a massive brick home. About halfway down, the driveway loops to the left, forming a circle drive that wraps around a large fountain. The steps lead to a high porch, covered in brown wicker furniture with bright cushions, in front of a large front door. Each corner is decorated with tall palms.

It's hard to imagine this is where someone lives, but then again, many houses here are enormous. Houses like these put Mississippi mansions to shame. I open the door and step outside, as does Ryland. He starts up the walk and I just stand here, staring.

When he notices I'm not right behind him, he turns toward me. "Are you coming? Logan is cool; his parties are usually packed. It shouldn't be hard to find something, or *someone* to get into," he says with a grin. It's only nine o'clock and from the cars parked everywhere I would say the place is already at maximum capacity. Here we go.

Walking through the door, the house is packed from wall to wall and we haven't even made it out back. Music is blaring from speakers built into the ceiling and a DJ is setup by the door. I'm assuming that leads to the pool. Ryland said after a while everyone usually ends up in the pool at the back of the house.

He nudges me in the arm. "You good? We'll go find the bar and then I may take off and find Presley in a bit." He looks at me, a cocky smile spreading across his face.

Even if I were uncomfortable, I wouldn't admit it. I have never seen him into a girl like this before. Plus, I've never really had a problem making friends before. I nod at him. "Yeah, man. I'm cool. I'll find something to get into. Let's go find that bar."

We get to the bar and there is a guy running the keg. Ryland slaps his hand and looks back at me. "Logan, this is my boy, Breyson. Show him a good time, yeah? He needs to see how Cali people party."

I look toward the guy and he extends his hand. "I'm Logan, and this is my crib. I'll show you around and introduce you to some people. What's your beverage of choice?"

I shake his hand. Usually, I stick to beer, but today I need something stronger. "Have any whiskey?" I really hope he has something worth drinking. I can't do girly drinks.

His lips tip. "Ah, finally. Someone is ready for some real fun." He turns and places his hands around his mouth to enhance the loudness of his voice and yells. "Who's ready for some games?" The crowd goes wild with excitement. What have I gotten myself into?

I turn to Ryland, who is looking around the room. I guess he's hunting that Presley girl. The boy has it bad. "Ry, what you want to drink?" He must've spotted her, because he starts to move in the other direction.

"Just give me a Miller Lite. Actually, make it two." He reaches in his pocket and pulls out his keys, handing them to me. "If you get ready to go, just head to the house. I doubt I'll be home tonight. I think Presley's parents are out of town for the weekend. I'll probably just crash there and get a ride home in the morning. You cool with that?"

"Yeah, man, I'm good. Just give me a call if you need a ride." He bumps his fist with mine and takes off in the direction of the pool. I turn back around and Logan has a table set up, pouring shots.

After three rounds of quarters, I'm slightly past the point of intoxication. I stand, cutting myself off, because I have to drive home. Quarters is my favorite drinking game and I'm good at it, so I never get very drunk. I walk into the living room that has been transformed into a dance floor.

Upon entry, I see the back of a head covered in platinum blonde hair, grinding on some guy. Jealousy and rage course through my body. Before I can stop myself, I rush across the room and grab the girl's arm. When she looks at me with a look of disgust, I realize my mistake. I'm staring at a pair of hazel eyes. Wrong girl. I don't have the chance to apologize before a fist connects with my jaw.

Stunned, I come to and realize everyone has stopped dancing.

What in the hell is wrong with me? I'm normally laid back. This is completely out of character for my normal behavior. I've got to get out of here. If I can't control myself, I may be cutting this trip short as well.

I stand and look at the girl, wide-eyed and hidden behind the guy. Rubbing my hands over my face, I look at them. "Look, I'm really sorry. I'm a little drunk and thought she was someone else. I meant no disrespect."

The guy almost looks like he feels bad and the anger fades from his face. "It's cool, man, but you may want to double check before doing some shit like that again. You'll get yourself killed messing with someone's girl around here."

I nod my head in understanding. I deserved that hit, but I have to get out of here and clear my head. I've been here barely any time and I'm already doing stupid shit. Only one place comes to mind. The place that started all this shit. The beach.

But I can't drive just yet. I'm not one of those idiots that get behind the wheel drunk. Too many people get killed over self-absorbed idiocy. My older cousin Beau, Ryland's brother, was one of them. He went off to college and joined a fraternity. One night he got drunk and got a call from another frat brother that his girl was out with another guy. He was drunk and not thinking, so he took off after her and was speeding on a curvy road. He came around a curve going about sixty and wrapped his mustang around a tree. He was killed on impact and that was three years ago.

I take off, not saying anything else. I head outside toward the pool to sober up a bit. There are several people in and around the pool. I'm not sure what I want to do until I can drive, but I'd rather be alone to sort this mess out.

I turn to head toward the front when I feel a tug on the band of my jeans, then a body plastered to my back, rubbing her arms up my torso. "Hey, gorgeous, I remember you from earlier today at the beach."

I turn around and see a petite girl with short, black hair and a tan. Apparently, this girl lives in the tanning bed. She's cute, but not my type. She has now stuck herself against my front side, wrapping her arms around my neck. I grab her hands, pulling them from around me. "I'm sorry, who are you?"

"You're cute. I'm Lexi. I was with Presley and Kinzleigh at the beach this morning." Ah, Kinzleigh. Exactly who I would rather be stuck to right now. "We should go upstairs. I could show you a good time, California style."

She licks her lips and brushes her fingers down my stomach, stopping on my buckle, trying to unfasten my belt. *Whoa, not happening, sweetie,* I think, grabbing her hands and removing them.

"Look, you're cute and all, but I'm not interested. Actually, I was just leaving." I've got to get out of here. I think I am sober now.

She begins to pout. "What's wrong? Do you have a girlfriend or something? I'm sure what she doesn't know won't hurt her." She smiles and winks at me, going for my belt again. I'm pretty sure if I gave her the go-ahead, she wouldn't even be able to make it to a room.

Public foreplay is not my thing. Call me a douche, but I don't want my temporary girl or myself left out for the eyes of someone else's enjoyment. I also don't believe in sleeping with a girl that's clearly intoxicated. It's not my style. That's usually the guys that can't get any when the girl is sober.

"You seem like a nice girl and you look decent enough, if I wanted to go there, but I'm really not interested." *In you anyway.*

I hate to be rude to the girl, but begging is not going to make me change my mind.

"Fine, you're a jerk. See you around, I guess." She turns on her heels and stomps away toward the next contender. With that crap out of the way, I head for Ryland's truck. If I wasn't sober before, I am now.

I make my way through the scattered couples, some making out and some doing things I really don't want to witness, and get in the truck. Putting the keys in the ignition, I crank the truck and head for the beach.

THREE

Kinzleigh

I stand in front of the mirror, putting on the finishing touches of my makeup, trying to decide what to wear. Mom told me we were going to one of the nicer restaurants in town that requires a semi-formal dress code.

I walk over to my closet, fingering through my wardrobe, until I stop on my floor length, black satin halter dress with a sweetheart neckline. Mom bought it for me when she was in LA on a case a few months ago, but I've never had anywhere to wear it until now. I don't dress like this much. I pull the hanger from my closet and walk over to my bed. Removing it from the hanger, I step in and pull it up my body, securing the clasp behind my neck.

I take in my reflection. The dress does look perfect with my platinum blonde hair. I add my black strappy heels and pin the front of my freshly straightened hair back, securing it with the diamond-encrusted clip I received on my birthday. For the finishing touch, I add my diamond stud earrings that once belonged to Grams.

I used to constantly look at them, sitting perfectly nestled in

accepted FATE

the Tiffany Blue box each time I visited. Gramps gave them to her on their fiftieth anniversary. The Christmas before she died, she wrapped them and gave them to me. She said she had cared for them long enough and they deserve to get out of that old box, plus gramps would want me to have them. He passed away from a heart attack five years before grams died.

I really miss them.

After dabbing on my gloss, I sit on the bed to change out my purse when I hear a knock at my door. "Come in, I'm dressed." I call out, my voice carrying across the room. I expected it to be mom, but when the door opens Konnor is standing on the other side. He's wearing a baby blue button-down shirt and black slacks. The blue in the shirt really stands out with his short, inky-black hair and ice-blue eyes. He really is a handsome guy.

He comes in and shuts the door, placing his hands in his pockets. "Hey, Sis. You look beautiful, as always." He smiles a sad smile, but it doesn't reach his eyes. I could kill Sophia for what she did to him. If anyone deserves a happy ending, it's Konnor. He is the best guy I know, and I don't say that because he's my brother. He has a heart full of love and would give a stranger the shirt off his back.

I walk over to him, wrapping my arms around his waist to give him a hug, trying to hold back the tears attempting to fall free. My heart aches for him. I place my cheek against his chest. "I love you. You know that, right?" Looking up at him, he nods, answering my question.

My voice is barely above a whisper; scared he will break at any moment. I guess it would be worse to actually find someone cheating than to be told. Something about seeing it with your own eyes would make it more real and unforgettable, I would imagine. "How are you holding up?" We haven't gotten a chance to really talk since it all happened.

He clears his throat, as if he's holding back tears as well. "I've been better, but I'm okay. Stop worrying about me, Sis, it makes me feel worse. I'll be fine. I don't know when, but I have to deal with my own shit. It's mine to bear and mine alone. Now that I don't have to see her anymore, it should get easier. Maybe now I can finally get the image out of my head."

I can't stand this anymore. I hate seeing him in this much pain. I see it in his eyes—he's holding on by a thread. We have always been close. I can feel when he's hurting as can he with me.

I pull away and notice him staring at the wall behind me, checked out mentally. Grabbing each side of his face, I pull it down for his eyes to meet mine. "Konnor, look at me."

When he finally does, I can't help but to spill my heart out. "I hate her for what she's done to you. She doesn't deserve you. You're too good for her. I swear, Konnor, you better listen to me and listen to me good."

He's staring at me and nods so I know he's listening. Tears begin to fall, no longer controllable. "We all love you and I know you're in pain, but don't you dare do something stupid. Don't let that heartless bitch win. She's the one that screwed up. Show her what she's missing. She will regret what she's done one day when she ends up with a loser that will likely do the same thing to her. You know what else? When it happens, you will have already found someone that deserves your heart, someone worthy of your love. Sophia isn't it. She isn't the one for you. Bring my Konnor back. I want the real you, not the shell of a man you're becoming. This doesn't have to ruin you. One day, when you find that perfect someone, this will be just a bump in the road. I see how much this is breaking you. If you do something stupid, I will kill her. That is a promise. I will kill for you, Konnor. It's blood for blood in my book. Do you understand?"

A tear escapes his eye. The first I've seen since he was a kid. He pulls me in his arms and squeezes me tight. "You always did have my back, Sis. You're right, about everything. Just give me time, okay? I know you think love is just a crutch, but one day you'll change your mind. You may think you can control it by avoiding it, but you can't. When you meet that person, it just happens. You can't stop it like you think you can. One day, you're going to fall; just promise me you'll enjoy the ride down. You will make some lucky guy happy. I love you, baby girl; now stop blubbering before you get makeup on my clean shirt. Let's go. Mom and Dad are waiting downstairs."

He releases me and turns for the door. He's wrong about one thing. I will not allow myself to fall in love with some guy; the cost is too high. But for the first time in over a month I see a genuine smile. There is no way I'm killing it. Maybe I'm getting through to him after all.

We walk downstairs where Mom and Dad are waiting. I walk to my mom first, giving her a hug. "You look pretty tonight, Mom."

She's wearing a sleeveless, red, knee-length dress, pencil style that accents her small figure. Her long, black hair is pulled back in a neat twist, looking like perfection, as it always does. She has lightly coated makeup and glimmering green eyes, similar to mine. Every time she smiles, her dimples are deep set in her cheeks and she is wearing her favorite black pumps. She is a beautiful woman—one that has aged gracefully. Konnor looks like Mom, but with Dad's eyes.

Dad comes over shortly after, scooping me into his arms, giving me his usual bear hug and twirls in a circle. I always have been his little princess. Kissing me on the cheek, he smiles that heart-wrenching smile. "You look amazing, baby girl. Are you ready to do some celebrating?" He always could make me smile, no matter what mood I was in. Him and Konnor have called me 'baby girl' since I was old enough to talk, and it stuck.

I'm an exact replica of my dad, although, I received Mom's eyes. It's funny how genetics work, really. Dad is handsome, athletic, and tall. He is dressed in gray slacks, a black Giorgio Armani button-down, and the watch we got him for Christmas when I was seven. He never leaves home without it. He says, every time he misses home, he just looks at the time. He's quite the philosophical one, I must say. He's got the same blond hair as me, short, and gels it up in the front.

I was blessed with the greatest parents on earth. Not many kids can say that, but I can, because they have earned the credit. They have always been a part of mine and Konnor's life, no matter how hectic work got for them.

They never missed a game, cheer competition or school activity. They always tried to bring home a positive attitude. Dad always said that work should be left at work and home left at home. Never mix business with pleasure and you'll go further in life. I've rarely heard my parents fight, because they chose to be role models for us. My mom always told me to never go to bed angry with someone you care about in case a new day never comes. Live as if today is your last day. She has lived by that motto my entire life.

I've always looked up to my parents. They are completely and passionately in love—a once in a lifetime love. When you're granted a love like that, you're never given it a second time. I figure if you don't get it to begin with, then you don't have to worry about losing it. I smile at my dad as he sets me back down on my feet. "Ready as I'll ever be."

We pull up at valet and exit the car. We're seated at our table almost instantly. The restaurant is beautiful with high ceilings, low lighting, and candlelight dancing from every table.

Once we're seated, Mom and Dad order a glass of white wine as we glance at the menu. The waiter soon takes our order and the four of us enjoy a bit of small talk as we wait for our food. We're having a really good time, but I feel like my parents are avoiding something. My mom mentioned having to discuss some important news that they have yet to bring up since we've been here. I'm starting to wonder if it's something bad.

Now nervous, I pick up the crystal glass and take a sip of my water, trying to calm down. I look up and find my parents staring at each other with this look, as if they are talking in some code. Yes, I know that look. It always comes when they are preparing to tell us something we're not going to like. I look over at Konnor, but he just shrugs, knowing exactly what I'm asking him.

The waiter sets our food down just as it looked like Dad was about to speak, breaking the moment. Dad must sense my nervousness, because he smiles as if nothing just happened and starts eating, along with Mom, and Konnor following suit.

I'm seventeen years old and my parents still act as if we can't read them like a book. They never were good at hiding things, maybe because they are such honest people.

I'm picking at my food, when finally, I can't take the suspense any longer. My stomach is a ball of knots, no longer allowing me to eat anything. Clearing my throat, I look to my parents. "Mom, Dad, what was the big news you wanted to talk to us about?"

Dad finishes chewing the mouthful of food he was working on, looks to my mom, and nods. Okay, this is really starting to get weird.

Dad lets out a breath and then puts down his fork. "As a family, we're about to make some big changes. I signed a contract that will extend over the next five to ten years. It's going to change the face of the company your grandfather has built from the ground up."

I'm starting to feel relieved, because that wasn't near as bad as I was expecting, but then I realize there is something else. "Dad, how is this going to require us to change? You have new contracts all the time."

This is when my dad starts to look nervous, because he begins rubbing the back of his neck. "The contract is for us to build strip malls across the southern region."

My brows come together as he's still not making this clear. "Meaning, what?"

Mom jumps in to relieve Dad as she usually does when he's afraid of upsetting us. "We're moving."

I sit here, wide-eyed and in shock. There is no way I just heard that correctly. My parents would not do this to me right before senior year—the most important year for me. I have always done the right thing; never made them worry, never stayed out late, and worked my butt off in school. I just made cheerleading captain and have been checking out various cheerleading programs at colleges across the country. Our squad is the best in the state and top five in the country, which pretty much guarantees me a spot on any college squad of my choice. They cannot be doing this to me. "I'm sorry, what did you say?"

Mom begins rubbing her temples—a habit she developed when her anxiety starts—and then looks back at me. "Honey, I know this is unexpected, but this is a great opportunity for your dad. He has always supported us, as will we for him. We are a family."

Now she is going to play the guilt card? Because I of all people know my dad deserves it. I close my eyes, trying to process this.

Okay, Kinzleigh, think this through. Maybe this is all just a dream, and you're going to wake up, with everything completely normal. Think, think, think.

I look back up at Dad. "Who is going to run the company here?" He starts to look a little relieved. "Uncle Danny is going to run the company here. I will build up the southern offices, while getting the first project off the ground."

This makes no sense, whatsoever. Uncle Danny's kids are grown. Why do we have to uproot our lives and start over? I'm really starting to get angry, something I never do with my parents. "I don't understand. Why can't Uncle Danny move and start up the company there? His kids are grown and self-sufficient."

My dad is back to rubbing his neck again, turning it red. "Uncle Danny doesn't have the experience to expand the company into an entire new region. It's too much for him to handle. He will serve me better here. Stop letting the negative in. This could be a good thing for you. You've always been good at making friends. You will adjust in no time at all."

I feel like I'm in a nightmare I can't wake up from. Like the ones where someone is trying to kill you and you try really hard to escape, but can't? This feels like one of those times. "Mom, what about your job, my cheerleading dream, or Konnor's football scholarship? We can't just change our whole lives when we have everything planned out. This isn't fair. I've always done everything you guys have asked of me. I've never been in trouble. I make straight A's at school and I work hard in the gym. I don't even date for goodness sakes. I never cause strife. This is going to destroy all of my plans. Where are we even moving?" I'm starting to raise my voice at this point, causing the surrounding tables to glance in our direction.

I can see the defeat in Dad's eyes. He always did hate to upset me. Maybe I should calm down some. I'm about to apologize, when Mom holds up her hand, stopping me. "Kinzleigh, I know this is a lot to take in, but you will not take that tone with us again. I think we can all agree that Dad has only ever had our best interests at heart, but regardless, we are a family and we will continue to live that way. Are we clear?" I nod, because when Mom gets frustrated the best thing to do is remain quiet.

I take a deep breath, trying to process everything they are saying, and Mom begins again. "This is going to affect all of our lives, not just yours, and we understand that. I'm not all that thrilled with leaving my job and friends either, but family supports each other, and this is what Dad needs right now. We are not going to be selfish with all that he's done for us. You have until the end of June to spend time with your friends and say your goodbyes. If, after your senior year, you decide you want to go to college back here, then we will evaluate at that time. We are not trying to crush your dreams, Kinzleigh. It's just one year of high school. You can cheer anywhere. I know you are my little planner and can't seem to function in chaos, but sometimes the unexpected happens and you just have to roll with it."

She then turns to look at Konnor, who is just sitting there, as if nothing abnormal is even happening. "Konnor, as for you, you are eighteen now and ready to start college. Dad and I understand you have made a commitment to UCLA for football. You have two options. If you want to continue with that commitment, that's fine. You'll be in the football dorms anyway. If you want to be closer to us, Dad will do everything in his power to get you set up at your first-choice school. It's your decision, but you need to think about it before it's no longer an option. You have a week to decide. Dad has already contacted the coach at Alabama and pulled some strings.

accepted FATE

There are walk-on opportunities. If you choose that option, then we will absorb the cost of your school and provide you with housing as we've always planned. I know the SEC conference was your original choice for football, because they have some of the best football programs in the country, but you chose to stay in California for Sophia. Since that is no longer the case, maybe you need a change too, sweetie."

I'm sitting there in complete shock. This is actually happening. Before I can stop myself, I blurt out, "Where are we moving?"

Dad finally appears to be calming down. He looks at me, placing his hands in front of him on the table. "We're moving to Mississippi." My mouth drops and my eyes go wide. I'm speechless. This is not just my worst nightmare, but also Hell on earth.

Tears begin to fall. I can't hold them back any longer. I look from Mom to Dad, mouth quivering, trying not to cry hysterically. "You're sending us to live in a place with a bunch of red-neck hillbillies? Do they even know what cheerleaders are? Dad, you've seen on television the kind of people that live there. Please tell me this is a joke."

He is beginning to look angry, as if I've offended him. "Kinzleigh, I'm very disappointed in you right now. You know your mother and I have always taught you to never judge anything or anyone by hearsay or appearance. Things are rarely as they seem. Do you really think I would move my family somewhere unfit? I should have earned more respect than that."

I feel like I'm going to be sick. I've had enough bad news for one night. I need to get out of here, to think all this through. Usually, I work out my stress and frustration in the gym practicing, but it's too late. I'll have to go to the one place I always find peace and serenity—the beach.

I wipe the tears from my face as best as I can and place my napkin on my plate. Scooting my chair back, I stand. Looking at my parents—the two people I adore the most other than my brother—who have just hurt me worse than ever imaginable, I ask, "May I be excused? I really need to be alone right now."

Both parents nod their heads, excusing me from dinner, before Mom says, "You can go for now, but we need to finish this conversation later."

I can't imagine it being anytime soon. "I'll be home later. Don't wait up, okay? I'll get a cab." I grab my purse, turn, and walk as fast as possible until I get to the door of the lobby.

I reach the outside of the restaurant before my breaths become short and quick. I bend forward, placing a hand on each knee, trying to breathe. I'm on the verge of a panic attack; one I haven't had since Grams died.

Breathe Kinzleigh, breathe, I repeat to myself over and over, trying to calm down. I finally catch my breath enough to stand upright. I walk to the curb and hold up my arm, trying to hail a cab. Thankfully, it's late enough I don't have to wait long.

Getting in the cab, an elderly, white-haired man wearing a beret turns to me, tipping his hat. "Miss, where would you like to go?"

I probably look like a hot mess. I pull out my compact mirror to try and fix myself and look back at him. "The pier please."

FOUR

Kinzleigh

The cab pulls in about a half-mile from the pier. The driver turns to me, placing his arm over the back of the seat. "Is this okay, Miss?"

I nod and hand him a twenty. "This is fine. Thank you. Keep the change."

I open the door, placing my right foot outside, when I hear the driver clear his throat. "You look like you've had one of those days. I hope things get better for you."

I step out of the car, before sticking my head back inside. "It isn't looking that way, but thank you for your kindness. It's a rare quality these days."

I shut the door and watch the driver pull back onto the street, before turning around to face the sand, luminescent in the moonlight. Holding onto the rail that leads down the steps to the beach, I pull off one shoe, followed by the other. I have enjoyed the tranquility of the beach since I was a kid. The waves crashing against the shore always had a way of melting the stress away.

I walk down the steps toward the shoreline, my silver clutch hanging from my wrist with my shoes in one hand, holding my dress up with the other. The sand, squishing between my toes, is still warm from the hot day. I make it to the water's edge and stop.

Placing my shoes down in the sand, I release my dress and look up at the sky. It's a beautiful night. The stars are twinkling as if they know I'm here, enjoying their beauty. My hair and dress begin dancing in the breeze. For a summer night, the temperature is perfect. It's dark being so far away from the street lamps, but I welcome it.

As I look out across the water, the Pacific Ocean looks black, with just the reflection of the moonlight sitting on top. I close my eyes, enjoying the sound and the feel of the water crashing against my ankles, completely at peace. The bottom of my dress gets soaked from the waves washing ashore, but I don't care. I begin walking out farther into the ocean as if it's calling to me, but decide against it. I still have to get home and I don't have a change of clothes.

The half-mile strip from here to the pier is usually free from locals or tourists, aside from the occasional fisherman. That's why I love it here. I can come here and enjoy being free from worry or stress or heartache. It's an escape for me. The only person that knows I come here is Konnor.

The night I found out Grams died, I took off and came here. He was worried and ended up finding me here when I didn't come home or answer my phone. That's the last time I had to come here at night—my safe haven. I'm really going to miss this place.

I pick up my shoes from where they're sitting in the sand and start to walk toward the pier. I don't understand why I have worked so hard to be good and yet somehow, Fate has turned against me. I walk the half-mile along the shoreline when I reach the pier.

I climb the steps and begin walking toward the end, along the worn wood planks that are suspended and run about a mile out into the water. The pier is enclosed with side rails and a roof overhead, perfect for whatever the weather has planned. At the end, there is a bench on the right and a bench on the left, followed by a section that is uncovered, but continuous railing for fishing.

I finally reach the end and sit, placing my legs over the side, but because of my height they do not reach the water. The night begins to replay through my mind. I can't believe my life is crashing down around me. Everything I've worked so hard for is being taken from me.

Being squad captain is something I've dreamed of since I started cheerleading. Even if this Hicksville town, Mississippi has a cheerleading squad, will they have room for an additional cheerleader this close to the start of another school year? Do they even compete or is football games it? Now, I'm going to have to work harder just to get a tryout at the colleges I'm interested in.

Why would my parents just pick up and move us across the country when I have one year of high school left? How do they expect me to just leave everything I know behind and start over? I have friends and family here. That has to mean something to them. This isn't fair. Maybe I can think of a way to stay behind. I have to. My parents have to understand what this will do to me. It will crush me. I so desperately want to wake up and realize this is all a bad dream. All I can do is stare out at the ocean, lost in thought.

All of my emotions finally catch up to me and the tears start to fall, heavier this time. I can't stop them anymore. I don't know what to do. Everything was going great in my life and now the misery is about to begin. I don't even try to wipe the tears away anymore. I just let them flow.

I don't understand why, out of all the states in the continental U.S., my parents have to choose some po-dunk town in Mississippi. I can't imagine the kind of people that reside there. After that big hurricane—Katrina I think—they had people on television walking around barefooted and missing teeth. Do they even have shopping malls and designer clothes, I wonder, or is it full of trailer parks and cow fields? My stomach turns at the thought.

I'm not sure how long I've been sitting there, staring at the water, but my back is beginning to hurt from my position and I'm growing tired from crying. I can't stop the constant draining tears that continue to fall.

I should go home and go to bed, but I'm not ready to face my parents yet. I know they will still be up and wanting me to talk. That I cannot do yet.

I lay back against the pier, arms outstretched to my side, looking up into the sky. It's dark, but the sky is clear; the perfect shade of onyx marked by the speckled pattern of stars, glittering across the horizon. The moon glows like a spotlight, lighting up the pier. It's beautiful glancing out at all the stars, shining brightly as if each holds a story of their own. It's also a full moon tonight.

I remain flat against the warm wood and allow myself to enjoy the starry night. I wonder, if you were to talk, would there be someone to listen up there? Maybe there is a keeper of the sky, assigned to keep the stars in perfect order and change the days to night. Maybe he gets lonely and just wants to listen. At least then, all my secrets would be safe.

Listen to yourself, Kinzleigh. A sky keeper? Really? You're becoming quite the delusional one.

A strange peacefulness washes over me, causing me to close my eyes. Clearly, my mind is not in normal territory, because I would never close my eyes late at night on a public beach. There are too many creeps out there, but I suddenly just feel the need to sleep, like someone or something is watching over me.

I couldn't have been lying here but what seems like a few minutes, in the midst of a new dream, when I hear footsteps along the pier. I must've dozed off, but instead of my eyes bolting open at the sound, I just incorporated it into my dream. That is, until, "Mind if I join you?" flows through my ears in a deep, raspy, southern voice. My eyes pop open and a tall familiar face is standing over me, looking down with a smile on his face.

I panic and sit up in a hurry, embarrassed at being caught sleeping on a pier. Embarrassment is a rare trait for me, and this guy has brought it out twice in one day. "I'm sorry. I don't usually do this, but it's been a bad night. I'm a little more tired than usual."

I look back out at the water, gripping the side of the pier as if the most beautiful boy isn't standing behind me. He stuns me. Right then, I can feel his breathing on the back of my neck, quickening my heart rate. In the short time of his presence, he has managed to squat behind me, placing the inside of each knee resting against my sides. I don't even think he's trying to touch me, but the contact is making my body do things I don't understand.

He whispers in my ear. "May I keep you company for a while? I'll be quiet if that's what you need." His breath is so light it tickles my ear. I can barely breathe, let alone speak, so I just nod. Would I even be able to tell him no if I wanted to? My head is fuzzy and I can't think when he's this close.

He pulls up his pants legs and sits beside me. He removes his shoes, placing his feet in the water. I'm finally able to exhale the breath I've been holding. "How long have you been here?"

I turn and glance at him to find he's staring at me. I don't know where this guy is from and I don't really care, but he's gorgeous. I never take an interest in a guy. It's one of my few rules to avoid falling into the never-ending cycle of the love-struck patrons, but following rules have gotten me nowhere, obviously. I'm not thinking clearly anyway, so I guess I can break my rule and enjoy his company for a while. He's fun to look at; especially those lips. He's leaving soon anyway, and right now I need a distraction from all this bad news.

He reaches out slowly as if he's afraid I'll run away, placing his hand over my cheek. He begins rubbing his thumb underneath my eye, freeing it from the wetness of my tears. I fall into his touch like a cat being petted. Great, I have no idea what I look like right now. "I needed to clear my head and came to the beach. I saw you standing by the water earlier and didn't want to leave you out here alone. Are you okay?"

My eyes close at the warmth from his hand. I should be mad he followed me, but I'm not. I just want him near me. His voice soothes me, but no personal questions are allowed. I don't need him to know me or what makes me tick. I don't need any complications.

I open my eyes to him staring at my lips. "Can we just exist together without trying to exchange personal information? Let's enjoy casual company—two people needing nothing from each other. Clearly, you're not from here, meaning you'll be gone soon. I'm not one of those girls that needs or wants to know everything about you, nor do I want to spill my entire life to you. We don't have to pretend with each other. Let's call this what it is—a moment to avoid being alone. Can we do that?"

He stares at me as if he's trying to figure me out; like I'm a book full of secrets in another language. He seems lost in my eyes—amused, confused, I don't know. We sit there staring at each other as if we can't pull away. As if we don't want to.

He doesn't say anything; just bites his lip as if he's trying to answer his own question, or to decide. I'm about to get up and walk away when his other hand reaches behind my neck, pulling me closer as he closes in. His lips stop in front of mine, close enough to touch, when he whispers, "Beautiful girl," and crashes his lips to mine.

His lips are soft and full, but needy. I don't know what I'm doing, but for some reason the act comes natural with him. Our lips fit together as if they were molded for the connection. His warm tongue slips through the opening of my lips barely, requesting entry. I open up to him, granting his request. Our tongues touch, taste, and dance together. He tastes as good as he smells. I always thought it was kind of nasty to imagine exchanging spit, but with him, I want more. The senses coming at me are overwhelming.

A moan, barely more than a whisper, escapes my lips. I run my hands across his arms and up his neck, into the back of his hair. My heart is beating wildly. Foreign emotions are running through my body. I have entered into the depths of the unknown. I've never felt this need before, but it's as if my body needs more. Suddenly, I feel like I need to cross my legs from the spasms down below. What is he doing to me? What does this mean?

He turns, laying me against the pier. He has one hand on my waist and the other beside my head, holding his weight above me, like when we were at the beach. He continues to kiss me, taking my bottom lip into his mouth, lightly sucking. His hand slips down, brushing against my butt. When it does, he makes a low growling sound from his throat. I'm not sure why until I feel his need pressed against the bottom of my belly, making my eyes go wide from surprise. I tense. Oh no, I can't go there. As if he can sense my panic, he stops. He kisses me one last time softly and releases my lips.

He looks me in the eyes, a smile growing across his face. He brushes his fingers through my hair, down my arm and grabs me by the hand, interlacing his fingers with mine. "Nothing personal, huh? I think I can do that."

His lips brush mine quickly once again, before he moves back to his place on the pier, pulling me by my hand to sit between his legs. "I promise I'll be good for the rest of the night. I've just wanted to do that all day. Since the second I laid eyes on you actually."

I'm completely and utterly speechless. I have no idea what I'm even doing. I never do reckless or unplanned things like this. I have no idea who this guy is, really, and now I'm sitting on the pier making out with him for the entire world to see. I need to get my head back in the game. I always think everything through before I make a decision. Like mom said, I'm a planner. It's my quirk, I guess, but it's what keeps me sane. I need it like I need cheerleading. Being around him takes away my ability to process. Right now, there are so many unknowns, but what I do know is that I'm not ready for it to end just yet.

I sit here between his legs, staring out at the ocean, completely at peace and trying to replay what just happened. I would have never imagined a first kiss like that. At Presley's thirteenth birthday party, we played spin the bottle and I was forced to kiss Brantley Cooper. It was awkward and over in a second. We didn't even touch inside each other's mouths. Since then, I haven't been the least bit interested in boys nor kissing.

Presley thinks there is something wrong with my girly parts. Maybe it's because of all the risk involved. In Family Dynamics class, we had to listen to nurses present a slide show and talk about

accepted FATE

sexually transmitted diseases and teen pregnancy. I was utterly grossed out. Who wants to deal with that scary mess? Not me. After that, my immature sex drive took a hiatus and never returned.

That, though, was worthy of locking away in my memory bank and never forgetting. That kiss set me up for all future kisses. Nothing will ever be able to compare. My body feels like it's housing an electrical current. My heart feels like it's on some kind of speed.

I lay my head against his chest and realize his heart is beating fast as well. Maybe he has the same reaction to me as I to him, but what does that mean? Whatever it means, though, right now I'm content to just exist, no words or thinking required.

He lays his chin on my head and places his arms around me, nestling me in the cocoon of his curled-up body. I feel so small and protected like this. The water is completely still and calm. This has been the strangest day. It has gone from bad to worse to a little bit better. If someone would have told me when I woke up this morning that I would be in the arms of a sexy, southern boy by midnight, I would have laughed, yet here I am. I begin to shiver, but it's not from being cold. Actually, it's pretty warm outside, being it's June.

He holds me tighter, the rhythm of his breathing soothing me, melting away all of the built-up tension from earlier. He rests his cheek behind my ear and whispers against it. "Are you cold? I can take off my shirt."

"No. Thank you, though. I'm okay," I say. He really needs to keep that shirt in place. I'm in no kind of place to be seeing the muscles I remember from earlier. Having them pressed against me in this state of mind is dangerous. "The kind of day I've had is still surreal. I'm just upset."

"Want to talk about it? I'm a pretty good listener." He brings his head down to rest on top of my shoulder, cheek to cheek.

Should I talk about it? I wonder if it's a good idea. Maybe it would help to get some of this built-up anger and frustration off my chest. I still don't want to talk about anything personal. A friend wouldn't hurt, though. I suppose it would be best to talk to someone I will never see again.

I exhale. Here goes. "My parents told me tonight that we're moving at the end of June. It may not seem like a big deal, but I've spent my entire life chasing after a dream. One I've wanted since I was a kid. My brother has always loved football. From the time he was old enough to throw a ball, he would drag Dad or me outside to throw with him. He was always trying to be like the big boys—the pros."

I breathe and continue. "When I was eight my parents asked him what he wanted to do for his birthday. He didn't even have to think about it. He wanted to go see the San Diego Chargers play. It was October and my parents made a whole weekend out of it. Everything was so big and exciting. We got in the stands and took our seats between Mom and Dad. I looked down at the field and saw the cheerleaders taking their place on the sidelines in their amazing showy outfits. They were beautiful. The entire game I couldn't look away. I sat there and watched them cheer and do amazing stunts the entire time. From then on, I knew what I wanted to be when I grew up—a professional cheerleader. My mom, being the amazing woman that she is, noticed me in complete awe the entire game. When it was over, she somehow managed to get a meet and greet with one. There was this girl that had blonde hair like me. I remember asking her how I could become like her when I grew up."

I start to cry again, thinking how my life is about to change. I love everything about California. "She bent down in front of me, so we could be the same height. She looked at me and placed her finger to my chest and said, *always follow your heart and work hard. You'll find your way, but don't let anything or anyone stop you. When you think you're working hard, work harder.* See, that's what I have always done. I have always been the good girl. I hung the picture I took with that cheerleader on my mirror and always remembered what she said. I've worked extremely hard for years on the best squad around. You don't just up and move your senior year. Squad tryouts are always held at the end of the previous year. I don't know what I'm supposed to do now. My heart has always been with California."

He sits here rubbing my arms. "I don't know anything about you, but from what I've seen so far, you'll find a way to make it happen. If you have worked this hard, then continue to work hard like she said. Make it happen. My dad used to always tell me the best things in life never come easy. If you want something bad enough, there is always a way to obtain it, no matter how out of reach it seems. I understand why you're upset. We work for years to be seniors. We're supposed to have seniority not be brand new. But there are always some pros with starting over in a new place where you don't know anyone. You can be anybody you want to be. Even if you think the door has closed for you, there is always a way to burst through. We have the power to control our outcome, no matter what problems arise before we get there."

I turn around, now kneeling on bent knees between his legs, placing my arms around his neck. "Aren't you just Mister Insightful tonight . . ." I tease. "Are you always this deep?"

He holds me by the waist, rubbing my ribs with his thumbs, a smile taking place. "Only when I'm trying to cheer up a beautiful girl." He reaches up, removing the tears from underneath my eyes. "I meant it, though, Kinzleigh."

"Maybe I just needed to hear it from someone else. I was rude to my parents when they told me. Oh, crap, what time is it? They are probably worried. I never stay out late. When I told them not to wait up they probably took it as a joke." I start to stand so I can go get my phone from my purse on the bench to check the time, but he grabs my waist, stopping me.

Breyson has his eyebrow cocked. "You've never stayed out this late?" He pulls his cell from his pocket and unlocks the screen. "Kinzleigh, it's only eleven o'clock. You can't be serious." He laughs, as if he thinks I'm lying.

"What is so funny? I don't drink and that's usually all that goes on around this time. I have to keep my body at its best if I want to have a chance. Alcohol is not going to do anything for me. I've seen the stupid things people do while intoxicated. I only go to parties on very rare occasion if Presley drags me out, and I'm always home by now, if not before, because hanging around drunk people sober isn't fun to me."

I take a breath, before driving my point home. "I don't date, ever, so I don't have to worry about someone else occupying my time with other activities. Like I said, I'm always home by now. Plus, my brother threatens his friends with life or death when they come over. If I'm not at school or cheerleading, I'm with girlfriends. I only hang out with male friends on the rare occasion when we all have a group trip. But usually, I hang out with friends during the day or early evening and practice at night, unless I go to a concert or something."

Something different has replaced the look that was previously on his face, but I'm not sure what. I have never been good with reading people.

"Don't go yet, in case I don't get to see you again before I have to go back home." He brushes my long hair over my shoulder. I know I should go, but how can I tell him no? He has the most handsome face and he has been nothing but nice to me.

"What do you want to do?" The breeze is picking up and with the bottom of my dress still damp, I'm starting to get cold. Goose bumps take place along my arms.

"I don't care. We'll find something. Come on, let's get you warm. I have Ryland's truck." He slides back to stand, never letting go of me. When he gets to his feet, he helps me to mine and wraps his arm around me. We start back toward the beach, picking up my shoes and clutch along the way. Something tells me that as much as I'm trying to avoid complications, I'm already headed for trouble.

"Okay. I guess I can stay out a little bit longer, but I need to text my mom once I get to the truck." What on earth am I going to tell her? I can't exactly tell her I'm with a boy she's never met. I have to be on the verge of a mental breakdown, because I can't believe I am about to get in the truck of a guy I just met earlier today. He could be a rapist or serial killer for all I know. I have never even been on a date before, so how can I tell my mom I'm going out with a guy this late at night. She'll think I'm losing it.

We get to the beginning of the pier and he gets to the bottom of the steps first, holding out his hand to help me. "So, what's there to do around here for fun at night?" I take his hand, trying not to be rude, but quickly release it once I get to the bottom. I don't want him to think he's going to get any more of what happened earlier.

I fold my arms over my chest, shrugging my shoulders. "Just depends; mostly parties or concerts at night, and sometimes bonfires on the beach. Other than that, whatever is open." I'm not sure what to do honestly. I rarely stay out this late. I wasn't kidding.

"I just came from this guy named Logan's house party. We

could go there if you want," he says nonchalantly as we make our way down the beach.

"I can't go to Logan's," I say quickly, hoping he won't ask any further questions. I absolutely will not have anything to do with Logan after what he put Konnor through. He has pretty much been a member of our family since elementary school, and to know he ruined a long-term friendship over meaningless sex is enough to steer clear of him for good. Don't guys have some kind of stupid motto, 'bros before hoes?' Obviously, their head reigns over their heart and I don't mean the one with the brain.

He furrows his brow as if he wants to ask, but doesn't. "Are you hungry?" I feel relieved, because I won't explain my reasons for not going to Logan's. It's not my place to tell Konnor's business.

As if on cue, my stomach growls. I guess I am hungry. I didn't get a chance to finish dinner with my parents. "I could eat. I didn't have much of an appetite earlier," I say, trying to smile.

We finally make it back to the parking lot. What I see when I get there is a huge, silver GMC truck with blackout tinted windows, a pair of matching black running boards and a black front grill guard. Complete with big tires and black rims. Wow. From what I remember Ryland has a southern accent too. I've never really hung out with him. And our school is big. This must be a country boy thing, because most guys around here like their sports cars or luxury vehicles. "So, this is it?" I ask, looking around the parking lot, thinking there is going to be something else around.

A smile begins to take place on his mouth. "You have been in a truck before, haven't you?" He unlocks the doors with the remote and opens the passenger door.

"Only my dad's company truck, because he is a contractor and needs the bed to haul supplies. There aren't exactly a lot of these around here." I laugh nervously, wondering how I'm supposed to get in this thing. It's so high off the ground I'm not sure I can. I am on the shorter side. I go to grab the door handle with both hands, trying to step on the bar. My body weight is offset, causing me to slip. "Crap," I say, and begin looking to see if there is another way.

He places one hand on my left side, cupping my waist, and grabs my right hand. He is now completely touching my entire backside with his body, causing my heart to race. His voice comes out low and deep beside my ear. "Try it this way."

He places my hand in the handle above the dashboard beside the doorframe. "Now place your foot on the bar."

I do as I'm told, and he runs his hand down my right arm, causing me to shiver. He places it on my right side, mirroring the left, and lifts me, helping me into the truck.

My stomach is in knots. I sit down after he releases my waist, turning toward him. "Thanks," I say, not sure what else to say at this point. He is staring at me, clenching his jaw with a predatory look in his eyes. He stands there for a good while, not turning away from me, before he finally shuts the door and walks around the truck.

He gets in and shuts his door. Putting the key in the ignition, he looks over at me. "Where to? Lady's choice."

I'm not sure what the look on his face means. He looks guilty, as if he's doing something he shouldn't, but wants to anyway. Maybe I should just go home. "We don't have to go anywhere. You can just take me home or I can call a cab. I don't live that far."

"No way. You need to eat. I wouldn't have asked if I didn't want to." Now he acts like he's scared I'm going to back out. He is confusing the heck out of me by his sudden change in facial expressions. I feel like it's giving me whiplash.

"Okay, what about *BJ's Restaurant & Brewhouse*? I think it stays open until midnight." Everything should be closing down soon, leaving not much but partying and late-night movies.

"Lead the way," he says and turns the key, firing up the engine. The truck roars to life. I jump. I didn't even know trucks could sound like that. He chuckles in amusement.

"What's so funny? Do all trucks sound like this where you're from?" I look at him in wonder. I don't know why anyone would want to listen to all that noise while they drive.

He shakes his head, still silently laughing. "No, all trucks don't sound like this. Ryland has *Flowmaster* pipes installed. It's a country boy thing, I guess."

This southern thing, I have to admit, does have my interest piqued. I roll my eyes, teasingly, as he finally backs out of the parking lot and heads for the restaurant. I pull out my phone and quickly send Mom a text.

Kinzleigh: Just letting you know I'm fine. Heading to BJ's to eat with a friend. Be home in a little while.

Within five minutes I get a response.

Mom: Okay sweetie. Thank you for letting me know. I'll leave the front light on for you. We will talk tomorrow. Love you.

Kinzleigh: Love you too. Goodnight.

I place my phone back into my clutch and put on my seatbelt. We're heading down South Coast Highway when we pull into the restaurant. BJ's is still pretty busy for being so late. I look down, just now remembering I'm a little overdressed for this type of restaurant. "Maybe we should just order something to go. I'm not really dressed for this place."

He smiles and takes my hand, looking me over. He shakes his head. "You look perfect. Let's go."

He steps out of the truck before coming around the front to open my door. I put my heels back on my feet and turn toward the door, carefully placing my feet on the step bar. He is standing in the doorway. I place my hands on his shoulders and he picks me up by the waist to help me down, not straining at all.

He starts to close the door when I realize my purse is inside on the seat. "Wait, I need my purse."

I start to reach for it, but he takes my hand, shaking his head. "I invited you. Why would you need your purse?"

"Why would you pay for my food? This isn't a date." I begin twirling my finger in my hair, staring at him in curiosity. Usually when we go out as friends, whether a group or just a couple of us, we pick up our own tab, except for the people in relationships.

He begins running his hand through the back of his hair, looking lost in thought. He then shuts the door. "Date or not, where I come from girls don't pay for their food when a man is around. If my parents knew I took a girl to eat and didn't pay they would have a heart attack, and my dad is a cardiologist, so he's a health nut."

By the look on his face there is no point in arguing. He seems pretty sure of his stance on this subject. "If you insist, but it's really not necessary," I say. He sounds the alarm, locking the doors.

His smile comes back. "I insist," he teases. "Come on. Let's go eat. I'm pretty hungry myself." We begin toward the door of the restaurant, side by side.

He opens the door, allowing me to enter first. "Welcome to

BJ's Restaurant and Brewhouse. Is it just the two of you dining tonight?"

We come to a stop at a podium and see a tall slender girl with short, blonde, pixie-like hair. She looks from me to Breyson, stopping on him, and she bites her lip when her eyes look him over. For some reason the look she has toward him bothers me. I look at her and narrow my eyes.

I'm not jealous, but it's rude to look at a guy that way when he's with a girl. She has no idea I'm not his girlfriend. I did just kiss him, so that has to give me dibs for the night.

She is still staring at him and doesn't seem ashamed of it at all. I'm starting to get angry and I can feel the look on my facing showing it. "It's just the two of us. Can we get a seat somewhere private please?" Breyson asks beside me.

HA! Time to get a move on it, sweetie. The stare fest is over.

I start twirling my hair again as a competitive smile begins on my lips. It's a nervous habit I developed years ago. I turn to look at Breyson and he is staring at me, barely acknowledging the hostess, with that cocky grin on his face.

Dang it!

I really need to pay more attention to who's watching if I'm going to stare daggers at another girl enjoying the view of the man in my presence. He always seems to notice my stupidity. I can't even blame the girl; he's gorgeous and available. Come to think if it, he's probably a man-slut, so I'm better off not even thinking about it. The thought of him with another girl begins eating away at my thoughts. I have to think of something else.

The hostess quickly grabs the flatware and menus, suddenly seeming embarrassed by her behavior. "Of course, right this way." She then leads us to a booth in the back and sets the table. "Your server will be right with you."

We haven't been seated longer than about five minutes when a server appears. "Hi, I'm Anna, what can I get you kids to drink tonight?"

She's a little older, probably mid-thirties. Her brown hair is pulled back in a low ponytail. She has dark brown eyes and a set of dimples when she smiles. "I'll have a tropical tea, please," I say, glancing up at the server.

"Iced tea for me, please," Breyson adds, glancing over the menu.

"Tropical tea and iced tea," she repeats as she writes it down. "I'll be right back."

"Did your parents tell you where you're moving?" I look away from my menu at Breyson, who now has his hands crossed over his closed menu as if he knows what he wants.

Before I can answer, the waitress returns, setting down our drinks. "Are you guys ready to order or would you like another minute?"

"I think I'll have the seared Ahi salad, dressing on the side."

She writes it down on her notepad and looks to Breyson. "What'll it be for you, sweetie?"

"I'll have the grilled chicken club, light on the mayonnaise." The server takes our menus and leaves the table.

Breyson is looking at me, waiting on an answer as he adds sugar packets to his tea. I turn my nose up in disgust. He is going to end up in a diabetic coma doing that. I look back up and I shake my head. "No specifics."

"Oh, come on. Are we still at that? I just want to know a little bit about you besides your name and that you're a cheerleader with a brother." He raises his hands in surrender. "I promise I'm not a stalker."

He smiles at me. That smile I can't deny that makes me feel things I know I shouldn't.

Contemplating what I can give him to satisfy his desire for more information and my desire to keep it to myself, I sit in silence. I'm not one of those people that volunteers endless, meaningless details about myself to other people. There are some things even my best friend of seventeen years doesn't know. "Fine, if you must know. We are moving to the . . . south at the end of June. My father is a contractor and CEO of the family business my grandfather started right out of high school. He just signed a major contract to build strip malls across the entire southern region of the country. I guess this could change the face of the company, making it a multi-million-dollar enterprise. So now, Daddy dearest is moving my mother and me across the country and I'm not happy about it. Happy now?" I ask teasingly, hoping that is enough.

"All jokes aside, it might not be that bad. You might like the south." He winks playfully.

Of course, me, earning a D minus in the subject of Flirting 101, just sits here stupefied. Maybe it wouldn't hurt to get a few training tips from Presley. Oh no, what am I saying? That will never happen. "I'm guessing telling me the state in question would violate your confidentiality rule?" He raises a brow as he takes a sip of his tea.

"You catch on quickly." I laugh. Ask me what my reasons are, and to be honest, I'm not sure. Since I will never see him again after tonight, I don't really know what it would hurt to answer his personal questions, but if I don't answer his questions then I can't ask. The less I know about this sexy, southern boy, the better.

The server brings out our food and places it before us, along with the check. "Let me know if you need anything else. I'll keep a watch on your drinks. You kids have a good night and be safe."

accepted FATE

We enjoy our meal mostly in silence since it's almost closing time. Once Breyson pays for the food we stand to leave. I'm starting to feel the fatigue setting in. It's been a long day. "Is it okay if we call it a night? I'm really tired from today's string of events."

He looks disappointed, but nods in understanding. "Sure, just tell me where you live and I'll take you home." We get to the truck and he opens my door, helping me in.

Once in the truck, he starts the ignition. "How long are you here visiting Ryland?" I'm not sure why I asked since I don't plan on seeing him again. It just slipped out.

"I'm only here until next Friday, then I fly back." He pulls out of the parking lot and heads in the direction I instruct him.

We spend the remaining twenty minutes with casual small talk before pulling into my driveway. The censored lights come on at the garage. Pulling to a stop, he kills the headlights. I'm assuming, because there is something he wants to say. I gather my clutch in my hand and grab for the handle of the door. Turning to him I say, "Dinner was good, thank you. It was nice having some company aside from my friends."

When I start to open the door, he pulls on my left hand, stopping me. "Kinzleigh, wait. Is it okay if I see you again before I leave?" I get nervous. What am I going to say? I'm not sure I want to see him again. It's just going to further complicate things.

"I don't know . . ." I exhale, thinking. "I'll tell you what. If it's meant for you to see me again, you will. Obviously, we know some of the same people now, so we will see how things play out."

It's the only answer I can come up with. "You're not going to make this easy for me, are you?"

"The best things in life are never easy." I smile, repeating his quote from earlier, and open the door. "Goodnight, Breyson."

I reach the paved driveway and head for the front door, slipping inside and shutting it behind me. Placing my back against the cool wood of the door, I take a deep breath. After a few minutes, I hear him pull away.

Everything is dark but the spotlights over the fireplace, meaning my parents are in bed. Trying to avoid any questions tonight, I walk quietly to my room and shut the door. I am finally able to breathe easily for the first time tonight.

I walk into my bathroom and wash off my makeup, before changing into my favorite pink tank and a pair of short boxer shorts. I climb in my high king size bed, placing my phone on the bedside table to charge. As I slide underneath my pink satin sheets and comforter, my eyes grow heavy. I smile, remembering how much fun it was to do something out of the ordinary for once.

The last image I remember before falling into a peaceful slumber is two beautiful blue eyes and a smile to die for.

FIVE

Breyson

I pull away from Kinzleigh's house, heading back to Ryland's. My mind is in a cloud, running crazy. I doubt I'll get to sleep anytime soon and it's only twelve thirty in the morning. I would call Ryland, because I want more information on Kinzleigh, but I don't want to be a dick knowing he's probably at Presley's.

Surprisingly, Ryland only lives about five blocks from Kinzleigh. As I pull into the driveway I turn off the headlights— trying not to wake his parents—and park outside of the closed garage.

After killing the engine, I step out of the truck and walk through the fence to the backyard where the pool is located. It's a large infinity pool looking over a drop off. The house is set in the hills surrounding Laguna Beach. I love coming here, because it's so different than back home.

I stand in front of the pool, enjoying the view below and admiring the different lights gleaming throughout the hills. Most of the lights are off at his house, aside from the security lights.

Continuing across the edge of the pool toward the pool house, the door comes into view. I unlock it and open the door, stepping inside. His parents insisted this year that I sleep out here, so I can have my own space now that I'm seventeen and we're allowed to go out. Before, I always took the guest room down the hall from Ryland.

I didn't get a chance to come in here earlier, since we went straight to the beach as soon as I got here. And once we got back, I was busy catching up with Ryland and his parents before getting dressed in the main house.

Shutting the door, though, I realize his mom has already put my suitcase inside the door. I'm surprised Ryland hasn't called permanent dibs on this place as nice as it is. It's like having your own house.

The spotlights are dim over the fireplace wall, giving enough light to comfortably see. In the center of the large, mostly open room sits a black, leather sectional surrounding a rug and coffee table. Straight ahead on the center wall is an electric fireplace topped with a mantle and large, wall-mounted television.

The floors are all wood and to be what looks like bamboo, giving it an island oasis vibe. On the right-hand side of the room is a small kitchen behind a bar with stools, housing a stainless-steel refrigerator, some cabinetry, and a built-in cooktop, as well as a wine cooler fully stocked. Built into the bar is a sink and dishwasher, hidden by the bar top until you walk around it.

To the left-hand side of the furniture, there is a door leading to the back half of the pool house. There are small touches of decor all around that resembles the style of the main house.

I pick up my suitcase and head toward the bedroom after locking the entry door. When I walk in, a bedside lamp is lit on the nightstand next to a king size bed. It's covered in a white, down-filled comforter and made up with satin turquoise sheets and matching decorative pillows of different shapes and sizes; a few coral-colored ones thrown in.

    I walk over to the right and place my suitcase on the bench at the foot of the bed. The room smells like lavender and chamomile. I only know the scent, because I asked his mom when the smell had spread throughout the bedrooms of the house earlier. On the left wall there are two doors separated by a dresser. I assume one leads to a closet and the other into the bathroom.

    I grab my shower bag from my suitcase and head into the left-hand door. If I'm not going to be sleeping anytime soon, I might as well get the sand and feel of the beach off of me by showering again. I hate going to bed dirty. The sand leaves you feeling grimy and gritty.

    The bathroom has a long counter top with double sinks, ornamenting a basket filled with hand towels. Instead of the same bamboo floors throughout the rest of the house, they have tile in here. In one corner, cradled in a nook, is a Jacuzzi tub and a standing shower in the other corner, with a linen closet in the center. Across from the sink is a small closed in space containing the toilet.

    I remove a towel from the closet and throw it over the towel bar, then discard my clothes in front of the shower door, before turning on the water to begin warming it up. Getting in, I stand beneath the hot water, letting it run down my body, relaxing any tense muscles.

    My mind is running nonstop. I can't quit thinking about Kinzleigh. I don't know what it is about her that draws my attention. Maybe it's the mystery of her; the fact that I know nothing about her. Most girls practically throw themselves at me, dishing out any useless information they think I may grasp onto. It's no secret that girls like athletes, and if you're any good, that gives you an advantage.

She's different.

Most of the time I get bored with girls quickly, because most are all pretty much the same. I usually don't date seriously. I like to have fun. Go out with who I want. Natalie is the exception, because in high school it's frowned upon to sleep with a girl and ditch her, but after her behavior earlier today I remember why I avoided relationships in the past. I don't like restrictions. I like to be in control of myself and don't want to answer to a girl.

"Ugh!" I growl, aggravated, rubbing my hands over my face and through my wet hair. That's another issue I have to deal with. I want to spend more time with Kinzleigh before I leave, but it's not right to do that to Natalie no matter what the situation is. How much of a jerk would I be, though, to break up with her halfway across the country? And over the phone at that . . .

Do I really care? No, not really.

I *do* care enough I don't want to hurt her, but as a friend she deserves more than anything I will ever give her. I can't help that she thinks she loves me. In my defense, I tried to prevent it from happening by not getting close. She has never been around my family and vice versa. I don't call her and talk for hours at a time and we don't go on dates, not really anyway. Parties or places with a bunch of other friends, yes, but intimate dates like what I did with Kinzleigh tonight, no.

Personally, I have no idea how this happened. I don't give the girl much of anything besides my body. We have sex. That's about it. I know I'm going to be the biggest ass in the world, because as much of a friend as Natalie is, I want to see Kinzleigh again. It takes priority since my time is limited.

I shampoo my hair, trying to decide how I'm going to find Kinzleigh again now that I've decided I'm breaking it off with

accepted FATE

Natalie. The girl confuses the hell out of me. She seems attracted to me but refuses to release any information about herself. She is making this harder than it has to be.

Maybe I can get some information out of Ryland about her. I'm out of my league with her, because I've never had to chase after a girl's attention. Most of the time they are shoving their number at me or tracking mine down from someone else. That doesn't include the Facebook stalkers. I go to a large school, so it's not uncommon to go to school with people you don't know.

The most work I've ever had to put in is a little flirting or complimenting her looks, and just like that, I make it to at least second base, but mostly third. Some let me round the field and bring it home.

My dad has had me in sports since I was old enough to walk, particularly football. I've been the starting running back since my freshman year, and Dad has me on a strict workout program that keeps my body fitter than most guys my age. He's more hardcore than my coach.

I'm coming up blank on how to get to her. Maybe I just need to sleep on it and figure it out in the morning. I finish my shower and shut off the water. Securing my towel around my waist, I step out and dry off, before pulling on my black boxer briefs. Quickly towel drying my hair, I toss the towel and run my fingers through the damp strands.

As I'm getting ready to brush my teeth, Natalie's ringtone plays on my phone. My shoulders fall. I was hoping to get some sleep before dealing with this, but I guess it's better to do it sooner than later. I put down my toothbrush, about to walk into the bedroom to get my phone when the ringing stops. I guess I missed it. No reason to rush then. I quickly brush my teeth and head to the bed to get my phone.

Sitting on the bed, I grab my phone and unlock the screen. Pulling up the missed call from Natalie, I hit the call button and put it to my ear. It only rings once before she answers. "Hey."

"Hey, Nat, what's up?"

"Are you having a good trip?"

"I am. Look, Nat, we need to talk."

She sighs, her voice coming out a little off beat from before. "Okay... About what?"

This blows. I've never wanted to do this. It's easier to stay single. She is going to get hurt either way. I need to do this and get it over with. "Natalie, I feel like a dick to do this over the phone, but this relationship isn't working out anymore. The truth is we want different things. You've been a good friend for three years now, but I can't do this. We're stalling the inevitable and that's going to make it worse later. Next year we'll be going off to college... separately. I'm not looking to get married. You deserve to have what I can't give you, and there are plenty of guys willing to give it. But that guy isn't me."

She starts sniffling and I can tell she's crying. Dammit! Please don't do this to me. Just make it easy. "Breyson, please don't do this. If it's about earlier today, I'm sorry. Just forget I ever mentioned it."

"It doesn't have anything to do with... *that*; although, it did make me realize I will never give you what you want. It's okay to want love, Natalie, and to be loved, but that's not something I want. The feelings aren't there."

I can tell she's starting to panic at this point and the crying is getting heavier. "I don't need those things. Maybe I was just confused. I can be whatever you need, Breyson. You know we should be together. I won't let you throw it away. Whatever brought this on, we can fix it."

"Maybe not what you need right now, but it's what you want . . ." I wipe my hand down my face in frustration. "So stop lying to me, Natalie. You seem to forget I've known you for years. Stop settling for less than you could have to hold onto this relationship. I'm not even sure why you want to be with me when you know I don't feel that way for you. I never have. Our relationship is no different than friends with benefits but with an added title. I let you call me your boyfriend and don't sleep with anyone else."

"Oh, my god." The crying suddenly shuts off. "You've met someone, haven't you? Who is she?"

That wasn't part of the plan. I don't want to make matters worse, but I've always tried to be an honest person, even if it comes back to bite me in the end. "Yes and no. I did meet someone, but it's not like you think. Who she is isn't any of your business."

"Did you sleep with her?" Her tone is laced with venom. "That home-wrecking whore. Why would you allow some tramp to ruin our relationship?" She takes a breath. "You know what? Never mind. I forgive you. I know I'm not there to meet your needs. It's okay. Just please tell me you used a condom." I just sit here, eyes wide and in shock. She has lost her damn mind. Am I even hearing this correctly? No woman—unless she is a gold-digging whore—would be okay with that, and we are still in high school, so that can't be it.

Then my mind repeats what she said. A surge of anger shoots through my body at how she talked about Kinzleigh when she doesn't even know her. "Natalie, I'm going to say this one time, and you better listen closely, because I won't repeat myself. Don't ever talk about her or any other girl I may or may not take interest in that way again. You have no idea who she is or what she's like."

"But—"

"First of all, no, I didn't sleep with her. She isn't that kind of girl. But to be fair, I did kiss her. *I* kissed *her*. I admit it was wrong to do so before having this conversation. There, I said it. The rest was friendly. Secondly, what we will or won't do from here on out is none of your business, because you and I are no longer together. Lastly, my dick and whether or not I wear a condom is also none of your business unless I'm having sex with you. And I won't be anymore. You were my friend first, and I'd like for you to remain that way, but your behavior is borderline crazy."

"Ugh!" she growls out. "Fine, Breyson, go have your week of fun. Screw her and get it out of your system. I know I wasn't your first girl. I'm more worried about being your last. What happens in between doesn't matter. Don't think this is over for good. I didn't get you by giving up easily and I won't lose you that easily either. You're in a different place and she may seem like a new toy, but when you get home you'll come back where you belong. I'll grant you a pass this time and overlook your temporary stupidity. I'll even be faithful to you, because I want you to have the best. Just remember me when you're banging her."

What? It's almost insane enough to laugh. My maturity takes priority. I have officially had enough. If I had any doubts I would regret my decision, right now would confirm I don't. "Goodnight, Natalie."

I couldn't end the call fast enough. Throwing my phone at the end of the bed, I fall back on the pillow. Now I wonder if she's always been this crazy and I've somehow overlooked it because she's hot and I thought she was cool or if something just snapped.

Rolling over, I hug my pillow and close my eyes. All of a sudden, I'm exhausted.

SIX

Breyson

A beating sound occurs, waking me up. It must be the door. I rub my eyes with the palms of my hands. Who in the world could that be? It gets louder. "I'm coming. Hold on."

Throwing the covers off my body, I sit up, placing my feet on the floor beside the bed. Standing too fast, I sway a little, trying to regain my balance. I adjust my morning wood and walk toward the front door.

When I get to the living room and make it to the door, I pull it open. Ryland is standing on the other side, fully dressed in a yellow, nylon, button-down fishing shirt, khaki cargo shorts and boating shoes, topped off with a visor hat. He has a really big smile on his face. One that is not usually present on anyone this early in the morning. "Looks like someone had a good night," I say sarcastically, rubbing my stomach.

"Get dressed. We're going deep-sea fishing with Dad. Not even your smartass mouth can kill my mood," he says, that smile getting bigger. I don't even want to know what put it there, because I have a feeling I already know. Damn tail-chasing girl-loving boy.

"What time is it?" The sun isn't even over the clouds yet, so it can't be past like six or seven. "And how did you get home?" I run my hand through my messy hair, attempting to comb it.

"It's six fifteen. We have to be at the charter boat by seven." Jeez, how can he go out and party all night then be up ready to go strong at six o'clock?

"All right give me a few minutes. By the way, you owe me coffee for this."

He raises his brow in sarcasm. "Fine, I guess I'll take coffee duty, but hurry up Dad already has the truck loaded."

He pushes the door open and heads for the kitchen. Okay . . . I didn't think this kitchen was fully stocked too. I guess his mom thinks of everything.

Shutting the door, I head back to the bedroom in search of some clothes. It's been a while since I've been deep-sea fishing anyway. Fishing is one thing that has always relaxed me. Dad and me used to go back when I was a kid if he wasn't on call with the hospital.

Some of my fondest memories are just Dad and I sitting in a bass boat on one of our nearby lakes, making small talk and catching brim or bass mostly. Occasionally, he would take my brothers and I down to the coast and charter a boat for deep-sea fishing, but he doesn't have much time for that between clinic and call unless he requests off.

Even though Dad is a successful cardiologist, he always prided himself on raising active boys that had a love for anything and everything outdoors. He said even though he could comfortably provide for us, no kids of his were going to act like spoilt rich brats. He hated entitlement by association.

accepted FATE

He wanted us to learn responsibility and to know what it meant to earn money by sweat and hard work, so throughout the year but mostly during the summer, I help my grandfather on his cattle ranch. Fishing, hunting, work, and sports are things I know well.

I get to my suitcase and pull out my favorite khaki shorts and navy fishing shirt similar to Ryland's, along with my sneakers. I love these shirts. The material is thin to keep you cool, dries quickly when wet, and is vented at the back shoulders with a breathable mesh lining. Ten minutes tops and I'm dressed, all the way down to brushed teeth and deodorant—perks of being a guy.

Removing my polarized sunglasses from my bag, I pull the eyewear tether over my head, securing them around my neck, followed by sliding on my favorite ball cap. After losing several pairs between the river and ocean, I learned the hard way to buy a sunglasses strap.

I push my wallet into my shorts pocket. I remember I forgot to charge my phone, so I plug it in with the charger and leave it on the table. Now that Natalie is out of the picture, no one should need me. My parents and brothers know I made it. Grabbing up Ryland's keys from the nightstand, I head back in search of a highly needed caffeine fix.

Just as I'm walking toward the kitchen, Ryland meets me at the door, two to-go cups of coffee in hand. "You ready?" he asks, handing me a cup.

Taking one, I hand him his keys. "Yeah, I'm ready. Let's go."

"Keep them while you're here. There's a pool house key on them and I have an extra set. Mom is weird about keeping the doors locked, so you'll need them. I'll get them before you go home." He holds the door open, waiting on me to pass.

We get to his dad's brand-new Toyota Tundra to see him

standing against the hood with his arms crossed. As soon as he sees us coming he smiles. "You boys ready for some fishing?"

Ryland's parents are like second parents to me. Since we were next-door neighbors back home, we were also best friends, until he moved here three years ago, right after Beau died. Ryland is my cousin, as well as Beau's younger brother. Our moms are sisters. After he died they needed a change, a different place to grieve, I guess. Being around constant reminders of him was too hard for my aunt, so when Uncle Joe got a job opportunity they packed up and moved here.

"Yes, Sir. How's the fishing here?" I place my free hand in my pocket once I'm standing in front of him. Uncle Joe stands about five-foot-eleven with short brown hair and light blue eyes. He is a little heavier set, but not overweight, and wearing brown shorts with a red angler's shirt identical to ours, a straw hat topping it off. Uncle Joe is the fun, free-spirited one. He lives life to its fullest; always has. This move was good for them, because Beau dying sent a plague of depression for everyone around.

He wraps his arm around my shoulders, giving me a sideways hug. "I have to admit, it's not like Mississippi fishing, but California can hold its own." He winks and smiles playfully. "Let's go before we're late. I already put down a non-refundable deposit."

I walk toward the back of the truck and climb in the back seat, Uncle Joe and Ryland following closely behind. We start off toward the harbor where we are supposed to meet up with the charter crew.

Staring out the window, while watching everything pass by, I start to wonder what Kinzleigh is doing right now. She's probably sleeping with it being this early in the day. I want to ask Ryland about her, but now doesn't seem like the best time. I don't need the teasing from Uncle Joe that I've developed a crush.

I can't seem to get those beautiful green eyes out of my head. I don't know what it is about her, but I want to know her, even if just for a short time. She seems so closed off, though. I don't know how to go about it. Whatever it takes, I'm prepared to do. I have to hang out with her again before I head back home. If I don't, I know I'll regret it.

Lost in my thoughts, I didn't realize we were already at our destination. We pull into *Dana Point Harbor* and park in the mostly vacant lot. We must be the first trip scheduled. There are several boats still docked in the harbor, the water at a peaceful calm, standing still.

We get out and grab the things we brought for the day, starting with the cooler of drinks. We make it to the boat and meet the crew that's taking us out today. "Hello, it's good to have you all this morning. My name is Jeff and I'm going to be your guide today," he says, extending his hand to Uncle Joe. "You guys ready to get started?"

Jeff looks to be around his mid-thirties, taller and leaner around the middle than Uncle Joe. He has a tan that's only obtained by daily hours beneath the sun, his teeth whiter against the dark contrast of his skin. His jaw is long, his eyes bright, and his hair is the color of chestnuts, peeking out of his khaki fishing hat. Sea foam green tee shirt with the logo of his tour company and swim trunks reflect his easygoing personality.

"Absolutely, I've been waiting for this all week. I'm Joe Reeves. My nephew, Breyson, is visiting from Mississippi, so I want to show him how fishing is done in the Pacific Ocean." Uncle Joe says it with a smile on his face, looking at me. He then looks at Ryland and squeezes him on the shoulder. "This is my son, Ryland."

"I think we can handle that." the guy returns, shaking his hand.

He looks at me and winks. "Well, let's get started while it's still cool outside."

We walk onto the boat and the guide starts discussing the day's events as well as going over standard safety information for liability purposes. He hands each of us a life jacket and shows us to our spot, along with getting our gear in order for the day.

The boat pulls away from the harbor, so I utilize the time it takes to get to our first anchor to ask Ryland about some wanted information. We're standing on the deck, elbows resting on the railing, looking out at the ocean as the boat begins churning through the water. "Hey, Ry, can I ask you a question?"

He looks at me, studying me with curious eyes. "Sure, what's up?"

"You know a girl named Kinzleigh?" Ryland was out surfing during the time Kinzleigh was at the beach, so I'm not sure if he knows who I'm referring to or not, but I am hoping he does.

"Kinzleigh Baker?"

Ahh . . . finally, a little more information on Miss Secretive.

"I don't know," I say. "I never caught her last name. She has light, curly blonde hair and bright green eyes. Perfect body . . ." I trail off at the memory of her.

"Yep, that's her. Why do you ask?" He now has his eyebrows pulled together as if he's honestly curious. He takes hold of his visor bill and begins moving it up and down across his forehead.

"Just curious I guess. I had a run in with her on the beach yesterday while you were out on the water. Then, last night I did something stupid at that party, so I took off to the beach to clear my head and found her crying . . ."

I don't even have the chance to finish before Ryland cuts in. "What the hell, dude? Are you holding out on me now? What happened at the party? All you had to do was call me, bro. Now I feel like shit for leaving you alone."

"It's not important. Besides, I handled it. I wasn't going to call you when you were clearly . . . busy. You never chase after a girl, so I know she must be something."

A smile takes form on his face before he turns serious again. "Wait, did you say she was crying? I have never, and I mean ever, seen Kinzleigh cry. The girl comes across about as emotionally breakable as a cement wall. She's a sweet girl but doesn't take crap off anyone. Is she okay? Presley didn't mention her being upset. The two are normally glued at the hip. The only reason she wasn't at Logan's was because of her brother."

What happened with her brother? "She said her parents told her at dinner they are moving at the end of June. She doesn't really like to give out information about herself, apparently. I couldn't get much out of her. What happened with her brother that would keep her from going to a party? Did someone do something to her?"

A flash of rage floods my body at the thought of someone trying to hurt her. I begin clenching my fists unconsciously. "Calm down, Rambo. If you just met her, what's up with the caveman act?" he asks raising his brows.

"Shut up."

"Moving, huh? That sucks. I wonder if Presley knows? That's going to be interesting to watch. If you didn't know any better, you would think they were twins separated at birth."

He laughs. "Anyway, about Konnor and Logan . . . I don't like putting people's business out there, but since you're leaving I don't see how keeping it a secret is relevant, just keep it to yourself. Konnor, her brother, and Logan, the guy you met at the party, were best friends until about a month ago. Konnor dated this girl Sophia for three years. He was obviously pretty crazy about her from the way he acted. In my opinion, the girl was a whore in training by the way she flirted with *everyone* when he wasn't around, but what do I know? The guy is way better than her anyway. He's too nice and everyone loves him. She was a classic spoiled rich girl that always made sure she got what she wanted, regardless of what it did to anyone else. Not to mention, he's the best quarterback around these parts. He's a football star, kind of like you and Braxton."

"He dominated the rankings all four years he played. I'm really not sure how they lasted as long as they did, thinking about it now. She was like two different people. The perfect little girlfriend when he was with her and always flirting behind his back when he was away. And I mean like bent over, tits hanging out cleavage or rubbing on a guy's thigh in class under the table, even with his friends and teammates. But no one had the heart to tell him. Sophia could do no wrong. He was sickly in love with her."

He pauses. "God, some girls can manipulate . . ." I know where he's going, but he continues. "It wasn't because he couldn't get anyone else either, because the guy could get any girl he wanted. I overheard conversations at parties when he walked into the room and saw the stares. They were all lined up waiting for them to break up. Long story short, someone, names shall not be called, finally got tired of her whoring around behind his back and tipped him off. He came to Logan's in an angry panic. I guess he thought it was a joke at first, but after seeing the look on everyone's shocked faces he burst through Logan's locked bedroom door and found them going at it. Logan was trashed, so I don't even know how he was able to get it up, but Sophia didn't seem all that drunk at all.

accepted FATE

I'm telling you, she's a bitch. He freaked out and went all ape shit, put the guy in the hospital. I still would be surprised if that was even the first time she cheated. No one would say after they saw what he did to Logan. It was brutal. They haven't spoken since. The asshole hasn't even tried to apologize. He just keeps telling people he doesn't remember anything until Konnor walked in. Maybe him not pressing charges was his fucked-up apology. I actually like Logan. He's cool as shit and throws good parties, and I get it. I've been that drunk before, but fucking your best friend's girl, whether accidentally or purposely deserves an apology. Could you imagine that shit? Walking in on your girl riding another guy's cock... That shit is messed up. Kinzleigh and her brother are really close, so she cut her ties with anything Logan related."

Great, now I feel like a dipshit for going. Sounds like a charming guy, I think sarcastically. That's going against all bro code. "I want you to help me see her again. We went and ate at BJ's last night after we talked on the pier for a while. The girl is harder to crack than embedded code."

He's shaking his head, trying to hold back laughter. I don't see what is so funny. "Dude, there is no way you're getting anywhere with Kinzleigh Baker. Do you know how many guys have tried, me included? The girl doesn't date. She doesn't even flirt. I'm pretty sure she is still a virgin. She's a really nice girl, but all she does is cheer and practice flips or whatever it is that cheerleaders do. I actually think she despises guys, with the exception of her brother. If she didn't before Logan screwed up, she does now."

"Well, considering I kissed her last night, maybe I can knock down some of those man-hater walls. If her tongue in my mouth was any indication of how she felt about guys there is hope, for one, at least. I don't usually kiss and tell, but I'm getting aggravated. Are you going to help me or not?" I don't want to hear about all the guys that have tried to seduce her or get with her, and some that possibly slept with her. I can feel my veins popping out of my neck.

Ryland is staring at me with his mouth wide open, as if he's in shock. *My interest in her isn't so funny now, is it?* "Are you joking? You kissed Kinzleigh Baker? How the hell did you pull that off? I'm pretty sure she hasn't ever kissed anyone; none that I've heard about anyway. No one would keep that a secret. How did *you* manage to be the one to get to her?"

He seems genuinely curious, but I have given him way too much information already. I am a very private person. I don't get into the gossip ring of sharing worthless information just to showboat with other guys. Most of the guys that sit around talking about their conquests are lying anyway. I've seen too many girls' reputations get ruined because of a stupid guy running his mouth. "Ryland, you're my cousin and best friend, but *how* is really irrelevant at this point, don't you think?"

"You're really serious about this? If Konnor gets word, he will be at my doorstep the second he can get to you. He knows she's a good girl and her virtue is still intact, so he takes his protection of her overboard. I've seen the guy in action. Do you really want to deal with that over some girl? Wait, don't you have a girlfriend?" I'm getting tired of all his questions, but he's my only option at getting anywhere with this topic.

"Yes, I'm serious. I wouldn't be having this conversation if I weren't. I'm not trying to sleep with her. I just want you to help me get to the same place as her. If her brother needs to discuss anything, you can send him my way. I have a little sister, so I can handle a man-to-man conversation. Not that it's any of your business, but I broke up with Natalie last night."

"No joke? Why? I thought that was a sure thing. Plus, you're only here until Friday and then you'll be thousands of miles away from Kinzleigh." I am really starting to wonder about the questions. He seems awfully persistent in trying to sway me away from this subject, almost as if he wants her himself. He did say he tried. Now, I'm getting pissed, but he's my cousin.

"It was coming and needed to be done, regardless of Kinzleigh or not. So, you going to help me, or do I need to go another route?" I raise my brow questioningly as a smirk takes place, mirroring his earlier.

"Bro, you know I will help you; just getting the facts down. Presley is having an end of the year pool party tomorrow. She should be there. I think Presley said they leave for Cabo in a few days or a week. I can't remember."

"Are we invited?" I really hope we are, because I may crash it regardless.

"To the pool party? You know it," he says with his cocky grin in place.

"Okay, awesome. Let's catch some fish." I need to pass the time until this party.

We head back over to the rest of the group to bait up our lines and get everything ready for a day of fishing. I usually do well at anything I try, given my competitive nature. Today we're fishing for Blue Marlin, my favorite. Since it's heavier fish and bait than normal small game fishing, the charter provides all the fishing rods and bait.

I'm standing on the deck and I cast out my line beside Ryland. Uncle Joe and the rest of the charter crew are on the other side. The sun is coming up, so I pull my sunglasses over my eyes from where they are dangling around my neck. Looking across the water, I try to formulate a plan for this pool party.

I want to get Kinzleigh alone. She doesn't seem to open up at all around other people. She acts like she has some kind of phobia against males. Remembering her perfect body and the things Ryland said about guys trying to get with her, I know it's probably going to be a challenge. I can't stand the thought of another guy putting his hands on her. I barely know her and I already feel protective.

My knuckles turn white, grasping the pole. The thought of another man putting his lips on her and touching her in intimate places is like toxic venom running through my blood. I can't breathe and I feel weak. I don't even notice the tug on my reel.

"Breyson."

My eyes see nothing but the reels in my thoughts of her biting her soft lips and her big, beautiful eyes closing in pure ecstasy at the pleasure of someone else. How many guys have tried to sleep with her?

"Breyson!"

My vision turns red and blurred. My fists hurt from how hard I'm grasping the rod in them.

"Breyson, what the hell? Sink your line before the fish gets off!" I finally realize where I am and what is going on. Dammit, I've got to get a grip. This has never once in my entire life happened to me. I don't know what is wrong with me. I prop the bottom of the pole into my lower abdomen for support and jerk the line to sink the hook into the mouth of the fish.

Quickly, I begin reeling in my line. I can feel the fish playing tug-o-war as I use all of my strength to get it to the boat. From the weight on the other end and the amount of strength it is taking, I can tell it's going to be a good size catch— a prize.

I finally get the fish close to the boat and Ryland scoops it into the net. He cuts the line from the fish and places it in the storage compartment of the boat, not even wanting to measure it. Placing his hands on his hips, he narrows his eyes at me, as if trying to figure something out. "Mind telling me what is going on with you? I've never seen you spaced out like that and you looked like you were seconds away from breaking that rod in half and ready to stab someone."

I lock the rod into the pole lock on the deck of the vessel until I re-bait my line. I rub my hands over my face in aggravation. "Dude, I don't know. I can't get this girl out of my head. It's driving me crazy. You know me. I never get this way. Maybe it's because she's not easy like the rest of the girls I usually mess around with. I don't know, but I've got to fix it. I can't handle all this shit in my head."

He looks at me and a knowing smirk takes place over his face. He grabs me by the shoulders. "You, my friend, have the hots for Kinzleigh Baker. The one thing every guy that has crossed paths with her has had, but never actually been able to obtain. She's every man's dream, but that's all it's ever been for the rest of us—a dream. I'm going to be honest, so you don't get your hopes up. Several have tried and gotten nowhere. I'll help you get on her radar, but man, I'm not going to lie. You're going to need a lot of luck, because I've seen many crash and burn when it comes to her. Maybe you'll be different for her. For your sake, I hope you are."

He is not helping the situation any. The last thing I want to hear is the many failed attempts of men trying to make her theirs. "Man, would you shut up? That is the last thing I want to know." I pull my cap off and throw it down the deck.

He watches me act like an idiot, not saying a word. I've been known to have anger problems. "Be realistic, bro. Even if she gave you the time of day, what are you going to do when you have to leave six days from now? Kinzleigh is not the kind of girl you screw and run back to Mississippi with another notch in your belt. She's the kind of girl you take home to meet your parents; the kind of girl you marry. She is a rare find; a diamond in the rough. Once you get a girl like her, you try everything in your power not to screw it up, because chances are you won't find another one like her in your lifetime. Don't think about yourself, think about her. It wouldn't be fair. You know every girl in your clutch falls for you. Am I wrong? Look at the way things turned out with Natalie. If you want to have a good time, I'll introduce you to the right girls, but she's not it."

I pull away from his grasp and cross my fingers behind my head, exhaling for relief. If I really think about it, he makes sense. I didn't think this through. What am I going to do when I go back home? Most grown adults don't keep up anything long distance, much less high school kids. I'm definitely not anywhere in the realm of marriage.

Running my hand through my hair, pulling it in different directions, I sigh. "You're right. I guess I haven't really thought about it. We'll just go to the party and have fun. There was a cute girl last night that came on to me. Maybe I can revisit that offer." I try to smile, but it isn't real.

"Nice, who was it?" He crosses his arms over his chest.

"Lexi, I think. I wasn't really into it then."

He bites his lip a little, trying to hide a smile. "Now we're talking something that can be done. Piece of cake."

"Aight, cool. I guess it's settled then." I try to get in a good mood, but it was just slaughtered. "Let's get this done. You know I can't go home until I beat you." My competitive smile takes place.

Ryland stands there and studies me a few more seconds. He seems to be contemplating something by the way he is rubbing his chin with his fingers. "Let's do this."

We spent the rest of the day fishing. Once I got my head back in the game, I did pretty well. Ryland ended up with a catch of five at the day's end and me with seven. Uncle Joe had four. We're headed back to the house and it's about four forty-five in the afternoon. I'm staring out the window, index finger propped over my lip and thumb resting under my chin with my elbow on the door, lost in thought.

"You boys have fun?" Uncle Joe asks while looking in the rearview mirror.

"Sure did, Uncle Joe. Thanks again," I say, never looking his way. I can feel Ryland staring at me, but I can't bring myself to look away from the window. I can't concentrate on anything, nothing but her. It's starting to anger me at this point. I feel like hitting something. I tap my knuckles against the window, trying to relieve the tension before I actually do hit something.

Everything Ryland said was true, though. I have to figure out a way to forget about her. I can tell she isn't just a hook-up kind of girl and that seems to make forgetting her more difficult. Maybe we can just be friends.

Friends are better than nothing at all; although, I don't know how I'm supposed to do that after getting a taste of those sweet lips. I have never been much of a kisser before. Personally, I think it's too intimate for what I'm generally interested in. It screams commitment. It's just an easier way for a girl to develop feelings. Girls at my school know by now relationships aren't my thing.

Natalie is the closest I came to one and it was evident what that was.

With Kinzleigh it was different. It was like I couldn't control myself around her. The first thing I wanted to do and the last was to kiss her. Getting a taste had to be the smartest and stupidest thing I've ever done. Like a drug addict thinking he can be done after one taste of his potent poison.

Maybe Ryland is right. Maybe I just need to find the closest hot girl and get her out of my system. That's exactly what I'm going to do. I've made up my mind. The problem is trying to get my mind to actually believe it'll work.

We pull into the drive and start walking to the pool house when Ryland breaks me from my thoughts. "Hey, cuz, you want to go out tonight? I know a few things going on."

We get to get door and unlock it. "I'm kind of beat. Mind if we just stay in tonight? Watch some movies maybe . . ." I say. His mouth drops a little. I guess I do sound like a total douche. I'm usually the first one to be up for a party, especially on Saturday night. Walking in the pool house, I head toward the couch and grab the remote as I sit down.

"You're really bummed about her, aren't you? I thought you were just hot on her, dude. I didn't know it was like *that*. Crap, man," he says, removing his visor and running his fingers through his longer, messy hair, curled in all the right places to add to his whole surf boy vibe.

"Nah, you're right. It wouldn't be right. She's just different from any girl I've come across. I don't know, maybe I do just need to hook-up with someone. Maybe it's all this Natalie crap coming at me. I just don't feel like partying tonight."

He grips the back of the couch with both hands. He's staring at me as I browse through the channels. I can see him through the corner of my eye. "I'm about to head to *Redbox* and get some DVDs. Any requests? I'll get a pizza on the way back. Drinks should be in the fridge."

"Okay, cool. Just no chick flick and I'm good." I go to grab for my wallet, but he starts shaking his head.

"Keep it. I got it this time." He pulls out his phone and starts touching the screen before holding it to his ear. "I'll be back shortly." He turns and heads for the door, but right before he shuts it I make out the first few words of his conversation. "Presley, I need a favor."

I wonder if he's making a stop on his way. Didn't the guy just get some last night?

SEVEN

Kinzleigh

I've been hard at work since ten o'clock this morning with my cheerleading coach. I didn't even take a break for lunch. I have too much on my mind. For starters, the images that my traitorous brain decided to play like a movie during what could have been a peaceful night's sleep. I woke up in a complete sweat, scared to go back to sleep at the thought of returning to one beautiful half-naked body on top of mine, kissing me senseless. The best way to control its wandering abilities are to focus on my stunting.

Coach Andy grabs me by the waist and throws me into a liberty. My knee shakes as I try to lock my right leg into position. "Stick it, Kinzleigh!" he yells as he struggles to hold me steady. I'm always the flyer, because of my size, and I'm really good at it. I rarely have problems sticking and for the first time I feel like an amateur. As I'm pulling in my left foot toward my knee to finish, I lose my balance and fall, Coach catching me on the way down. "Where's your head at today, girl? You're never this clumsy, and I've worked with you for seven years now."

Those are words I never hear from my coach and it infuriates me. Nothing ever gets in my way of cheerleading. "Just a slip up, Coach. My center was off a little. I must have gone up unbalanced. Easy fix. Let's go again."

He repositions on the mat behind me, placing his hands around my waist again. "One man stunt this time. Are you ready?" he asks into my ear.

Andy has been my coach since I was ten. He's about an average height at five-foot-ten and has light blond hair and honey colored eyes. He's the strongest person I know. He is about thirty now and takes coaching very seriously. He has the body to prove it. He also coaches the university squad nearby. Once Mom realized the cheerleading dream was not going away, she looked up the best coach around. She told me if I was serious then I was going to be trained by a professional. I think most of it was to keep her baby safe from trying to do my own stunts, but turns out I love him.

I nod, slightly squatting to give me some extra height in my jump and place my hands on his wrists. "What kind?"

"Just go into a tuck once you're in the air, but don't forget to lock on your way down. I want it clean and flawless. Got it? One, two . . ." He lifts me by the waist and throws me high into the air. I perform the perfect tuck before he grabs me by the middle of each foot at chest level and extends his arms high above his head. "Tighten your form, Kinzleigh," he says, looking up at my arms wavering slightly in the 'V' position. "That would be a deduction on your score at competition. You need to pay closer attention. You're really off today. Get ready to de-mount." He lowers me back down to chest level and tosses me just high enough to cradle me in his arms.

He sets me on my feet. Crap! This freaking sucks, and I won't allow myself to screw up. I can't remember the last time Coach had to correct me, especially not more than once in a matter of twenty minutes. "I want to go again."

"Maybe we need to call it a day or work on something else. I think your mind is elsewhere and it's showing in your form."

"No, Coach, I'm good. Let's go again." I refuse to show weakness, especially in front my coach. "What about the scorpion? You up for it? I need the practice now more than ever. You know I have tryouts coming up in a few weeks for the national all-star squad. I cannot fail. I've been working for this too long."

This is one of the things I have been waiting on for several years now. This is the one thing I have trained and shed sweat and blood for. My parents will not take this away from me. I don't care where they move me. I have been waiting for my tryout invitation since I applied freshman year and I have only had my acceptance invitation since last December. They send out invitations six months before tryouts to give you ample time to train. I was so excited, because it came the week before Christmas.

There are four divisions across the country. Usually, it's based on the territory that you live in; however, it is not a rule. Trust me, I have seared them to my memory bank. To even try out you have to apply and then after extensive review of your application and credentials, wait on an invitation. The board of judges only picks the best girls in the country and there are only a limited number of open spots each year. They only invite high school seniors and college age applicants for tryouts and they compete all over the world.

To even get a tryout says a lot about your skill level and talent. If I make the team, I will have experiences most people only dream about. Plus, every win, members get a bonus of cash and prizes.

Before, I wasn't really worried about the money, but now that my parents are trying to shatter my dreams, I need every penny if I want to move back to California after senior year.

"Kinzleigh, I've known you for years, so why don't you just tell me what's going on in that head of yours. It may help you practice getting it off your chest." Coach knows I never talk about my problems, so I don't know why he is even asking. Heart-to-heart chats make things awkward for everyone involved since no one really understands except oneself. Some things are better left locked away.

"Can we just practice? I don't want to talk about it. You know me, Coach. This is how I deal with my crap." I'm hoping this can be the end of this conversation. I never deal with problematic conversation well. It makes me nervous.

"Very well then. I guess we can do a few more mounts," he says, looking at his watch. "It's almost six. We've been at this since this morning. Are you sure you don't want to call it a day?"

He smiles, because he knows me better than anyone. Even covered in sweat, as I am, and feeling the soreness in my muscles, I could do this well into the night. The right side of my lip pulls up into a slight smile as I shake my head in response. "I didn't think so."

He winks and turns to walk to the trampoline. "Come on. We're done with lifts for the day. We can practice on your tucks and back handsprings for a while. You may be small, but I've been lifting you since you warmed up this morning. My arms need a rest," he says teasingly.

I follow him to the trampoline and hop on. I begin securing the halter from the bungee cords that hang from the ceiling beams. We always practice on the trampoline if we're tired or learning something we haven't done very much and then take it to the ground once we're ready. I'm securing the last strap when I hear shuffling feet behind me.

"There's my favorite bi-atch!" That's a voice I would know anywhere—the one and only Presley Dunagin. Why is she here? I have a hard-enough time getting Presley here when she has to practice for the team, much less during her summer vacation.

I turn around to face her. By the looks of her wardrobe she isn't here to practice. She has her hair curled in big waves down her back and her makeup is heavier, as if she's going out. She's wearing white denim shorts and a black low cut, three-quarter sleeve top with tan wedges. Her cleavage is peeping out of her neckline. I shouldn't be surprised. Ever since she came to school freshman year bearing full C-cups, she has them on display whenever possible.

"What are you doing here? I thought I was supposed to meet you at your house tomorrow morning to help get everything ready for the pool party." I quickly scan my memory, trying to remember if there was something I forgot I was supposed to do. My mind has been on overload lately, so it's definitely a possibility, but nothing comes to mind.

She walks right past me with her eyes set on Coach Andy like she's a woman on a mission. On top of Coach being the best around, he's also young, attractive, and a hunk of muscle. I'm used to the drool plastered on females when in his presence. Even with Presley in all her promiscuity, this is a new one for her. She is not even eighteen yet and Coach is thirty.

I turn back to face Coach in complete confusion. The look on his face is as if he just saw a ghost. He looks nervous, and knowing Presley's reputation for getting what she wants, I can understand why. Poor guy. He has always been nothing but professional. She stops in front of him, barely leaving a space between them. "Presley, do you mind telling me what's going on?"

She turns back to look at me with a guilty gleam in her eye. Oh no, what has she done? "I just came to borrow you for the rest of the evening. Something suddenly came up." A seductive smirk takes form on her face, before looking back to Coach Andy. She places her index finger right over his navel and begins lightly trailing it up his torso. "You wouldn't have a problem with cutting this practice session a little early, now would you, Coach?"

He looks over to me, turning a little pale. "We'll pick this up in a couple of days, Kinzleigh. Just give me a call to set up the details, okay?" He starts backing away from Presley, looking side to side. I imagine he is terrified of another parent seeing a seventeen-year-old rubbing up on a grown man. Rumors can ruin a perfectly innocent person now days, and I don't have a problem admitting that Presley is jailbait.

I sigh, defeated. I might as well see what Presley is up to. She always gets her way. I know this by now. I look to Coach apologetically. "Okay, Coach. I guess we'll call it a day."

As he turns and walks rather quickly toward the office, stopping only long enough to gather his belongings, I start to unstrap myself from the harness that I'm still standing in. I think I was in such shock by the series of events taking place that I couldn't remove myself from the confinement of the trampoline.

Presley is making her way toward the entry of the trampoline. Her face now appears totally serious, as if nothing out of the ordinary just happened. What did just happen? I have no idea, but I'm going to find out. "Presley, what the heck was that? Do you want Coach to stop training you? It isn't like he needs the money with the mile-long waiting list of other girls wanting to train with him. What are you doing here? I was a little busy. You could have called."

She's smiling, setting me off further. My small, five-foot-two body comes flying off the trampoline, arms wailing in every direction as I yell at her. "If you need me to be backup for you to get with some guy, fine, but ask. Some of us have actual important things going on in our lives," I say harshly, sounding a little angrier than I meant.

"Are you done yet?" she asks sarcastically, as if daring me to continue. "This right here," she says, waving her finger in my direction, up and down my body, "is exactly why I'm here. Look at you, Kinzleigh. Do I really need to elaborate?"

Now calming down from my earlier burst of anger, I look myself over, trying to figure out what is wrong with my clothes or body. I wouldn't think workout clothing is anything outside of the realm of normal. I'm wearing black yoga shorts and a neon pink sports bra.

The only place I dress this way is practice or training with Coach, because it is easier to stunt and flip in fitted clothing. My hair is pinned up in a tight bun on my head to keep it out of my face and I'm barefooted with my black ankle sleeves on to keep from twisting an ankle. I'm glistening with sweat, but I've been practicing all day, for goodness' sake.

Now I'm confused, which isn't uncommon around Presley. After seventeen years of friendship, I still am not sure what all goes on in that head of hers. Her thinking is unlike anyone else. Her brain should be left to science one day. "What's wrong with my clothes? I always dress like this for practice," I say, walking to my gym bag to grab a towel. Presley is following closely behind, making a loud noise on the floor with her shoes. I grab my hand towel and begin wiping the sweat from my forehead and the rest of my face, then around my neck. I throw the now damp cotton back in the bag and grab my bottle of water.

Taking a refreshing sip, coating my dry mouth, I sit on the small set of bleachers utilized for family watching practice. Standing in front of me, Presley crosses her arms over her chest and narrows her eyes at me. "You really don't get it, do you? Look around, Kinzleigh. It's Saturday night and we're on summer vacation. Look where you are. You're wearing gym clothes, no makeup, and covered in sweat from head to toe. I get that you have the national tryouts coming up and you want to make the squad, but come on, Kinzleigh, you know you're going to make it. You're the best cheerleader around. The most driven. You don't have to have sex and drink alcohol if you don't want to, but you need to get out more. You need to experience life while you're young. I try my best to leave you alone, but it's time I put my foot down. You're my best friend, and it's my duty to keep you from wasting away like an old maid. This is supposed to be the best time of our lives, and I'm not letting you waste it away by practicing and staying at home with dear ole Mommy and Daddy. You won't get a do-over of your senior year."

She comes to sit beside me and grabs my hand. I look down at our hands fitted together. This is definitely awkward. That's one reason Presley and me get along so well. We are not emotional people. We don't entangle our hearts to men or anyone else like the rest of the girls do.

It's easier to keep your heart to yourself, to worry about one heart instead of two. If it makes me seem like a heartless person then so be it, but at least I know it will forever be intact and completely mine. Maybe when I'm older and have accomplished all of my dreams I will consider sharing it. Call me selfish. I don't really care.

She sighs as she stares off across the building. It's a large warehouse packed with mats, trampolines, harnesses and swings. There is a small lobby up front and an office. "What are you afraid of, Kinzleigh? I get that you want to keep your heart out of the equation, because you and I are one and the same, but you don't have to fall in love to have fun, you know."

Presley, of all people, should understand. Corey was as close as she has ever come to giving her heart away, and I am quite positive she wasn't in love with him. It was more so *we've been friends since kindergarten kind of I love you.*

Besides, look how that turned out. She ripped his heart out and stomped it to pieces, because they didn't share the same type of love. He has loved her since childhood. He finally got her to notice him in a way other than friends sophomore year. He unintentionally smothered her and became overly jealous and controlling. No man will ever control Presley. The girl has a mind of her own and isn't afraid to use it. She's beautiful and bold and turns guys' heads everywhere she goes.

If he were smart, he would have embraced her qualities. In return for his behavior, she ruined him for all other females while she carries on unaffected. It's sad really, how one person can forever change the life of another.

Love is cruel that way. Two people passionately and completely in love are the minority in a pool of people who love one they can't have. The best thing to do is avoid it at all costs. Protect your heart from heartache by caging it up and keeping it hidden from anyone else.

From anything I have ever seen, getting involved with someone does nothing but emotionally drain you, so why lead someone on when you have no intention of putting your heart out there for the taking.

So many indulge in love, hoping to get the fairy tale they read in books and see in movies, but that's not reality. Reality is hard, ugly, and painful. It doesn't take one with an experienced broken heart to know that's the way it is. Just look around you. You will see pain-stricken and brokenhearted people everywhere. I just think it's easier to avoid it than try to pick up the pieces after it's said and done.

She snaps her fingers in front of my face. I guess I was lost in thought. I turn toward her and straddle the bench. I shrug my shoulder at her. "I don't know what you want me to say, Presley. I just have other priorities in my life right now. I get that you're worried, but my parents have put a lot on me and I need to remain focused. You're just like me, but instead of focusing on cheerleading you focus on guys, in the plural form, to keep from giving your heart away. That's okay, but that's you, not me. I don't need a guy to make me happy."

I reach into my bag to pull out my pink *Fudpuckers* t-shirt. In the bottom of my bag lies a brochure size BJ's menu. How did that get in there? I wonder, my brows coming together before I am reminded of last night?

Suddenly, I imagine what Breyson is doing. The boy has a gorgeous smile and body from what I saw that day at the beach. I have never seen a guy my age that built and defined. Maybe he is as involved in something as I am with cheerleading. My lips tingle like they did after he kissed me. I begin fanning myself. Gosh, it's really hot in here. I guess Coach forgot to turn down the air.

"I call bullshit," she says, a little snippy.

"Excuse me?" Now what is she talking about? She still hasn't told me why she is actually here. I slip on my shirt and designer flip-flops, before removing my keys from my bag, zipping it up.

"You may have everyone fooled, Kinzleigh, including yourself, but I know you better than anyone and I know you were affected by a certain southern charm. Get up, you're coming out with me. I'm not taking no for an answer."

I drop my head down, resting my forehead into the heel of my hand. "Presley, I'm not even dressed to go anywhere. I've been sweating, and I would imagine I don't smell pleasant, even with deodorant. Can I please just go home?"

Her mischievous look comes on and she shakes her head. "I thought you might say that, so I grabbed some clothes and your makeup bag from your room. The bag is in my car. You can shower in the locker room."

She must have planned all this out. I stand, as does she. "When did you go to my house?" She throws her arm around my neck, towing me toward the door.

"Now, now, how did you think I knew to come here? If you don't want to be found, you should become less predictable." I roll my eyes as we walk closer to her white Mercedes convertible.

She bends over into the car to retrieve my bag from the passenger seat. The top is down. As she reaches over the driver's seat, her pelvis resting on the rolled down window, her feet lift slightly off the ground, leaving her rear in the air. I chuckle lightly. Presley can't do anything the easy way. Could she not have just walked to the passenger side? "Where are we going, anyway, that is so important? Some big summer party you forgot to mention? A concert?"

She pulls the bag across the seat and lifts it from the car, turning around. Extending her hand toward me with the handles resting in her palm she says, "Uh uh uh. A girl never tells her secrets. You go get fabulous and leave the rest to me. I will be right beside you to keep you company, so don't even think about bailing on me," she says, and pops a piece of gum in her mouth.

"Oh, heavens, what would I ever do without you?" I roll on the sarcasm thick, before grabbing the bag and turning on my heels, walking back inside toward the locker room.

She skips up beside me, slapping me playfully on the butt like baseball players do, catching me off guard. I yelp. "Lucky for you you'll never have to find out. Get a move on it, sister. We have places to be and people to see."

Walking into the locker room, I set my duffle bag on the countertop. There is no telling what Presley packed. The girl doesn't have conservative in her vocabulary. I exhale and begin sifting through the bag. I pull out necessities for showering, my makeup bag, the folded bundle of clothing, and my shoes.

Surprisingly, it isn't as bad as I expected. She packed white denim capris, a coral and salmon candy-striped, open shoulder sleeveless that meets at the neckline, front and back, and my favorite coral sandals. "Not bad, huh?" she says, leaning over behind me, directly beside my ear.

I jump. "Crap! You scared me. Do you have to do that?"

She moves beside me and turns her back to the countertop, gripping the side with her hands and jumping slightly to sit on top. "Oh, don't be such a baby. I may be dealing with the socially impaired, but I know how you like to dress, doll. You know I take care of my girl. Baby steps. One of these days I'll bring out the sex goddess I know is in there, but for now, getting you out of that pretty little shell is top priority."

She smiles, kicking her dangling legs back and forth. As much as I hate to admit it, I'm really going to miss her when I'm gone.

I don't know how I'm supposed to leave her behind, or any of it for that matter. Why couldn't this wait one more year? One thing about Presley that only I know is that she acts all tough, but deep down she has a heart of gold. Everyone thinks she is this outgoing, emotionally disabled heartbreaker, but most of it's just an act.

What she doesn't know is I know the one thing that can break down her barriers. I guess the one person is more appropriate. I've watched her pine after my brother, hopelessly, for years. He is the real reason she could never fall for Corey. It's kind of depressing, to be honest.

She is only promiscuous to take her mind off the one person she wants but can't have. It's why I don't judge her. I think some of it is to even try and get his attention; to show him she isn't the little girl that follows him around anymore. He never gives her a second glance, though; not really anyway. I'm sure like many guys he thinks she's hot. I see him glance her way occasionally, but that's all it is.

The truth is, Konnor and me made a pact a long time ago. When I was becoming a teenager, he made me promise not to date any of his friends and in return he wouldn't date any of mine. I think he only did it trying to play the big brother role and protect me from being used and thrown away, as so many girls are, but the thing is, Konnor never breaks a promise. He never has.

At the time, I was selfish and didn't want him dating my friends, but after watching her all these years and seeing how Sophia treated him, maybe they deserve each other. Maybe that's why she is letting out this emotional side to her I've never really seen. Maybe it's because of Konnor being single. I wonder if she is allowing herself to feel in hopes that he will notice her and make a move.

I don't know how or when I'm supposed to tell her I'm moving.

Thinking about everything, maybe I need to lighten up on Presley some. I'm sure I'll wish I did when I no longer have her around nagging me all the time. "Babe, are you going to shower or stand there looking at me all night? I know I'm a sight to see, but we really need to get going," she says, a smirk turning up on one side of her face.

And she's back.

One good thing about having curly hair is less prep time when you're in a hurry or being rushed by one impatient but charming best friend. Thirty minutes later, I'm dressed and putting the finishing touches on my makeup. "You look gorgeous, baby girl, as always. Now let's go. I'm tired of waiting."

I'm putting my stuff in my bag and I turn to gaze at Presley. She is looking at her phone again. She has been texting nonstop since I got out of the shower. "So, who are you texting? They have been blowing up your phone for thirty minutes." I pick up my bags and start for the locker room door, where she is standing against the doorframe.

She looks up, locking her phone, as I get closer. "Just Corey being Corey," she says, as if it's a normal thing. I can tell she is lying. Presley is the worst liar for two reasons. One, she is blatantly honest, so when she tries to 'lie' it is obvious. Two, Corey doesn't text her anymore. He gave up when rumors started flying of her random hooks-ups over Christmas break. I guess the guy figured groveling wasn't getting him very far. If she were a good liar, she would have known not to use that excuse. I would have actually believed it was Konnor first. They've always been friends, just nothing more.

"Uh huh," I say, not believing a word she just said. "You ready to go?"

She links her arm with mine in the way she always does. "I thought you'd never ask." The rest of the walk to the car is silent.

When we get to the parking lot, I remember we both drove. "I need to take my car home and let my parents know I'm going out."

"We'll drop it off at my house. It's on the way. I've already talked to your mom. You're staying with me." The little vixen has thought of everything to keep me from backing out.

"Fine, let's go before I regain my sanity and change my mind. I'm sure I'll regret this later." I get into my car, tossing my bags into the passenger seat.

She sits in her car, waiting for me to leave. I roll down the window. "Are you really going to follow me there?"

She nods her head. "I know your little games, Kinzleigh Baker. Get a move on it." I roll my eyes. I guess we're going to act like we're five. I pull out first and head for Presley's house.

Approximately ten minutes later, I pull into Presley's driveway. She lives in a large, three-story house with a four-car garage, the exterior walls all cream stucco with lots of windows, because there is one thing you don't block in Laguna Beach, and that's the views. All four doors are closed, so I park my Range Rover in front of Presley's garage door. As I'm getting out of the car, Presley pulls behind me, pressing on the horn. "I'm coming! Could you be a little more patient?" I ask, opening the passenger door and getting in.

"I've been waiting on you long enough. I'm starting to feel gray hair coming through," she says sarcastically. Always the dramatic one...

"Are you ever going to tell me where it is we're going?" She pulls away, staring straight ahead, never once glancing back at me.

"You'll find out soon enough. Don't get your panties in a bunch." She smiles, but continues to watch the road. "It wouldn't be a surprise if I told you, now would it? Let's just say it's a much-needed outing."

She reaches in her console and pulls out a small makeup bag; her emergency kit, nonetheless. Driving with her knee holding the wheel, she unzips the pouch and pulls out her famous pink lip polish. She never leaves the house without it. I'm more of a natural girl myself, but I guess the vibrant, shimmery pink does fit her personality.

Looking in the mirror, she smears on a coat and tosses it back in her makeup pouch. She then takes out a small bottle of perfume, the sweet but clean smell permeating the air as she applies a spritz to her neck and wrist. She then hands it to me. "Put this on. It's amazing and my favorite."

One of the things Presley and I have in common is our need and obsession for girly things, designer brands even more.

I spray myself, and as I'm handing it back to her she pulls into a gated driveway. She stops at the keypad and enters some random code. The gates slowly open. I raise my brows, looking at her. "Been here much?"

I don't even know whose house this is and she knows the gate code. That's pretty personal if you ask me. It's a gorgeous house, as most are around here, but I don't recognize it from any of the people we hang around. The garage doors are closed, so I can't scope out the vehicle.

She pulls up behind the garage door, closest to the fence that leads to the back of the house. Before killing the ignition, she presses the button to raise the top of her convertible, turning to me. She bites her bottom lip, trying to hold back a smile. "Maybe a time or two. Come on."

I step out of the car, leaving my purse in the passenger seat, but first remove my iPhone and slide it into my back pocket. I'm a little uneasy about this whole situation. I've never been the extroverted one in new places or when meeting new people. I've always been shy. I've gotten a little better over the last two years, because Presley is usually dragging me along on all her spontaneous endeavors, but I'm nowhere close to outgoing. I look up at the entryway and exhale, shutting the car door. "Okay, let's go."

Instead of walking to the front door, Presley cuts to the right and opens the gate of the privacy fence. It leads into a fairly large backyard with a huge pool. That says a lot considering we live in California. You pay a hefty price tag for outdoor living.

You can see for miles over the hills. I stop briefly, admiring the view. It's beautiful up here. I'm dying to know who lives here. "You coming, girlie?"

I turn around and Presley is standing at the door to what I assume is a guesthouse. I nod and begin making my way to the door beside her.

She knocks. It's only been a few seconds and I can hear footsteps getting closer. I begin fidgeting with my top—stupid nervous habit. I don't know why I'm shaking. Presley is standing against the doorframe looking down at her phone.

I'm about to ask what she is doing when the door opens. Turning toward it, everything begins to make sense. Oh . . . my . . . Every thought has completely left my brain. All I can see is six feet of solid muscle, standing in all its half-naked glory. It s . . . *him.*

He's barefooted, wearing nothing but gray cotton sweatpants. The elastic band of his underwear is sticking just above the top of his pants. I nervously bite my nails as my eyes adjust to the magnificent sight before me.

His chest rises and falls to the rhythm of his breathing. His stomach is like a piece of artwork, smooth but solid, revealing each abdominal perfectly, as if they are sculpted from stone. He has the slightest trail of blond hair that travels from his belly button downward, disappearing into . . .

My eyes follow it, landing on his . . . Oh gosh, am I staring at his crotch? I slap my hand over my eyes, trying to contain them from wandering. This is humiliating. "I'm going to let you two catch up." I can hear the laughter in her voice. Great, I probably look like an infantile schoolgirl.

Presley passes by him, walking inside the house, most likely with a big smile on her face. She loves to humiliate me. "Let's get this party started," she says. "What are we watching? Please tell me you got *Pacific Rim*. Charlie Hunnam is so sexy, and I heard there is a shirtless scene. I wouldn't mind having dreams about that sexy piece of man-candy tonight."

I can hear the sound of the leather moving as she plops down on the couch.

I separate my middle and ring fingers to peek and see if the coast is clear. That's a negative, ghost rider. Now he is standing in the middle of the doorframe with both arms raised, gripping the top in his hands, causing his muscles to flex. His hair is damp as if he just got out of the shower and he has a rather large smirk on his face. I'm such an idiot. I will not let his cockiness affect me. I'm around good-looking guys all the time and it never fazes me. Why he is different I have no idea. That is the million-dollar question.

I drop my hand and try to look into the house. I give myself a second to calm my heart rate before attempting to speak. "Hi," I say, giving him a slight wave. "So . . . I take it this must be Ryland's house?"

I slide my hands in my back pockets, not knowing what else to do with them.

He begins walking toward me with that same cocky grin still in place. It may even be bigger. I back up. He is looking straight into my eyes, as if he is on the prowl. "I guess I found you," he says in a low, sexy tone. He has one hand in a fist and the other flat, swinging them together in front of him, kind of like a pendulum swing, as he continues forward. He is already completely out the door, having shut it behind him.

"I guess you could say that," I say, smiling nervously. My stomach feels like it's full of butterflies fluttering around. I keep backing up until I can feel the edge of the pool. I look down and I'm one step from falling in. I'm trapped. Now what am I supposed to do? "Presley mentioned we're watching movies? What are we watching?"

He grabs the thin fabric of my shirt in between his thumb and index fingers, slightly pulling me toward him. "Come in and I'll show you what we've got. I promise I won't bite, unless you ask."

He winks, taking hold of my hand and turning back to the house. He has a tattoo between his shoulder blades. It's script in another language. I wonder what it says or what it means. Most people our age don't have tattoos, unless it's significant or you have parents that don't care about anything. You can't even get one unless your parents sign a consent form or you get by with a fake ID.

Tonight should be interesting. I don't usually hang around with guys, except in a large group. Sure, I get asked out on dates, but I've never had a problem declining . . . until now.

Somehow, though, I have to stay strong. I have to find a way to keep my distance from him. He could potentially ruin *everything*.

EIGHT

Breyson

At first, I thought I was seeing things. That surely my mind was deceiving me. The girl who's taken residence in my mind is standing before me. I had watched TV for a while, mindlessly flipping through the channels but not really paying much attention to what was on. Ryland came back a little while later with two large pizzas and a handful of DVDs.

I had finally decided Ryland was right. In a few short days, I was going to be heading back to Mississippi and I would likely never see her again. No matter how much it sucks, that's the way it is.

Ryland ran to the main house to get some more blankets and pillows. He said he had a couple of girls coming over to hang out and watch movies. He never did tell me who, so I just figured it was that girl from the party.

I had just gotten out of the shower when I heard a knock at the door. The first thing I found was my sweatpants, so I quickly pulled them on and went to answer the door. I definitely wasn't expecting to find what I did on the other side of that door.

I owe Ryland for this. I'll gladly do whatever he wants after tonight, because standing on the other side of that door is the most beautiful sight I've ever seen. Each time I see her she gets more beautiful. Honestly, I never knew that was possible. I was temporarily at a loss for words when I saw her standing there.

I quickly recovered when I saw how shocked she was that it was me who opened the door. I guess she was as surprised to see me as I was her. She's so shy that I can't help but to smile every time I'm around her. Presley just scored one of the top five spots in my book of the best girls for bringing her here. What makes her even better—she left us alone, no questions asked.

I can tell Kinzleigh is attracted to me too, but also how much she fights it. I've got my work cut out for me if I'm going to get anywhere with her, and I have a short time to do it. But she's here tonight, and that's a start.

This girl is becoming like a drug to me. Comparable to that first high you always hear about. She's my gateway drug. I may go back to Mississippi and spend the rest of my life searching for that same first high, but right now I'm going to savor the real deal, and that's her.

God, I love it when she gets embarrassed. I can't help but to play with her. The way she blushed when she realized she was looking at my crotch will forever be engrained in my memory.

I pull her into the house and shut the door. "Do you want anything to drink or eat? Ryland picked up some pizzas." She's standing beside the door, looking around the room as if she is afraid to go any farther. She's twirling a lock of hair around her fingers. I've noticed she does it a lot when she seems uncomfortable.

She looks at me, her cheeks a shade of pink. "Pizza sounds good. I accidentally skipped lunch today." How does someone forget to eat? I'm always thinking about food. Girls are weird about eating, especially around guys. That's not something I wanted to hear. She has a beautiful body, but she is small enough. She doesn't need to be missing meals. I walk over to the kitchen and take a few plates from the cabinet. I nod my head for her to come to where I am.

She walks over to the edge of the bar and pulls out a stool, sitting down. "Do you do that often?" Her eyes are focused on the place setting in front of her like she is afraid to look at me. I don't know why a girl as hot as her is so shy. "Kinzleigh, look at me."

She looks up at me slowly, her cheeks changing to a more prominent shade of red as she scans up my naked stomach. "I was training with my coach all day. It slips my mind sometimes when I'm at it for hours at a time." Her voice comes out just above a whisper, as if she is having trouble catching her breath.

I put a slice of pizza on each plate when Ryland comes barreling through the door, arms full of blankets and pillows. He looks at Presley lying on her belly on the floor, digging through the DVD collection. Kinzleigh turns around on her stool. "Hey Ryland. How's it going? I haven't seen you in a while." She smiles. Ryland looks at her and up at me with that knowing grin rising from his lips. I can't help it that I'm grinning ear to ear knowing the hottest girl in all of California is sitting right in front of me. He knows I owe him one for this. I can see it written all over his face.

"Kinzleigh." He nods. "I'm glad Presley got you to come. You guys up for some movies?"

"Sure, what are we watching? Nothing scary, right?" I take some glasses from the cabinet. When I turn back around Ryland is looking at me with a guilty expression. I know exactly what he's thinking and for once I like where his thoughts are going.

"I think one or two of them are horror. Is that okay? I've been dying to see that new movie *The Conjuring*. I missed it in theater. Presley and I can take the floor and you guys can have the couch. Will that work for you?" Only I know that tone is Ryland's form of sarcasm. To everyone else it sounds genuine. If I didn't like the idea of getting her close to me I'd slap him in the back of the head for doing her that way.

Her eyes widen, and she looks unsure. Ah hell, I can't do this to her. I'm about to tell him to put on *Pacific Rim* when Presley rolls onto her back, props up on her elbows with a big smile on her face, and says, "You'll be fine, Kinzleigh. You're staying at my house tonight, so you shouldn't have any nightmares. I haven't made you watch one since *The Ring*. A little fear is good for everyone every once and a while."

"Okay then. I guess it's settled." She turns back toward me and I set her plate in front of her, as well as a glass of ice.

"What do you want to drink? Soda or water?" I set my plate down beside hers and start to walk toward the refrigerator.

"Water, please." She suddenly looks a little embarrassed. "Do you have a fork?"

Grabbing a water and soda, I shut the door and set them down, my brows coming together, a little puzzled. "A fork?"

She smiles. "I don't like getting the grease on my hands. It makes me feel gross. Sorry, it's a little strange, I know."

Her embarrassment is such a turn-on. Usually, girls that look like she does ends up being a complete bitch, but not her. "I have to admit, I don't usually witness someone eating pizza with a fork, but I'm always game for something new." A smile spreads across my face. Ryland comes over and grabs a plate for him and Presley while she gets their drinks.

Presley stops before returning to the sitting area. "You have ten minutes to get over here or I'm coming to get you, whether you're finished eating or not," she says, a goofy grin on her face to show she's joking with her.

I look at Kinzleigh. "We can watch something else if you don't want to watch a scary movie. Don't listen to Ryland. He can watch it later. We did get other movies."

She begins cutting up her pizza, making me smile. She looks like she has to put some muscle behind it to get through the crust. "It's okay. I'll never hear the end of it if I don't. Plus, I'd rather watch it first and get it over with. That way, by the time I go to bed I'm thinking of something else. If you stick around long enough, you'll learn there is no use in arguing with Presley."

I'd love to stick around long enough, but there is no way I'm going there with this conversation. I may have the hots for this girl, but I'm not a pussy. I don't like to sit around and talk about my feelings to a girl; trying to fill her head with garbage in hopes of getting laid. It's not my style. We finish eating and head over to the couch, just as Presley is skipping through the commercials.

I finally remember I'm not wearing a shirt. I'm not used to having to cover up after a shower unless I'm going somewhere. Ninety percent of the time this is how I'm dressed around the house, because I never have girls over. When girls are around, I'm at a party or in my truck and the night usually ends with me removing clothes, not putting them on. Her pattern of barely looking at me and constantly blushing now makes sense.

I walk to the back bedroom to grab a black sleeveless shirt and pull it on. When I return to the living area, Kinzleigh is sitting on the couch, barefooted, with her legs crisscrossed. I grab a couple of pillows and a blanket from the stack Ryland brought in, placing them on the couch beside her.

As she notices my shirt a smile occurs. She takes a pillow and places it in her lap. "Thank you . . . on both counts."

I pull the bottom of my shirt back up my stomach, toying with her. That smile quickly fades and her eyes go wide. I laugh, because I can't help myself. She almost acts younger, and with girls, I'm generally used to the opposite. Between the well-matured body and the clothing and makeup adding to it, you can't tell who's your age and who's older anymore. Her cheeks turn a soft shade of pink. I'm about to sit down when she smacks me in the face with the pillow she's holding.

She laughs softly at the startled look on my face. I love her laugh. "Behave yourself or you can sit on the hard floor," she says with a playful look in her eyes, pointing to the floor. She's finally relaxing. I knew she had a feisty side. It just needed to come out.

I hold up my hand, index and middle finger pointed upward in unison. "Scouts honor," I say in return. "Is this seat taken?" I point beside her, only joking, because I'm sitting there whether she invites me or not. She looks down the vacant couch and back to me, sucking her bottom lip between her teeth, shaking her head. "Good, because I was prepared to vacate it if necessary."

I take a seat beside her and Ryland pops his head up from the bed he made with blankets on the floor that him and Presley are sharing. "Dude, are you going to turn out the lights? Last one standing gets the job and you know it. Hurry up, we're waiting on you two to start the film."

"Could you not have told me sometime in the last ten minutes I've been standing here?" I get up and turn off the lights. As I sit back down the opening credits come on. It has that creepy music always used in horror films. I look over at Kinzleigh and she has pulled her knees to her chest and spread a blanket over her body, the top clutched in her hands right below her nose. She is staring at the television with one eye open and one eye closed. I have to bite my tongue to keep from laughing.

I grab the side of the blanket and lift it, scooting underneath it closer to her. "You really don't like scary movies, do you?" I talk low, trying not to be too loud. She looks at me, shaking her head. I scoot close enough to her that our sides are touching and put my arm around her shoulder, pulling her toward me. "I promise I'm not going to try anything," I whisper against her ear. "It makes it less scary feeling another body close to you."

She looks up at me and raises a brow questioningly. "Who told you that?" She doesn't believe me. I can tell by her tone.

"I used to have nightmares when I was a kid. My mom would come and sit beside me when I woke up in a sweat screaming. I think she called them night terrors. She used to sing and pull me close enough I could touch her. She said as long as I could feel her near, the nightmares would go away. Maybe it was a load of crap, but it always worked." I shrug nonchalantly.

Her face softens. She grabs her hair in the fist of her hand and pulls it to the opposite side, laying it to rest over her shoulder. She places her head on the top of my shoulder. "Okay, I'll give it a try. I just have really colorful dreams; always have. That's why I avoid scary movies."

I can't describe the feeling I have with her body touching against mine—peacefulness maybe. I've never wanted to be this close to a girl before, aside from sex, and that's just long enough to get off and get her dressed. For the first time in my entire life, I just want to be near her and do nothing but talk to her. Don't get me wrong, I'd love nothing more than to experience all of her, but it's not a priority with her, which surprises me. I feel the need to make her mine in every way possible, somehow, some way. Only thing wrong with that picture is come Friday we'll be on two different coastlines. Maybe I can somehow get out of her where she is moving. Anywhere in the south is closer than we are currently.

We are about forty-five minutes through the movie with nothing major happening at this very moment. Kinzleigh is still buried beneath the blanket, folded into my arms. Out of nowhere, an image jumps on the screen, causing Kinzleigh to scream and bury her head into my side. I bite my tongue in an effort not to laugh out loud at her burst of terror. I bite down so hard I can taste blood. I love her nestling into my side. It makes me feel like I'm protecting her.

Ryland and Presley didn't even budge. They haven't come up for air the entire movie. From the sounds and the movement under the cover they won't be anytime soon.

I look over at Kinzleigh, barely peeking out of the blanket. I can tell she is really bothered by the movie. "You want to go to the other room? There is another television in there. We can put on *Pacific Rim* or *We're the Millers*." She looks like she is about to decline when a moan comes from Presley's mouth, causing her eyes to widen as big as saucers.

I don't know what it says about me that I like she is uncomfortable in sexual situations. The thought of her making sounds like Presley from another guy sends my blood boiling. "Okay, will you grab the movie?" She keeps eying the mound of blankets moving in different directions and the doorway to the other room.

I nod, and before I can get up from the couch she grabs the pillow and bolts in the direction of the bedroom door. I shake my head in laughter and get up to grab the DVDs.

When I walk in the bedroom she is laying on her stomach with her legs crossed behind her in the air. She has her phone in front of her and doing what appears to be texting. I wonder if she is texting a guy. The thought plagues my mind and embarrassingly I want to grab it and find out. I want her for myself.

I rub my hand through my hair. I need to get a grip. *What the hell is wrong with me? Is this what jealousy feels like?*

I have never cared who a girl talks to, not even Natalie. We basically had a 'don't ask don't tell' policy as far as talking goes. I like to have fun. Since I started driving, I only needed them for one thing, and the type of girls I usually hung around it was understood they liked the same kind of fun—easy to give it up too. I don't like this at all.

"What will it be?" I hold up the movies from where I stand in front of the bed. She lays her phone down in front of her, looking up at me. She props her chin on the heel of her hand, wiggling her fingers above her upper lip as if she's thinking. "I think *Pacific Rim* is the better option of the two. Konnor said it was really good and we usually like the same movies."

"Great choice," I say, putting down the other DVD, so I can open the cover and put it in the Blu-ray player. "Will you see if the remote is in the drawer by the bed?"

She sits up on her knees and turns toward the drawer. She bends over, resting on her right palm, rummaging through the drawer of the nightstand. Her shirt comes up slightly, revealing the bottom of her back. Just above the band of her jeans sits two perfect dimples. My eyes lower, lingering on her perfect round bottom. I need something to take my mind off of her before I start undressing her in my mind. Knowing that it's there, I look down and confirm my hard-on. Quickly adjusting myself, I try to think of something to calm my raging thoughts. "So Konnor is your brother?" If talking about another guy isn't an erection kill, I don't know what is.

She pulls out the remote and turns around, sitting crisscrossed on the bed. She points the remote at the television, turning it on. "Yeah," she sighs and pulls her knees against her chest to wrap her arms around them, dropping the remote on the bed. "He's going through a lot right now. He just told me he's at a tattoo shop picking out a new tattoo. He asked if I wanted to come and watch."

I remember Ryland telling me about his ordeal, but I don't want her to be mad at Ryland for telling me, so for now I'll keep it to myself. "You don't like tattoos?"

She is a little spaced out as she stares down at her knees, lost in thought. "It's not that." She shrugs. "I don't know. It's his second one in a month. At this pace he's going to be covered in a year from head to toe. They aren't small ones either. He's never been the 'bad boy' type. He's just becoming very . . . different, and fast. Each tattoo represents something different and it's not the happy reason to get a tattoo. He and his girlfriend recently broke up after three years of dating. What's going to be next? He turns into the rest of the jocks at school and sleeps with everything that walks? Breaking hearts along the way or becomes the bad-boy rocker man-slut seducing women with his voice? I'm scared he's going to regret it when he finally gets over all of this. He really loved her, I guess." Her nose scrunches in disgust.

Point one—she obviously doesn't condone sleeping around. Point two—it's making me want her all the more. I don't know what to say, because I've never been in that situation. I learned years back not to trust a woman with your heart. It will only kill you in the end, Beau being the example in that lesson. I have no idea what that feels like, and from the looks of her she doesn't want to go into any further detail. I finally got her laughing and having a good time,

accepted FATE

so I'm perfectly fine with steering away from this conversation.

I nod in understanding and turn to put the DVD in the player and then return to the bed after turning the lights off. "Do y'all have a curfew?" It really isn't that late, but according to what she said last night she's never out late.

She shakes her head. Her smile is slowly coming back. "As long as Presley's mom knows where she is and it's someone's house she can stay out until two in the morning. Anywhere else she has to be home by twelve." She leans back against the pillow and starts to shiver. Ryland keeps it cold. Last I checked the thermostat was set on sixty-five.

"You can get under the cover. I promise I'll keep it PG-13." I grin. I like messing with her.

She raises her brow at me and plays with her curly hair as a smirk forms. "I think you better keep it G-rated or I'm kicking you off the bed. I know how to fight."

Oh, would I love to see that.

I might give it a go for that very reason. "I'd like to see you try," I say playfully. I can't imagine her tiny body being able to do much damage.

"My parents wanted me to learn self-defense, so I had to take classes when I was fourteen. I'm quite experienced in taking down an attacker. Don't let my size fool you." She pauses and then smiles. "Didn't your mom teach you not to judge a book by its cover?" She is getting more comfortable around me and I like the sassy side that seems to be trying to break through.

I place one knee on the bed, followed by the other. Feeling playful, I grab her by the ankles and pull her across the bed to meet me. Kneeling between her legs, I release her ankles and grab her hands in mine, pinning them to the bed. "Is that a challenge?"

I lean forward, getting closer to her face. I can feel her breaths coming out short and quick. I can tell I'm having an effect on her. She brings her knees up beside me, the bottom of her feet flat on the bed, opening her spread wider. Her eyes are slightly hooded. I place my mouth right beside her ear. "One point for me."

With a big grin on my face, I release her hands and sit back up, grabbing the remote and pressing the play button. She quickly sits up and moves back to the head of the bed. I'm starting to worry she's mad, but then she smiles. "Not a chance. Payback's a bitch."

We lay here watching the movie. It's mostly quiet with occasional small talk. Things are easier now than when she first got here. The more I talk to her, the more I realize how down-to-earth and likable she is. We seem to have a lot more in common than I originally thought.

I look at her, lying back on a pillow watching the movie. Her hair is fanned out behind her head. She has one leg bent in the air, the bottom of her foot flat against the mattress with her hand resting on the thigh of her bent leg while the other is lying flat against the bed. I notice the same anklet she was wearing at the beach. It must be her favorite piece of jewelry or either something meaningful. She's beautiful. I wish I could take a picture with my phone without it seeming creepy, so I'll have something to remember her by when I go back home.

"Ryland said something about a pool party Presley is having tomorrow. Are you going?" She rolls onto her side and turns toward me, propping her upper body onto her elbow.

"Yeah, I have to help setup. She has one at the beginning of every summer. Her parents go all out and have it catered. It's kind of become a tradition. Pretty much everyone from school will be there. Presley has me running around picking things up while she sets up at the house. I guess you could say I'm the chauffeur for all the supplies."

"Do you need some help? I don't have any plans tomorrow. I think Ryland said he had some stuff to take care of for school before the party anyway, so I'll just be stuck here or following him around."

She's looking me in the eyes. She doesn't answer for a moment. I wish I knew what was going through her mind right now. She finally answers, smiling. "Yeah, okay. I could use some of your muscle."

We haven't heard much out of Presley and Ryland since they changed the movie in the other room. I assumed they finally finished taking care of business until we start hearing Presley calling out his name. Kinzleigh looks at the door. "You have got to be kidding me." She looks back at me. "Does it take everyone that long?"

Her face flushes at the question.

I glance at her lips being sucked between her teeth. Her innocence shows more and more as I get to know her. I like it more than I care to admit.

I meet her eyes with my own. "Depends on the guy . . . If you're dealing with a man it does. A man cares about the pleasure of his girl before his own. A man waits on his girl to be satiated first. A man holds out as long as necessary, regardless of what he has to do. And on the occasional slip, he goes again. Only a boy lets himself get off first and then is done."

I notice the slightest moan escape her lips. It's so low I wasn't even sure I heard it. Presley starts up again, louder this time. I can tell Kinzleigh is getting really uncomfortable. Me—I'm not bothered by it. Being on the football team you hear and see so much it doesn't even faze you after a while.

There is a door in the bedroom that leads outside. "Come on," I say. "Let's get some fresh air."

We get up at the same time and she follows me outside the door. The door comes out on the side of the house so, we walk back to the pool. "It must be nice to have views like this every day," I say, standing at the edge of the pool.

"It is," she replies. "I love it here. I'm going to miss this place. I plan to try to come back after senior year for college." She stops behind me. My tattoo must be slightly showing from the neckline of my shirt, because she starts tracing the outline. The light caressing of her finger sends chills down my arms. "People our age don't usually have tattoos. What does it mean?"

I don't talk about my tattoo, because it's mine and mine alone. Something I don't want shared with the world. I've never told anyone what it means; not even Ryland. That's the reason it's in Latin. She whispers, "Infragilis."

For some reason, though, I want to tell her. "Unbreakable. It's Latin." I expect her to ask a lot of questions, to quiz me on the meaning, but she surprises me when I hear nothing at all.

Only a sigh of contentment.

She runs her finger down my back. She then clasps her small hands around my waist. The feel of her so close makes me close my eyes. I try to turn around when she shoves me off the side, causing me to fall into the pool.

I come up for air—completely soaked—to her bent over laughing. "What was that for?" I'm trying hard to sound mad, but her laughter is contagious and before I know it I'm laughing along with her.

She stands upright, placing her hands on her hips. "That's for earlier." She winks. "I don't get mad, I get even."

I come to the edge, placing my palms flat on the cement, pulling myself up. She doesn't realize she just made this a game. I can do this all night. It's in my competitive nature. I'm trailing water as I stalk toward her. She is still laughing a little until she looks me in the eyes. Her eyes widen as she realizes what I'm doing and takes off running.

I chase after her around the yard. She's pretty quick to be so short and dainty, but no match for me. Back home, I play baseball and football to be close to each of my brothers and I'm one of the fastest guys on the team. I'm not even breaking a sweat and I'm on her heels. I'm giving her a few minutes lead just to toy with her, allowing her to think she's won. Right before she gets to the gate, I increase my stride and wrap my arm around her waist, causing her to scream out. When she realizes it was a little loud, she slaps her hand over her mouth, trying not to cause commotion with Ryland's parents.

I pull her backward toward me and scoop her into my arms, cradling her. She places her arms around my neck for stability, but begins kicking her legs, trying to break free from my grasp. "There's not a chance I'm letting you get away now, sweetheart. I love a good challenge."

She looks at the pool getting closer with each step and turns back to me. "You wouldn't dare." She narrows her eyes. "Breyson, no!"

"Oh, but I would," I say, and take off running toward the pool. I jump off the deep end with her in my arms. Breaking through the water, I release her, so we can each come back up for air.

She breaks the surface, brushing her hair back out of her face, laughing. "The water is freezing," she says, teeth clattering. "I can't believe you did that!" She splashes water at me. "I didn't bring any extra clothes."

Her thin, satin top is clinging to her body, revealing the outline of her bra and cleavage. For the top to be so conservative—reaching all the way to her neck in which it connects with the back fabric—this is by far the sexiest view I've ever had. There is something to be said about a girl that leaves a little to the imagination. When it's all out there for the world to see, for some reason it's less appealing.

"I wouldn't worry about clothes. I'm sure we can find you something." She is wading in the middle of the pool and I am closer to the farther side. I begin making my way toward her, my eyes never leaving hers. She has the slightest smile on her face. When she sees me coming toward her, she begins swimming backward, slowly. "You trying to run from me?"

I grin, because she is getting closer to the side, leaving less room for her to go.

"You trying to catch me?" she counters sarcastically. You got to love a girl with a little spunk. Her back finally reaches the corner of the pool, not far from the diving board. She turns around, noticing she is now trapped and I have her right where I want her. She bites the corner of her lip.

I stop right in front of her, grabbing the edge of the pool on each side of her. "Maybe I am. I know a good catch when I see one."

Her eyes are slightly hooded like earlier, giving me the answer to the question in my head. She is giving me confirmation that she feels the way I feel right now. I close the distance between us, the warmth from our bodies mingling around us. The water isn't so cold anymore. I wrap one leg at a time around me to support her against the wall. I remain holding one edge of the pool and place the other hand on her neck.

I lean in closer, our lips just a breath apart. "Stop running, Kinzleigh." Her eyes close as she releases a sigh. I can't stop myself anymore. I don't want to. I don't care if I have to go back home in a few days. I would rather have a few days I'll never forget than spend the rest of my life in regret.

I softly kiss her lips, before sucking the droplets of water from them slowly, savoring her taste. They are full and soft. She slowly relaxes, letting me suck and pull at her bottom lip. I can feel her inexperience with every movement. She allows me to lead her lips where I want them. I lightly lick her lips, requesting entry, in which she grants. As I slide my tongue inside her mouth, I seek out hers. It's warm and moist, entangling with mine.

I run my hand from her neck down the seam of her body, stopping at her waist, just before testing the water and cupping her bottom. It feels as good as I envisioned it would feel and it's covered in denim. I can't imagine how it would feel bare.

I continue to kiss and suck her lip, guiding her tongue in the perfect rhythm with mine. As she slides her tongue inside my mouth, I clench it with my lips and suck it, then release. The lowest moan escapes her perfect lips, as if she's afraid I'll hear her.

My hormones are raging. It's unavoidable. Holding her by the butt, I pull her closer at the waist. My erection is pressing between her legs. Even in this pool of cool water, I can feel the heat radiating from inside the opening at her thighs. A growl comes from within my chest, causing her to slightly bite my bottom lip. Oh damn, for the first time in my entire life I feel like I could come, and she hasn't even touched me. She brings her arms up around my neck, interlocking her fingers at the back.

I lightly rub my erection over the material separating us. She rolls her head to the side, giving me access to her neck. I kiss just below the lobe of her ear and run my tongue lightly down her neck, stopping at the top of her exposed shoulder.

She gets a little bold and sways her hips from side to side. "If you keep doing that, I'm going to lose my control, and this will end up going further than you likely want."

She lifts her head and looks at me, smiling mischievously, and kisses the area on the front of my neck between my collarbones. She lightly trails kisses higher up my neck. "Kinzleigh, you're playing with fire." I warn. She clamps her legs tighter behind my back and clenches the muscles between her legs that are pressed against my sides.

I can't take it anymore. Without thinking, my hand goes for the button of her pants as I take her lips, more roughly this time. I finally pull away to look her in the eyes. I rest my forehead against hers. "I'll have to go inside and get a condom from my wallet if you want to go any further."

I look into her eyes and her breathing is quickening. She looks like she is thinking about it, which only tells me one thing. "Kinzleigh, you have had sex before, right?"

I thought Ryland was blowing smoke up my ass when he was talking about her being inexperienced with guys, but I didn't think he meant literally none. I will not be the one to take her virginity. That's a connection and attachment I stay away from. Plus, she doesn't deserve that. Her first time should be with someone who has a warm beating heart, someone who'll take his time, make it memorable. Mine turned to ice a long time ago.

She isn't looking at me. As a matter of fact, she is staring at the water. She releases my neck. "No, I haven't. Does it really matter whether I have or not? Since when do guys care about that sort of thing? It's just sex, right? Maybe it's time I stop trying to be so perfect. Look at where it's getting me. Nothing is going the way I planned. A few weeks from now my life will be over as I know it. Maybe I should just live for myself and have fun like everyone else.

It's perfect really, if you think about it. You can help me get it out of the way and then we won't ever see each other again once you leave. No lies, no expectations; just fun."

Dammit! Why in the hell does she have to be a virgin? I run my fingers through my wet hair. I want her; so bad I can't stand it. I've never turned down a girl that looks even half as beautiful as her and I'll probably hate myself for this.

She may not want any attachments, but I can't do it to her. She deserves better. I want to claim her as my own, to mark her in the most absolute way, but at what cost? "Let's go inside and change clothes and we'll continue this there." I kiss her softly and lift her to sit on the side of the pool. I lift myself out of the water, and once standing, I reach for her hand. "Come on, beautiful."

Walking into the bedroom, I grab two towels from the linen closet. I hand her a towel, along with a pair of boxers and a t-shirt. "Thanks. I'll be right back," she says as she turns and disappears into the bathroom. I remove my wet clothes and put on a pair of dry boxers. I sit on the edge of the bed, leaning forward, resting my forearms on my thighs. How fucked-up is it that I can't stand the thought of someone else being her first? But for once, sex alone isn't enough; at least not with her. This time, I can't be selfish. I have to think about her and not me.

The door to the bathroom opens. She saunters toward the bed. She tied her wet hair up on top of her head. As she gets into bed, she yawns. I pull back the comforter for her to lie down. Crawling in, she lays down on her side, facing away from me. I wrap my arm around her waist, placing my hand against her belly, and I pull her toward me until our bodies are aligned. "What time is it? I should probably check on Presley, so we don't miss curfew."

Pulling the blanket over our bodies, I nestle her in the nook of my curled body. She fits like a glove, like we were cut from the same cloth and now coming back together. "Just lay with me for a while, please." She doesn't say another word; just relaxes beside me. If I were breakable, this girl is possibly the only thing that could do it. That scares the hell out of me. That's my last thought before falling asleep with her in my arms.

NINE

Kinzleigh

I'm having the most peaceful night's sleep until I'm jolted awake by someone shaking my shoulder. I rub my eyes, trying to wake up. "What time is it?"

Presley is standing over me beside the bed, talking in a hushed whisper. "It's almost two in the morning. We have to get going or my parents are going to ground me before my pool party."

I then realize there is an arm wrapped around my waist, holding me tightly, as if to keep me from going anywhere. I can't see the look on Presley's face, because it's dark, but I'm sure I'll hear about this later.

I lift his arm carefully, slipping out of the bed as quietly as possible to avoid waking him. Tonight was probably one of the best nights of my life. I'm not quite ready for it to be over yet.

Maybe I can spend a few days with him and then everything will go back to normal. He makes me feel things I never knew you could feel, and I haven't decided if that's good or bad. I want to feel him out some more. He's easy to talk to and I'm myself around him. I don't have to pretend to be someone I'm not.

Maybe it wouldn't be so bad to be friends with a guy. I can't deny I'm attracted to him. It sounds like neither of us want to pursue anything more after hanging around each other for the time he's here, so maybe having a little fun won't ruin everything. At least when I have to leave this place, I'll have something to take with me. "Can you grab my clothes from the bathroom?" I continue her charade of whispering in hopes we can ease out of here without being caught.

"Yeah, but hurry up," she whispers, walking to the bathroom. I walk around the bed to Breyson's side. I only have one thing to give to someone and that's my body. My heart will never be owned. That's the way it is and the way it has to be. I will forever hold my own heart in the palm of my hand.

But if I'm going to give a piece of myself away to someone else, I want it to be him. I've made up my mind. It may be stupid to lose my virginity without my heart involved, but that's the way I want it. I won't risk everything in my life for something that will never last. It's time I do something for me instead of making everyone else happy.

I'm standing over him, looking down. He looks so peaceful. I bend over and whisper in his ear. "Thank you for tonight." I kiss him on the cheek and he stirs in his sleep. I still until he stops moving and head for the door, following behind Presley.

We quietly walk out of the door and tiptoe in a running fashion toward Presley's car. I can finally see her with the sensor operated floodlight shining from the edge of the house. She looks at me, examining my clothes with a big smile on her face. "Shut up," I say, smiling back at her. "I don't want to hear what is about to come out of your mouth. By the way, next time you want to rendezvous with a guy, can you at least be more private?"

She unlocks her car and we get in. She starts the engine before saying anything in return. As she pulls out of the drive she decides to respond. "If what I think is about to happen, happens, you'll find out being less vocal is not always possible. That boy is one good piece of ass." She looks at me with a smirk in place.

"Do you have to be so crude about it? It's really awkward." The smell of Breyson's clothes passes through my nasal passages. It smells so good. It's a really clean smell of laundry detergent mixed with only his smell, like when you walk in someone's house and there is a distinct scent to each one that can't be replicated. I think I may keep this shirt.

"It's only awkward for you, love, but by the looks of you smelling that shirt, that may change soon." Crap, I've been busted. I didn't even realize I smelled it noticeably.

We pass through the mostly dark streets in silence. "Presley, can I ask you a question without getting a bunch of crap from you about it?"

She glances between the road and me. "Sure, babe, what's up? You know I only give you heck because you're my bestie, right? I'm always here if you need to talk. No judgment."

"What's it like?" She scrunches her brows, showing she is clearly confused as to what I'm talking about. "Sex, I mean. Is it worth it? Losing your virginity."

"Whoa, Kinzleigh, are you thinking about giving him your V-card?"

I shrug my shoulders. "I don't know. I'm just starting to wonder why I'm still hanging onto it is all. Most people with it still intact are saving it for the person they intend to give their heart to, but I don't plan on giving mine to anyone. He's just . . . different, and maybe after tonight I'm a little curious. I've never been interested in anyone before. What better person than that to give it to? He's leaving in a few days, Presley. It could be one of those awesome weeks you have and then remember it forever."

She is watching the road, deep in thought. "I don't know, Kinzleigh. Your first time hurts if the guy is even average in size. If he's big you can count on it. It isn't really enjoyable when you first start out, which is why most people do it in a relationship. It sucks until your body gets used to it and that can take a few tries. Are you sure you can give something like that away without any emotion involved? It's harder than you think to go that far with someone and not develop an attachment. Even with my experience, I have to set myself in the right mind frame to not let emotions get in the way. It's human nature. What if you regret it? One day you may decide love is not your worst enemy."

I look at her, pulling my mouth up in disgust. "Um, no thanks. If I do this, it's for the point of avoiding that stuff."

We pull into Presley's house with a minute to spare. Parked behind my car is a white Porsche 911. As Presley kills the engine, I grab my wet clothes and walk toward the porch with her by my side. "Whose car is that?"

"Preston's. He just got home for summer vacation. He made the dean's list third year in a row at UC Berkeley. Since he's Dad's clone and will soon take his place in the Dunagin Empire under Dad after graduation, I guess Dad is bribing him—or motivating as he calls it—to finish his business degree at the top of his class. Granddad is really on Dad's case about stepping up as CEO, so he can retire. We all know that means Preston will become CFO in Dad's place. It was set in motion when he was born." She shakes her head. "He doesn't shut up about that hefty bonus Preston will get when he joins them.

I think he's terrified Preston will go his own way."

We get to the door and stop. Before Presley turns the knob, she looks at me. "Be quiet, because I don't want my parents to see you dressed like that, not to mention Preston. Definitely not Preston. All I'll hear is how bad of an example I am for you. You know he's had a killer crush on you for years. If he could ever take the Kinzleigh goggles off, he might actually stop sleeping around with every hot unattached girl that walks in that frat house of his and settle down. He seems to think if he just has fun and stays single you'll come to your senses and see that he's the best guy for you. I'm pretty sure if you gave him the go ahead, he'd have a massive diamond picked out and purchased the day he graduates college."

I roll my eyes. Presley is always giving Preston crap about having a crush on me. I think she is one severed string away from insanity, but what do I know? What I do know is there is no way Preston Dunagin is waiting around to date me. He's gorgeous with the same brown hair and blue eyes as Presley.

He reminds me of an *Abercrombie* model the way he's built. He's attractive and he knows it, making him cocky. He's sitting really high on the preppy scale—a pretty boy. He has that rich-boy persona down pat. He also tends to whore around a little too much for me. Plus, I've known Preston all my life.

I'm not ever settling down, most likely, and nothing good comes from dating a friend of the family. It would ruin everything, because it's destined for failure. Our families are too entwined for that to happen. I'm not interested in screwing things up for my parents and will not pretend that I am, no matter how happy it would make our moms.

We walk inside and quietly shut the door. All the lights are off, so obviously everyone is asleep. We tiptoe across the marble floor to the large staircase in the center of the even bigger room. Presley is already halfway up the staircase to the second floor when I step on the bottom step. I grab the rail and make my way to the second floor. When I get to the top, we turn right and walk down the hallway to Presley's bedroom.

When we get inside, Presley shuts the door and turns on the light, letting out a sigh of relief. She looks at me, and smiles. "So . . . I want details, and lots of them. How did you end up dressed in his clothes, asleep in his bed with him wrapped around you, and still holding onto your V-card?"

I knew I wasn't going to get away with keeping it to myself. She is always ready for the latest juicy gossip. "I'll tell you, but first I have to pee, so you're going to have to wait." I walk into the bathroom and take care of my business.

I'm standing at the sink, bent over, washing the smeared makeup off my face when I feel two hands wrap around me from behind. I have soap all over my face and my eyes are closed, so I can't see who it is, but I have an idea.

Presley and Preston's bedrooms are connected by a bathroom they share. They have their own counter space, though, making it ideal. Since he lives on campus Presley has taken over the space, but they share when he's home for holidays and summer. As I'm trying to rinse the soap off my face, a body aligns to the backside of mine. "I'm glad you're here," he says in a low whisper into my ear.

I grab a hand towel near the sink and stand upright, drying the water from my face. When I open my eyes, staring into the mirror in front of me, I see Preston towering over my short body in a pair of blue and gray plaid pajama pants and a gray shirt with the college logo on the front. I turn around, standing against the counter. "Preston, what are you doing?"

"Something I should have done a long time ago." He leans forward, placing each palm on the counter, entrapping me, making us eye level. He is really close to my face, making me slightly uncomfortable.

I look off to the side to put some distance between us. "Are you going to make me chase after you forever? Stop being difficult and give me a chance? You know we'd be good together. Our moms are dying to find a way to combine our families. I graduate in a year and I'll take my dad's place. I could take care of you and give you everything you want."

Is he on something? He has always been flirty, even throws lines out there that make me wonder sometimes, but never all this. Maybe Presley isn't crazy after all. I never considered the fact that they may talk like Konnor and I do. Preston has always been a busy guy between school and social events, parties, the like.

I turn my head back to him, but try to lean back so he's not practically kissing me. "What are you talking about, Preston? Where is this coming from? Are you drunk and scheming to get in my pants, because it's not happening? You have plenty of other girls willing to give it up trailing after you that you don't have to lie to."

It doesn't work. He grabs me by the waist, picks me up, and sets me on the counter, continuing this debauchery. "You've known me your entire life, Kinzleigh. Quit pretending you don't know how I feel about you. Do you really think I'd tell you this to get laid? I would never do that to you. That's not even my style with other girls. I want to be with you, Kinzleigh."

He scoots me to the edge of the countertop. "I have wanted you since I was twelve and you were nine and you came barreling into my fort demanding to be included. I've never wanted anything the way I want you."

I'm sitting here, blinking as if my brain stopped working. He looks dead serious. "That's never going to happen, Preston."

He looks agitated. "Why the hell not? Just give us a chance. I could make you happy. I know you better than anyone."

"That's a disaster waiting to happen. I'm young. I have goals and dreams. None of them entail being a trophy wife and bearing sons to carry the family name. I highly doubt I'll get married at all. I don't even date. And it's only going to get easier to avoid the older I get."

His eyes are roaming over my body. He must just now realize I'm wearing male clothing—clothing that does not belong to him. He clenches his jaw. "Whose clothes are you wearing, Kinzleigh? Was this Presley's idea? One of her schemes to practically pimp out your body? Is she trying to drag you into shit again? Are you sleeping with him? You're better than that."

Now I'm starting to get angry. "How is any of that your business? What if I am? I'm not yours to have and control, first of all. Secondly, you sleep with everything walking that's female, pretty much, so how dare you question my sexual activity."

He stands upright, closes his eyes, and rubs his hands over his face, releasing a breath in aggravation. "You're right. I just care about you. She's always trying to get you to do stuff you don't want to do. It frustrates me. But I won't give up until I convince you. We belong together. And I know you'd want to take it slow. You may not think so now, but I'll show you. I've waited for so long for this. I know about your cheerleading dream and I can help give that to you. I will make you mine. I don't stop when there is something I want, and you, Kinzleigh, are what I want. You don't want me to sleep around . . ." He walks closer, cupping my face in his hands, and lifts my head to look at him. "Consider it done. I don't need another girl to satisfy me. I was just biding my time until I could have you. They aren't satisfying me anymore anyway. You're almost eighteen now." He lines my body with his. "I will claim you as mine sooner or later. You deserve the best and I have the means to give it to you. The sooner you realize that, the sooner we can stop playing these games and I can start giving it to you."

I'm stunned. Speechless may be a better word. He brings his head in closely, tilting his head. "I want you to be mine. I always have." He touches his lips to mine and I try to pull away, but I can't even move. His lips aren't as soft as Breyson's. He kisses a little rougher and faster. He slides his tongue inside the opening of my lips.

I can't bring myself to kiss him back. It doesn't feel right. None of this feels right. He nibbles on my lower lip and then releases my lips from his. "It may come as a shock to you now, but one day you will kiss me back. I will wait. I won't try to kiss you again until then, but know that I will never stop trying until you're mine."

Good luck with that.

Presley walks in the door. "Babe, what on earth is taking you so long? Did you fall . . . Oh." She looks the way a person would look who just walked in on her parents going at it, terrified and freaked out. "Am I interrupting?"

She is standing with one hand on the doorframe and the other on the doorknob. "No, I was just finishing up in here."

I push Preston by the chest so he will take the hint and move. As he backs up, I jump off the counter and take off toward Presley's room, almost knocking her over to get through the door. "Think about what I said!" he calls out as I come barreling through the door.

Presley peeks into her bedroom before she walks in the bathroom door saying, "I'll be right out. Find something to watch okay?"

I nod, and the door clicks shut. I have no idea what she's up to, because all I hear are hushed whispers. I can only imagine what that looked like with him standing between my legs, holding my face in his hands.

I sit on the edge of the bed and place my hands over my face, shaking my head. What just happened? Is he insane? He can't possibly think I'm going to change my mind. Could he? Somehow, I need to rectify this, or our family gatherings are going to be really awkward.

After all that the first thing that passes through my mind is Breyson. His kiss was perfect, not rushed. My lips tingle at the memory of his touching mine. I'm really tired. I need to go to bed and maybe I'll wake up and none of this Preston stuff will be real. Maybe I'm asleep and just dreaming it all up. The subconscious can be a deceiving thing.

What time is it anyway? I get up to charge my phone and realize I don't have it. Maybe I left it in Presley's car. Thinking about it, though, I know exactly where it is; on the bedside table next to one hot country boy that's gotten my attention.

I'll just have to go get it tomorrow. I crawl up to the head of the bed, turning back the covers and nestling beneath them. As I close my eyes a smile forms. I get to see him again after all. Falling asleep comes much easier as the memory of tonight all comes flooding back.

TEN

Kinzleigh

The tide rolls in, crashing against the shoreline, birds migrating overhead. Their calls echo against the perfect, clear blue sky. I'm standing on the beach, sand particles covering my damp feet, wearing a white monokini swimsuit that gives an extra glow to my sun-kissed skin. My blonde hair is blowing in the breeze, but it's cut shorter—just below my shoulders.

I stare out at the water, enjoying the warm sunny day. I don't recognize this place. It's absolutely beautiful. The sand is bright-white and the water is crystal-blue, swirls of aqua mixed in, revealing the ocean floor at a glance from the shoreline. Coral and seashells litter the sea floor.

Two arms wrap around my waist, resting on my stomach. "You make this place even more beautiful than it already is." I love the sound of his voice. It's so soothing. I close my eyes and rest my head against his chest, placing my hands over his.

"You're too good to me." I sigh in contentment. He picks me up, cradling me in his arms. I interlock my hands at the back *of his neck, sunlight reflecting off my left hand with movement, making the diamond attached to my ring finger sparkle. Wrapped around my third finger lies a beautiful, large square cut diamond surrounded by small, round diamonds embedded in an antique style white gold band. It's has a vintage yet still modern design.*

I look around us. There isn't another person in sight, just a small hut on the vacant private beach. He walks me over to a wood frame canopy bed covered in white linens, sitting in the sand. The almost black knots in the dark-stained wood tell its story and the uneven planes give it a hand carved feel. Hanging from the canopy are sheer white sheets, blowing in the breeze. He lays me down gently in the center of the bed, before removing his shorts, and then kneels on the bed over me. "You're the most beautiful woman I've ever seen."

He pulls the straps of my swimsuit down my arms, slowly freeing them, before peeling the rest of it from my body. He lays over me, holding his weight with his arms beside my head. Without me having to make a move, he spreads my legs apart with his knees. He kisses me gently, not getting in a hurry. "I'm going to make love to you; today, tomorrow, and forever. Today has been the best day of my life. Here's to forever. I love you, Kinzleigh Abercrombie. Promise me you'll never leave me; until death do us part."

He slowly thrusts inside of me, and stops, knowing I'd be ready without question. I'm always ready for him. "Promise me."

"I promise," I say. "I'm yours forever."

He moves slowly, thrusting in and out. This moment—it's beautiful and it's ours, the first day of our forever. I bite my lip, trying to hold onto the tightening taking place in my body. "Let it go, baby." And just like that, I fall into an orgasm, contracting around him.

He picks up pace and a few thrusts later, releases his semen inside my womb. He leans down and kisses me, a smile across his face as he pulls my left ring finger to his lips. I love seeing him this happy. "I love you, Breyson, my husband."

My eyes pop open. The sounds of my heavy breathing are all that fills the silent room and I'm covered in sweat. I look around. The beams from the sun are peeping through the curtains. Everything in the house is completely quiet, meaning it's early.

I'm still tired from being up late, but after a dream like that I'm scared to go back to sleep. Why on earth I would dream something so horrifying? I can't even say the 'M' word, let alone image it for myself. Talk about your subconscious going haywire.

I look beside me and Presley is still sleeping peacefully, not a single limb moving; only the steady rise and fall of her chest signifying she's very much alive. I sit up and throw my legs over the side of the bed. Only one thing is going to make me feel better right now—to run.

I get up and walk to Presley's dresser. I know she keeps her yoga clothes in the third drawer. Pulling the handles toward me at a snail's pace, I slide it out slowly to keep noise down, and grab a pair of black yoga pants and a lavender racer-back tank. I fold the clothes I'm wearing and neatly place them on her dresser to take them home later. I tiptoe into her closet and grab a pair of running shoes and some socks. Thank God we wear the same size in everything.

Dressed, I walk to the door as lightly as possible since we're on the second floor, directly above her parents' bedroom. Opening the door, I peek out into the hallway, hoping Preston isn't anywhere to be seen. Everything is still dark and quiet.

Tip toeing down the steps, I make it to the front door. I look around one last time to make sure no one is up. Finally making it out the door, I relax a little as I take off running through the neighborhood. This is the best way to clear my head, because it's just the pavement and me. The sun hasn't fully risen yet, so the heat is still hibernating along with most of the residents.

I don't know how long I've been running and I don't care, because it's far better than my thoughts running into places it has no business wandering to. Just a few more days and a certain someone consuming my thoughts will be long gone and across the country. I'll enjoy having some fun and then everything will go back to normal . . . I hope.

The sun is now exposing itself fully and attacking my delicate skin with its rays. The heat is dry but torrid. My clothes are drenched in sweat. I finally stop running, my lungs working overtime to pull in air. I look around and realize I ran about ten miles from Presley's house. My stomach lashes out at me with a growl. I have no idea what time it is, and I still have to shower and pick up some of the stuff for the party.

I'm now realizing how long it's going to take me to get back and summer is showing its hand today. Crap! Leave it to me to end up ten miles from my car. I better get started if I want to keep a good time. I turn around and begin running back toward Presley's house when I hear a truck slowing to a stop. I don't think much about it until a door shuts, followed by shuffling of feet on the pavement.

"Kinzleigh, wait up."

I stop abruptly, turning toward the familiar voice. He is walking around the truck with his hands in his pockets. He's wearing a pair of shorts, a polo, and a pair of boating shoes. Just when I get him out of my thoughts he waltzes right back in and takes them over. "What are you doing here?"

"Presley woke up and you were gone. When she called your phone to see where you were it started ringing and woke me up." He pulls my phone from his pocket. "I saw it was her, so I answered it. She panicked since you were supposed to be picking stuff up for the party. I told her I'd come find you, so she could finish up there. She figured you wouldn't be far since your car is still parked out front."

Of course, she did. She knew good and well if my car was parked out front I wouldn't be far, unless I was kidnapped, and I highly doubt someone would take me and leave her if that were the case. There is only one street in front of her house. She could have looked herself. She knows I run to keep my body fat percentage down since I'm always a flyer in cheerleading, but instead, she sends him after me when I look awful, sweaty, and in need of a shower. "Will you just run me to Presley's to pick up my car? I can go home, shower, and meet you in town."

"There is no need for two vehicles. Ryland took the family Jeep and left his truck with me. I can come by and pick you up. Is that okay?" Whatever is fine as long as I can clean myself up. I don't usually argue with people; I never win. This is a tad bit embarrassing. I hope my deodorant holds up; although, it's Sunday and my parents will be home, so I'm not sure how to explain him. I better be figuring it out fast.

I place my hands on my hips. "That really isn't necessary. My parents will be home and possibly my brother. Unless you want to go through an interview, I can just meet you there." I can't even imagine how my parents would respond to me bringing someone home, because it has never happened.

He stands there, looking back and forth between the truck and me. He interlocks his hands behind his neck. I'm hoping he is going to make this less complicated and meet me there. "Nah, that's okay. I'll just come pick you up." I sigh, defeated. Well, this will be interesting. "Come on, get in."

It takes about five minutes to get back to Presley's. I hurry to my car, because Preston's car is still in the drive. I guess he is partaking in the party festivities today. After last night, I really don't need any drama from him.

I've known Preston all my life. Other than the age difference, I'm as close to him as I am Presley. With our parents being such good friends, we were constantly around each other growing up, so it comes with the territory. If it had been anyone else last night, I would have been thoroughly creeped out, but I know that's not how he meant it, so I will let it go. He is spoiled and a bit of a control freak, in the non-psychotic way, so when he is losing something he's after or it's not going his way, he tends to panic. And well, then he's kind of an asshole.

I pull out of the driveway with Breyson following behind. It took some maneuvering to get out, since Preston's car was behind mine, but I managed. I would hope that my parents are gone, but that's not going to be the case.

If I were one of those kids always sneaking out and getting into trouble, it would be easy, because my parents are predictable. They are always home on Sunday and we always go to church. They are conservative. My dad has always said that he's pulled the company this far, because he doesn't work on Sunday and he reserves it for a day of rest, as it was intended.

Pulling in my driveway, I glance in the rearview mirror. Breyson is pulling in behind me. I press the remote on my visor, raising the garage door. I might as well get this over with. I feel nauseous from the nerves when I hear him shut the truck door at my rear. My hands are sweating and my breathing is becoming impaired. I've never once in my life introduced my parents to a boy. I have no idea what to expect.

Closing my eyes and resting my forehead on the steering wheel, I breathe deeply, trying to calm down. A moment later, I hear tapping on the window. Opening the door for me to get out, Breyson is standing there with a cocky grin on his face. "What's the matter? Are you scared your mom and dad won't like me?" he asks, teasingly.

Walking toward the garage door and twisting the knob, I stop. "They may be a little shocked, since I've never . . . uh . . . brought a guy home before. I really hope Konnor isn't here," I say, opening the door.

Konnor is in a bad place right now and bringing a guy home for the first time, knowing he is going to think the worst, scares the crap out of me. The garage door leads into the mudroom and from there into the kitchen.

Opening the opposing door, Mom looks up at me from the kitchen island. She is standing over the cook top, stirring something inside a pot with one hand on her hip. She is wearing her glasses, which means she has been reading— probably case files or a book. "Hey, baby girl. Did you and Presley have a good time? You missed Sunday Mass." She gives me that look. I nod, knowing she's displeased. Breyson comes through the door, making himself known, and her jaw falls slightly.

She quickly recovers, placing a smile on her face. Yep, my absence at Mass is quickly forgotten. Wait for it . . . Here it goes. She places the spoon down on the counter and heads toward us. Looking straight at me, but closing in on Breyson, she says, "Who is your friend, honey?" Breyson is slightly behind me, off to the side.

I look at him apologetically, mouthing 'sorry', as she opens her arms to give him a hug. "It's so good to meet you, dear. Kinzleigh has lost her manners. I'm Leigh Baker, Kinzleigh's mom."

I stand here, speechless, watching the interaction. This is really awkward, to say the least. What am I supposed to say? I didn't think this through. How am I supposed to introduce him? *Hey, Mom, this is the guy I just met and may let de-flower me before he heads back home to . . . wherever he's from.* Not going to happen. But what are my other options? He's not my boyfriend and he's not really a friend either, so I'm at a loss. Nothing is coming to mind.

Breyson is looking at my mom with a grin on his face. "I think she may just be a little caught off guard. It's nice to meet you, Mrs. Baker. I'm Breyson Abercrombie, Ryland Reeves' cousin. I'm here visiting like I do every summer and met Kinzleigh at the beach Friday. I'm just helping her get everything ready for this pool party of Presley's that I keep hearing so much about."

She releases him and looks at me with a big smile on her face. "I do believe I know Ryland. He's a sweet kid and comes from a good family too. It's great to have you here, Breyson. I'm glad Kinzleigh is meeting new people. I'm cooking some lunch if either of you are hungry."

She releases him from her grasp and looks at me. "By the looks of you, you still need to shower. The food should be ready before you leave." No way am I sitting around the table having a family meal with him here. I need to hurry up and get showered, so we can be out of here.

"Mom, we're in a hurry. Rain check? We can just grab something in town." I look over at Breyson. "Right?" He doesn't even look uncomfortable. He should be very uncomfortable. Am I the only one freaking out right now?

He shakes his head at me, smiling, as if he knows what I'm trying to get out of. "Where I come from, you don't turn down home cooking for fast-food. Presley told me what time we need to be back and gave me the rundown on what your duties are. I think we have time to eat before we go." He looks back at my mom, and I can tell he's laying the charm on thick. "We'd love to eat, Mrs. Baker, thank you."

My mom wraps her arm over my shoulders, steering me toward the living room. I can hear the golf announcer coming from the television. "You go on and get dressed. I'll introduce Breyson to your dad and brother."

I bite my nails. "Konnor is here?"

Great. This is just what I need. Not.

I should have just showered at Presley's and borrowed some clothes. My mom looks at me as if I'm being ridiculous. "Of course, he's here. It's Sunday. Normally, you are too. We always hang around here on Sundays together. We haven't been home from Mass long. Everyone missed you this morning."

She stops in the doorway and turns back to Breyson, who's still standing at the dining room table. She waves him over toward the living room. He walks over and she wraps her other arm around his shoulders, towing us together. "Ken, we have company. Turn that television volume down."

Breyson looks over at me with a smirk on his face, raising his brow questioningly. I guess he figured out where I got my name.

Dad always wanted a little girl and when they got pregnant so soon after having Konnor, they thought it would be fitting to combine their names—Kinzleigh being the result. Ever the sentimental ones, those two are. Konnor was named after Gramps. George Konnor Baker was my dad's father, also founder of G. Baker and Sons Contracting, L.L.C.

Dad is sitting in his recliner, hidden behind the Sunday paper that is spread across his lap. He lowers the page, raising his brows as his eyes lock on Breyson. He looks at Mom. "Who do we have here, Leigh?"

Oh brother, he has that tone. He's not too thrilled. *Awesome.* Konnor turns around from the couch he's sitting on. One look at Breyson and I can tell he isn't pleased either. How am I supposed to leave him down here with these two vultures?

"Ken, this is Kinzleigh's friend, Breyson." She pats him on the back. "You know Joe and Susan Reeves. This is their nephew."

Konnor looks at him, his eyes slightly narrowed. "You're Ryland's cousin? I don't recall seeing you around here before."

Why do they have to make this a big deal? I've never brought home a guy before. So what? At the rate they're going, this will be the last time as well. Breyson walks toward my dad and brother. He stops at my dad first, holding out his hand. "Breyson Abercrombie, Sir. It's nice to meet you. I'm here visiting family for a week. Third summer now and I love it here."

I inch forward, but Mom grabs my shoulder, halting me. I look at her, but she shakes her head at me. "Go get dressed, honey. Time is wasting. He will be fine. This is something that every dad looks forward to. Don't take that away."

She smiles at me. "Run along. I'll supervise. I've been where you are. It'll be fine." No, she hasn't been here before, because Dad is the only man she's ever been with. I, however, have no intention of taking this further than a week and then I'm sending him on his way. Him meeting my family will just further complicate things, because Mom is already making it sound like he is a prospective boyfriend.

"Breyson, what are your intentions with my daughter since you will be gone in a week?" Dad speaks out, breaking me from my stare off with Mom.

"Dad!" I yell out, completely humiliated that this is happening. Why can't they just be normal and talk about football or something?

Konnor looks at me with a smirk on his face. "What's the matter, Kinzleigh? You know we have to keep your best interests at heart."

Breyson looks at me, giving me a reassuring smile. "It's okay, Kinzleigh, go get ready. I'll get to know your family a little." I don't feel good about this. As a matter of fact, I tried to avoid it, but what other choice do I have now? I can't go to the party like this.

I move toward the stairs, dragging my feet. "Dad, please don't embarrass me. Behave," I say, pointing my finger at him.

"Kinzleigh, I believe you have a shower calling for you. We'll be fine down here. I don't need tips on how to parent, but thank you for your concern."

Sighing, I run upstairs to get ready, quickly, so we can get out of here before he tries to give him the *Daddy with the shotgun speech* or something else completely crazy. Dinner with the fam was just crossed off the to-do list. I don't care what he says. Manners went out the window when words like *intentions* went flying through the air.

I'm standing in the middle of my room, staring at the clothes spread across my bed, showered and wearing my bra and panties. What do I wear? I already know I have to take my swimwear, but what do I wear until then? Now that I may want to go through with this *losing my virginity* thing at some point in the very near future, I should probably put forth a little effort in getting ready; as in what a guy would like versus what I like.

My two choices, as I stand here pondering, are my black one shoulder mini-dress that stops halfway to my knee and is fitted, but not tight, with a butterfly style sleeve opening as it falls. I usually pair it with my beige canvas wedges and gold hoops. The other choice is my chevron shift dress in mint green and white with three-quarter length sleeves that I usually pair with my white gladiator sandals topped off with a splash of red in my jewelry.

"Hmm . . . What to wear?" I say, tapping my index finger to my lips.

Mom slips inside my door. "You always look beautiful in the mint green one. It does wonders with your blonde hair and makes your eyes stand out. Plus, the flats will be more comfortable. All that walking may be hard on your feet in those heels. You don't want to try too hard. The black one says, *take me to dinner,* and the other says, *I'm cute but comfy.*"

I always did love my mom's eye for good fashion. Send us shopping and we always put a dent in Dad's wallet. He has limited our mother-daughter shopping outings to a minimum. Really, he just jokes, since Mom is a big shot lawyer and all, contributing a large portion of what's there. "You really think so? What should I do to my hair?"

"I know so." She smiles and comes to my side, brushing my curls off my shoulder. "It makes the green in your eyes pop. You always were my little princess. You're growing up so fast. At least you've waited this long to bring boys around. You're making me feel old, you know." She winks at me playfully and sits on the bed. "Now put on that dress and bring me that comb and some bobby pins and I'll do your hair."

It's been a long time since Mom has done my hair. It makes me feel like a little girl again. I pull the dress over my white, lace bra and panty set with baby pink trim. Grabbing the container of bobby pins and the comb, I sit between her legs on the floor. "What are you going to do to it?"

"You just sit still and let me worry about that. I will make sure that boy's jaw drops when he sees you." My hair is parted down the left side of my head, the biggest portion of hair laying over to the right. She begins to braid loosely from my part down the right hairline, beside my face. Just behind my right ear, she ties the braid with a small hair band.

I close my eyes, as the light tugging of my hair makes me want to go to sleep. She used to brush my hair each night when I was little. "What are they doing to him down there? Is Dad behaving himself? Is Konnor freaking out?"

She chuckles as she swoops all of my hair to the right side. She piles all of my curly hair, including the loose braid in one hand and ties it with a pony tail holder at the bottom of my hairline, below my right ear. She begins forming a messy bun with the ponytail. "Honey, every man dreads the day he has to share his little girl with another man. You'll see one day when you have a daughter. I would say Dad is doing pretty well considering he had no warning. Usually, it's when you're sixteen and come home asking to go to the prom, months in advance, and he has a chance to get used to the idea before a boy shows up at the front door. You've always surprised us, though, never going by the book on anything. As relieving as it is that you never give us an ounce of trouble, I was beginning to wonder if I was ever going to get to take you prom dress shopping and other mother-daughter things I have been waiting to do with you."

She almost sounds sad. I suppose this isn't the time for me to announce I don't plan on having kids, ever. Kids are a blessing from above and everything, but it's just not for me. I don't see that ever changing. I would think it's a desire you have at an early age if you're going to have it. I have too many dreams for myself than to be tied down to children or marriage. Traveling would be one.

She puts the last of the bobby pins around the bun to hold it loosely and gets up to grab the hairspray. "Come here. Let me finish you off."

I stand up and walk to the mirror. I have to admit my mom is one awesome fashionista to be a mother with two nearly grown kids. It's a loose bun of curls on the lower right side of my head, beneath my ear. "I have something for you." She pulls a handkerchief from her pocket, holding it in her hand. She unwraps the cloth, revealing a small pair of diamond hoops.

My eyes widen as they lay perfectly still, glimmering in the light. "Your father gave these to me one year from the day we started dating. I had them cleaned and put up for you for this occasion. The first day my little girl became a woman. To me, that day is today. You have blossomed and have shown your maturity, so I think you're ready."

I really feel bad that I have no intention of becoming serious about dating. "Mom, you don't have to do this. You know we're not serious, right? I just met him. I'm only showing him a good time and taking him around while he's visiting, nothing more."

She holds up her hand to stop me. "Honey, I know you're not holding out your hand waiting on a diamond ring, but this is a big step for you. Take them. They will look beautiful on you."

accepted FATE

I give her a hug. "Thank you. I love them." She releases me and watches me put the earrings on, one by one.

"You're welcome. Now, let's get you finished. You have one handsome boy down there waiting on you. You know how to pick a cute one. Hurry up or your brother may not let him leave with you in hand. He seems a little on edge." She winks again and sprays my hair. Just like that I pick up pace. I know Konnor and I've seen him in protection mode when his friends used to show an interest in me. I don't want to rehash those times.

Putting on my gladiator sandals, I grab my mint green clutch purse I bought to go with this dress and put my necessities inside. Handbags and shoes are my personal weakness among fashion. I have a bag for everything.

I run to my closet and pull my mint green and gold tote from the shelf. I place my black monokini swimsuit and matching sheer cover-up skirt in the bag, as well as my black shimmery flip-flops. Walking into my bathroom, I grab my black and pink beach towel.

As I come back out, Mom is standing at the doorway, holding onto the knob. "You look beautiful. He isn't going to let you out of his sight. You ready to go?"

Smiling, I nod and start for the door, trailing behind my mom. As we're coming down the stairs, everyone looks my way, standing to their feet. I feel like a princess being announced at a ball. It's strange. I don't usually like being the focal point, but right now, knowing I'm the focal point to a guy that looks like that, really isn't all that bad.

A big smile spreads across Breyson's face at the same time a scowl crosses Konnor's. I walk beside my dad and he puts an arm over my shoulder. "You're gorgeous, just like your mother," he says, kissing my cheek. He then turns to Breyson. "I expect you to take special care of my baby girl. You do that and we won't have any problems. Understood?"

Breyson nods. "Yes, Sir. That won't be a problem." He looks over to me. "You ready to go?"

I can tell Konnor wants to say something the way he is looking at me. I look him in the eyes, telling him I'll be fine. We've always had a way of communicating without actually speaking. He nods his head in response to my silent message.

I look back at Breyson, excitement fueling my response. "As ready as I'll ever be."

ELEVEN

Breyson

I wasn't prepared for what came walking down the stairs. Sure, I've seen her dressed in several different ways at this point, but what she looks like now barely allowed me to breathe. If I thought it was hard to contain myself before, it just got harder. This girl puts any other girl to shame, and today she's mine. Legs to die for. It brings back the memory of them wrapped around me in the pool.

I can't believe I'm at a girl's house, meeting her family. I'm not sure what that says about me when it comes to her. It's too intimate and gives off messages I don't want made, but this girl has a way of making me want to do things I never usually do without even trying. I have to admit that now I know why I never do this.

After sitting in the living area with her family, listening to the *I've got a shotgun and I'm not afraid to use it* speech, I wasn't all that disappointed to leave without eating. Not to forget her brother staring daggers at me like he wanted to kick my ass. I can't say that I blame him, though, because I have a fourteen-year-old sister. I imagine if a guy like me were thinking about her in the same way that I'm thinking about Kinzleigh, I'd want to beat his ass too.

We walk outside and get in the truck. "Do you realize how beautiful you are?" I'm not much for compliments, but if this girl doesn't realize how gorgeous she is, she needs to be told. It blows me away that someone hasn't tried harder to claim her. If I lived here, I wouldn't let her out of my sight.

The fact that she actually wants to give me her virginity gives me chills. Instead of it freaking me out, as it should be, I'm imagining how much I want to be her first, to go where no other guy has gone.

I've never been with a virgin before. I've always stayed far away from them; it's an unspoken rule of mine. A girl that loses her virginity is looking for love and I am not the place to find it. Apparently, she is one person that could make me change my mind. The thought of being her first is consuming my mind, and probably more much than it should. Is it normal for it to thrill me; give me an adrenaline rush?

She blushes as I sit here staring at her. I can't help it. I can't take my eyes off of her. "Thanks, I guess. Where to first? You said Presley gave you the rundown, so I'm assuming I don't have to?"

"Yeah, I got everything covered. Let's go." We pull out of her driveway and head toward town. According to Presley, we really don't have much to get. A catering company is delivering the food and a rental company is setting up all of the tents and tables. A DJ will setup his own equipment as well. I think it was mostly just extras and stuff for her. Presley said there was a party planner in charge of the decorations and making sure everything ran smoothly.

Personally, this is all a little new to me. Where I'm from, party planners don't put a party together. Most people just get together and do their own thing. I wish I could take her back home and show her how it's done in the south. The guys would be falling all over her.

Wait, what the hell am I thinking? That's exactly why I wouldn't want her back at home. I like not having to share her. I'm going to enjoy the extra hour with her alone before we head back to Presley's and I no longer have her all to myself. "I have to run to the mall and pick up Presley a new swimsuit," she says, breaking the silence.

"Knowing what Presley's house and car look like, I find it hard to believe she doesn't have a swimsuit," I say teasingly.

"Girl rule number one. Always have a new outfit for every occasion," she replies sarcastically with a smile on her face.

"You're telling me she hasn't already picked it out? Don't girls do that stuff weeks in advance?" I don't know much about girls other than physical anatomy, but I know enough from girls at school that those things are topics for weeks on end, prior to the event.

"Presley is a little . . . different, I guess. She knows the new swimwear line comes in today. She refuses to have on the same swimsuit as anyone else since it's her party. Don't ask me why, because I have no idea."

I shake my head. Girls are a species from an alien planet. You can't live with them and you can't seem to live without them either. "I'm just the driver; tell me where to go."

We come to a stoplight. Take a few right turns and Laguna Hills mall isn't far on the left. "You remember how to get to BJ's, right? It's in that same location." I nod and follow her directions.

It really doesn't take as long as I thought to get here. Pulling in the parking lot, I find a spot and kill the engine. "What all do we have to get again?"

She hops down off the side step, upon getting out of the truck. "Just pick up the party favors and Presley's stuff. That's all, unless something calls to me," she says with a smile on her face. "She called ahead for the party favors, so we just have to pick them up. It may be several trips, though, because the party favors alone will be three or four different stores. I think for the girls it's candles and cosmetics, and for the guys, I don't even know. I may have to call her. Probably sports memorabilia or watches or something."

"She puts a lot of money into this, doesn't she?" I don't know why it has to be so extravagant for a pool party. I'm out of my realm on this one.

We begin walking to the huge mall standing before us. "Well, her birthday is during the holiday season and cooler weather, so it's never a big deal. This is her way to make up for it. She's had one every year since she was fifteen. It's just become a tradition now. I don't know what everyone will do when she graduates. I guess her little sister Paxtyn will take over. By the time we graduate she will be in high school," she says, shrugging her shoulders.

As we walk into the mall, I notice just how busy it is. Making our way through the crowded interior I ask, "Where to first?"

She looks at me as she weaves through the mass of people. "I don't know. I guess *Victoria's Secret* is the best place to start."

I stop abruptly, before realizing there are several people following me. A woman pushing a stroller almost slams into the back of me. I walk quickly to catch up with Kinzleigh. "You did not say anything about *Victoria's Secret*. Victoria can keep her secrets, because there is no way I'm walking in that store."

"I don't know where you're from, but here you better keep pace or you'll become a floor mat." She laughs and keeps walking, not even fazed by the fact I'm silently, as well as outwardly, freaking out about walking in a lingerie store.

For such short legs she sure can walk fast. When I catch up to her she is at the edge of the store, about to walk in. "Well, are you coming?"

I stand here looking into the store filled with racks upon racks of lingerie and underwear. I have no experience underwear shopping; only removing the already purchased product. I run my fingers through my hair. I have never in my life been to a woman's lingerie store. Do men even go in these types of stores if they aren't married? She raises a brow at me. "Scared something is going to jump out and bite you?"

It baffles me that I'm so hung up over a hot girl I'm about to walk in this place. It's a little intimidating. Sighing, I say, "You owe me for this and once I decide what it is, I will collect."

She rolls her eyes at me. "Whatever you say, lover boy, now come on," she says sarcastically.

Funny, I actually like the sound of that. She is halfway through the store when I realize I'm still standing here at the entry. Putting my hands in my pockets, I walk quickly in her direction. Bypassing the store associates and other shoppers—all female—smiles turn up on each of them and multiple ask me, "Is there something I can help you with?"

Smiling politely, I pick up pace to catch up with her. Shaking my head, I reply, "No, thank you. I'm just along for the ride." The awkwardness is evident in my tone as I point at Kinzleigh flipping through the neatly arranged swimsuits on a table in the back.

I walk up beside her, smiling. "Now you owe me two things. Shall we continue to add favors?"

She looks at me, scrunching her nose. "Uh, how do you arrive at that assessment?"

"You just left me to fend for myself in a woman's lingerie store. The associates are eying me like flying vultures over road kill, waiting to swoop down and pick at me."

"Oh, don't be so dramatic. Your uneasiness makes you stick out like a sore thumb. They sense your nervousness. Just play it cool and watch," she says, holding up a swimsuit top. I eye it stupidly. How is this supposed to help? "Hey, babe, hold this for me, okay?" She says it loud enough that the store associate closest to us hears.

I awkwardly take the swimsuit, looking her in the eyes. She turns up one side of her mouth and has a mischievous look in her eye. "Okay..."

Sure enough, as I take the swimsuit, the girl closest to us wrinkles her nose in a look of disgust and stomps off like someone just stole her toy.

"You can thank me later," she says teasingly and goes back to rummaging through the pile of swimsuits. Thirty minutes later we're checking out with two armfuls—one for Kinzleigh and one for Presley.

This is not motivating me to want to do this again. I think I'll leave shopping to females. Usually, I just let my mom buy my clothes or run in one of a couple stores and have an entire new wardrobe in thirty minutes tops. The amount of money a girl can spend on underwear and swimsuits is insane to me. Five hundred dollars later, we're leaving the store, ready to finish getting everything for the party.

Two hours went by in a bit of a blur. Between hauling out hundreds of candles and other meaningless items, I'm ready to get to this party. If it wasn't for Kinzleigh being so freakin' hot, I would have never agreed to this. The girl has me doing all kinds of random things I would never in a million years do, without even asking me to do it; I volunteer. From all the constant trips back and forth to the truck, I'm sweating. We stopped about an hour ago and grabbed something to eat from the food court to replenish some of this lost energy.

Finally in the truck, I turn to Kinzleigh. "Please tell me we're done." At this point, I'll tell Presley personally that she can do it herself.

Kinzleigh shyly smiles over at me. "Yes, I'm sorry. I shouldn't have let you tag along. It was a lot of work." What she doesn't know is there was no way I wasn't coming along. Any excuse to spend more time with her, I'll take.

"Nah, it's okay, but Presley can do the rest herself. I'm not used to parties entailing so much work. Y'all do things a lot different around here. I didn't have anything better to do; I'm just giving you a hard time."

"We still have a little while until the party starts if you want to just drop me off at Presley's and come back later. She always times it to start in the afternoon and continue into the night, where she can turn on the pool lights and light up the tents." There is no way I'm letting her go this early. I can only imagine what dickweeds I'll have to go through to get her attention once everyone shows up. If what Ryland said was true, every male with something swinging between his legs will want to get close to her in a swimsuit.

The thought of someone else trying to touch her is starting to get to me. I let out a deep breath, trying to get a grip. "How about we drop this stuff off and you can come with me? I have to go by Ryland's and get my swim trunks anyway. I didn't think about it when I left this morning. Ryland's parents were going to some company BBQ, so it'll just be us most likely. We can hang out for a bit and change, then head over to Presley's a little before it starts to make sure she doesn't need help. I think Ryland said he was helping her."

"Are you sure? I don't want to take up your entire week here. I know there are probably other things you'd rather be doing. You don't have to occupy your time with the likes of me." The fact that she is humble enough to think she's keeping me from something better than being with her makes me like her all the more. The girl could likely have any guy she wants and she really doesn't see it.

"I'm sure," I say, pulling into Presley's driveway. That same Porsche is sitting in the drive from earlier, but now in the open garage. I wonder whose car that is. Just as I pull up, a guy walks to the driver's side door and opens it. He looks about twenty or twenty-one. When he looks at the truck his eyes focus on the passenger's side, clearly recognizing Kinzleigh. A snarling expression comes across his face. "Who is that?"

She sighs, as if not wanting to enter into this discussion. "That's Preston, Presley's older brother. He's home for the summer from UC Berkeley."

Hell no. She stayed the night with that guy in the same house? I know that look he's wearing. He wants her, and he is willing to do whatever it takes to get her. I've seen that look before. I want to hurry up and get her out of here. The way he is staring at her is pissing me off.

Ryland's yellow Jeep is sitting in the driveway beside me. "Will you be okay long enough for me to switch keys with Ryland?"

She nods, looking slightly confused. "Why wouldn't I be?"

"Well, for starters, that guy is still standing there staring at you, looking like he wants to tear my head off every time he glances in my direction." I look back over and see him standing with the door open, his fists clenched. I don't like to fight or start trouble, at least not over a girl, but if he wants to start anything over this one, I'm all in.

We seem to be having one of those man-to-man stare-offs. The one where you both understand what the other is after and she is the prize.

May the best man win.

My hands tighten around the steering wheel, my knuckles turning white. I may have to leave her to him in a few days, but right now she's mine. I will stake my claim if he doesn't back off. I hope this clown doesn't intend to hang around the party, trying to get her attention. He may be older and taller, but not by much and I'm twice his size.

"Preston won't hurt me; we just have some . . . unfinished business. It's fine. I'll go ahead and take my bags to the Jeep. Let Presley know her stuff is here, will you?" She looks at Preston and opens the door. Great, now I don't want to leave her side. The faster I go get those keys, the faster I can get back.

"I'll let her know when I tell Ryland to come unload everything. I'll be right back." I jump out and head for the backyard, where the pool is, in the opposite direction of the garage. I get to the back and see Ryland almost immediately. "Hey, Ry, come here, man," I say, waving him over in a sprint toward him.

"What's up? You okay? You look pissed."

"It's nothing; me and Kinzleigh are running by the pool house and we'll be back in about an hour. I need your Jeep keys. I'm going to let you unload everything from the truck."

Handing me the keys, he runs his other hand through his curly hair. "What's up with you? You cool?"

I keep looking back toward the front of the house, as if I could actually see what was going on with the two of them if I tried. "Yeah, man, I've got to go. I'll be back."

I grab the keys and take off toward the driveway. When I round the house, I see Kinzleigh leaned up against the Jeep with her arms crossed over her chest and that Preston guy has a hand on each side of her head, against the door of the Jeep. They seem to be having some kind of conversation. Seeing him that close to her has me raging to hit something. I close my eyes and pop my neck to the side, trying to calm down before I lay him out on the ground and freak her out.

As I approach the Jeep, I grab her bags from the ground beside her feet and look at her. "You ready to go?"

He pushes off the Jeep, but doesn't put any more distance between them. "Where are you going? You're not missing the party, are you?" His voice is deep, but he sounds a little panicky.

That's right, she's going with me.

She rolls her eyes as if she's slightly aggravated. "Preston, this is Ryland's cousin, Breyson. Stop being rude; it's not like you. He's visiting for a while." She looks over at me. "Breyson, this is Presley's older brother, Preston. I'm sorry, he's not usually like this," she says, crinkling her brows in confusion.

In a split second, his face relaxes, and he holds out his hand. "Kinzleigh is right. My apologies." He has a cocky grin and I know why. In all of that information he heard one thing— I'm visiting. He knows he has the lead, because I'm leaving soon, and he's not stupid enough to piss her off. Well, two can play that game.

I hold out my hand, grasping his. "Nice to meet you." His handshake says it all. My dad gave me a lesson on a man's handshake and what it means. He's overbearing in his grip. He's telling me she's as good as his. Well, assume away, because we will see who she ends up with. I tighten my jaw, looking him in the eyes.

Kinzleigh clears her throat. "I hate to break up this little bromance that's brewing, but we need to go if we're going to get back in time."

I can't help but to smirk, standing before him. I feel like a fighter that's just won his match. Yeah, she's coming with me. I drop my hand and open her door.

"I'll be waiting for you," he calls out as I shut the door, backing toward the garage, and just like that my temporary victory was shattered. I should have known better. Of course, he's going to hang around a bunch of high schoolers in order to be around her.

"I wouldn't count on it," I mumble after closing the door. I get in and start the ignition, backing out of the driveway.

The drive to Ryland's was short and silent. I was mad and trying to sort through all these emotions pumping through my body. I've never dealt with jealousy and rage when it comes to a girl and I sure as hell never had to compete.

As I park and kill the engine, she looks at me from the passenger seat. "Are you okay? You haven't said anything since we left."

I need to get my crap together. "Yeah, I was just thinking about some things. Come on and grab your stuff."

As we walk into the door, she sets her bag down. "We need to get going in about thirty minutes," she says, walking around to the front of the couch.

Awesome! I can't wait to get back to the spoiled little rich boy trying to one-up me. "We'll be ready." I sit down and reach for her hand, pulling her into the opening of my legs. "I just want to sit with you for a while. Will you do that?" She nods her head and I notice the slightest blush appear on her cheeks.

I grab her waist, pulling her closer to me. She places her hands on my shoulders, looking down at me. "What do you want to talk about?"

"Tell me where you're moving," I say. She starts to open her mouth, but then closes it again. Clearly it caught her off guard.

She shakes her head. "No specifics. Remember? That was the deal to hang out."

She is so stubborn. "What will it hurt? Maybe it's close enough to me that we can meet up some. It can't be too far from . . ." She slaps her hand over my mouth before I can say Mississippi.

"I don't want to know. Look, this can't go further than the time you're here. I can't afford any complications in my life. I've worked too hard for everything to let anything get in the way now. Me moving doesn't change anything. A year from now I'll be back in California. Nothing or no one, my parents included, will change that. My heart will always be in California. I won't give it away. I can give you my body and a few days while you're here and that's it. There is no reason to kid ourselves with some illusion that'll create an attachment that isn't necessary. I've thought about it a lot. I want to give my virginity to you, and not because I want anything from you, but because it's what *I* want, and the fact that you'll leave shortly after makes it less complicated. I always do the right thing. I'm doing this for me."

Well I'll be damned. I'm staring at the female version of myself. Of course, the one time I find someone exactly like me she has to be across the country. There are too many people blinded by the illusion of love. I know that, even at a young age.

I have finally found someone that doesn't care one thing about it. Someone who actually wants to live and go after the things she wants. I love that about her. I, on the other hand, have lived under my father's shadow all my life. He pushes my brothers and me to be doctors just like him and my mom, but I would rather play sports. It's something I'm good at. The one day of the year I wait around for is the NFL draft. During the fall I live, breathe, and sweat football.

To Dad, sports are just a part of high school and college—a way to keep you occupied—but nothing more. He is always riding me about keeping perfect grades. He loves sports just like the next person, but to him, professional sports are meant for the people that cannot excel academically, giving them a means to success. None of us stands up to him on how he believes. We all just go along with it. Since my mom is an OBGYN at the largest women's clinic in town, she's pretty much just like Dad.

To me, being drafted in the NFL my senior year of college would be a dream come true. It's an accomplishment only a small percentage of athletes attain. The main reason I'm Dad's lab rat when it comes to training and cardiovascular health is because I want to be recruited by one of the best colleges in the country.

I keep straight A's in case he has to pay for school at the college of my choice. Out of state tuition is expensive. It's among the many reasons a serious relationship isn't in the cards for me. I'll even major in biology like he wants as long as I can play football. All I have to do to keep dad happy is choose the major of his picking, then hopefully I'll get drafted before I have to worry with medical school.

I'm the fastest running back in our district and started getting college scouts last year. I've been first-string running back since freshman year. I haven't been benched a single game either. I have my list of top picks, but it's all about the offers. One more year and I'll be that much closer to my dream.

I just now realize I haven't said anything back, because I'm still shocked we're having this conversation. It's like someone handing you money and telling you not to worry about paying it back; no strings attached. "I don't know, Kinzleigh. As much as I want you, and believe me, the thought of having you before any other guy is appealing, but I'm not a virgin. I haven't been one for a while. In fact, I've been with enough girls you probably wouldn't want your first time to be with me. Isn't that supposed to be a special moment to share with someone else that's never done it before either?"

I can't believe I am actually trying to talk her out of this. Maybe I should check and make sure my dick is still down there. What red-blooded male turns down an opportunity like this? I lay my head against the back of the couch, looking her in the eyes, trying to read her emotions. She almost looks annoyed. "Are you done rambling yet? If you haven't noticed already, I don't usually follow what everyone else does. I would actually prefer this way, because I don't need it to be a gateway for anything, like dating. This is perfect," she says, as she straddles me on the couch, getting bolder. "You can teach me what I don't know and then you'll be free to go back home without worrying of me forming an attachment to you; to do whatever you want with whomever you please."

My breathing becomes ragged as I place my hands on each side of her waist. She grabs my hair in her fists, causing me to close my eyes. She lowers herself closer to my lap. A girl has never turned me on so hard and fast. I'm trying to calm myself down. I haven't even touched her yet.

My jeans are becoming so tight the seams could separate with one quick movement. The compression against my genitals is painful; it needs room. She lightly rubs against the zipper back and forth. She is experimenting, and I like it. A lot of people bitch about being used, but I can handle this.

A wave of heat radiates from between her legs, making it worse. She presses a cheek against mine, her lips barely touching my ear. "So, you up for it, or are you going to leave the job to someone else?"

She is playing with fire, as if she knows I can't stand the thought of another guy touching her. One specific guy comes to mind. It doesn't matter. I can't take it anymore. To hell with everything. I press her tight against my jeans, allowing her to feel what she's doing to me.

She is breathing hard, acknowledging that I'm having the same effect on her as she is on me. I take her face in my hands, looking her directly in the eyes. "Are you sure you want to do this? You have one chance to change your mind and I'll never bring it up again or attempt to kiss you."

I'm shaking and my voice is deeper than it usually is. I feel like I'm about to combust with need. "If you don't change your mind right now, this will happen before I leave. I will have your body. This is your one chance to back out and me forget this ever happened. You're making me crazy. After this, I will not be able to stop anymore."

I can't read her thoughts. She can hide them like a professional poker player. "I've never been surer of anything. I want you. I've never been interested in sex before," she says as her face flushes, her cheeks becoming a mild shade of red. "I don't know what these feelings mean or what to do with them. I may not be any good at . . . it, but I can learn if you will teach me."

That was the last straw. She hasn't even touched me there yet and she has me wound up so tight I feel like I can't breathe. I can't fathom her being bad at anything, especially sex. It then dawns on me. "Kinzleigh, have you ever had an orgasm?"

Her cheeks brighten in color. "I told you I've never been with a guy like that; that meant as in nothing at all."

It's appealing that she doesn't fully get what I'm asking. "I remember you saying that, but that's not the only way to orgasm. You have never given yourself one? You know, to learn your likes and dislikes." Her eyes widen and she bites her lip, shaking her head.

"I've never wanted to do that. It's weird to think of touching myself." I thought this conversation would calm these raging, Kinzleigh-induced hormones, but it's not. It's having the reverse effect.

"Kinzleigh, had you ever kissed someone before the night on the pier?" That conversation with Ryland is playing back loud and clear. I can't believe he was actually right.

She closes her eyes as I pull her closer to me. She is holding onto my wrists. When she opens her eyes, I have the answer to my question. I can see it all over her face. "Not since I played spin the bottle at Presley's thirteenth birthday party. I'm a quick learner, though; just teach me."

What she doesn't know is, I haven't kissed a girl since I lost my virginity at the age of fourteen. I haven't wanted to until her, and it was damn near perfect. I'm not interested in emotional attachments or acts so intimate it ties you to a person. I watched Beau lose his life over a girl. Me, him, and Ryland were really close. I saw how one girl could destroy an entire family, because she didn't have the decency to break up with him before she gave herself to another man. The day we laid him in the ground was the day I promised I would never let a woman break me.

I pull her in for a kiss. She will be mine—maybe only for a week, but a week nonetheless. Her lips are full and moist. I suck in her bottom lip. She tightens her grip in my hair. Slightly parting her lips, I slip my tongue inside. The menthol in her gum cools my tongue as it connects with hers. She twirls her tongue around mine, only plunging it slightly into my mouth.

I place my hand on the back of her neck and then run my hands down her spine, before stopping at the bottom hem of her dress that is resting on top of my legs. Taking ahold of her thighs, I trail my callused hand up her legs, beneath her dress.

Her skin is as smooth as molasses with a sun-kissed glow. I get to her perfect, round bottom covered in lace. She lightly bites my bottom lip, causing me to pull her closer to me in need. I run my tongue along hers. I kiss her chin and trail my tongue along her jaw line. When I reach the end of her jaw, I suck in her ear lobe, causing her to roll her head back, revealing her neck in full.

Her breathing picks up and she begins to rock back and forth in my lap. I continue kissing down her jugular vein as my fingers lightly brush up her body, continuing along the skin of her back. She arches, and her breasts press into my chest. Her bra must be made only of the same lace as her panties, because her excitement is noticeable through the thin fabric. Her dress travels upward, along with my hands.

I would not be doing this if Ryland's parents were home, but they aren't. She raises her arms, knowing what I want. I release my lips from her neck and I pull the dress over her head, revealing her body to me. Throwing it on the couch beside me, I pull back to admire the sight before me. "You really are beautiful."

She links her hands behind my neck, playing with the bottom of my hairline. "Shut up and kiss me," she says, closing in for more.

I minimize the space between us, lining my body with hers. She kisses me hungrily, as if she's just discovered something she likes and needs more. I unclasp her lacy bra, pulling it down her arms and off.

She nervously tries to cover herself by crossing her arms over her chest. Looking her in the eyes, I grab her wrists and pull them back around my neck. "Don't hide from me. You're the most beautiful girl I've ever seen. I mean it." I do mean it. She is just as beautiful naked as she is clothed. I'm lying. She's more beautiful naked.

I know she's inexperienced, so I want to go slow. I'm ignoring my own wants to make it memorable for her. I may be emotionally numb, but a girl like her doesn't come around often. She deserves to be treated with respect. She is different than all the other girls I entertain this way. I have four days to be different for her, and that's what I'm going to do. I'm going to drag this out.

I grasp her hips and rock her back and forth against the hardness that lies under the fabric of my jeans, rubbing the spot I know she needs stimulated. I continue kissing her with everything in me.

She begins to make little noises against my lips, but I can tell she's holding back, because she is shy and embarrassed. She doesn't know that as a guy, I need to hear it. I want to hear her confirm how good it feels.

Releasing her lips, I tell her, "Don't hold back, baby. It's okay to show me you like it. I want to hear you." She bites her lip and her eyes begin rolling back. "Do you feel that?" She nods in response. "Don't tense up. Let it go, baby."

I continue to rub her against the roughness of my jeans. I can't believe I feel like I could actually get off like this—just rubbing her against me and watching her get off. Her heart rate quickens and her breathing becomes heavier. After a few moments, she pulls tightly on my hair and stops moving, taking my lips in hers, moaning against them. I can tell she got her release by the feel of her underwear pressed against me.

She pulls away and lays her forehead on my shoulder, trying to calm her breathing. When her heart rate slows down she looks up at me. She has a nervous look on her face and I realize it's because I'm still hard beneath her. "Tell me what you like. I may suck at it, but I'll try my best."

I shake my head. I may be in misery the rest of the day, but it's totally worth it. This is about her. Just the fact that she is concerned with me having an orgasm is enough. "Don't worry about me. We still have four days. My plane leaves Friday morning. Let's go get changed for that pool party."

I grab her bottom and stand to my feet. She wraps her legs around my waist and locks her feet behind me. On the way to the bedroom, I grab her bag by the door.

Walking in, I make my way to the bathroom door and set her down. My eyes scan her body now that I have a full-frontal view. "I'll change out here in the bedroom. When you get *cleaned up* and changed," I say with a smirk on my face, "we'll be on our way."

Her cheeks redden, and she places one arm across her chest to cover up. I love how shy she is. It makes me smile. "Thanks," she says, closing the door.

This girl is going to be the death of me, and there is no way to stop it, I think to myself as I walk to my bag in search of my swim-trunks.

TWELVE

Kinzleigh

I place my back against the door and slide down to the floor. Wow. Is that what I've been missing? No wonder Presley has turned slutty and loving it. Don't get me wrong, I have no intention of being promiscuous, but dang it if that wasn't better than I ever thought it would be. I wonder if actual sex feels like that. Presley said it hurts, but I've worn tampons since my mom allowed me to at the age of fourteen, since my menstrual cycle can be rather heavy.

I've always been scared to go all the way or even think about it. Mom gave me the *birds and the bees* speech at the age of twelve. It was really awkward and scary. She had it drilled in my head that my dad would go to jail for murder if a boy ever tried to take that from me before walking me down the aisle like a lady. She said I had too much class to be loved and left or to whore around.

She also said the only purpose for sex was reproducing or making memories with my husband and I had no business making her a grandmother until I was married. To mom, reputation is everything. She came from a very traditional, Catholic family. She always took pride in telling me she waited until her wedding night to be intimate with a man—that man being my father. Birth control was an absolute no.

I have always followed my mother's advice and done as she instructed. Maybe it's time to make my own decision for once. Who knows, I may regret it and I may not, but at least it will be at my own risk. Besides, I have no intention of conceiving a child, ever, or getting married. My parents will have to rely on Konnor for grandkids.

I place my face in the palm of my hands, trying to calm down. I need to get it together before Presley starts calling my phone.

Standing up, I pick up my bag from the floor and place it on the countertop. Ryland's mom really has great taste. This place is decorated beautifully. I pull out the swimsuit I brought from home. Discarding my underwear into my bag, I step in my swimsuit and pull it up my body.

This is one of my favorite swimsuits. Mom doesn't care for it, because it's slightly revealing for her taste, but she tries to let me make my own judgment with my clothes within reason. It's a black monokini. The bottom is basically a standard black bikini bottom, but the top connects with the bottom by two gold hoops on my hips and it forms an infinity symbol from my neck to where it connects at the bottoms, covering only my breasts. I bought it to fit snug, because all it takes to reveal my chest is a pull too hard on the banded top.

I look in the mirror to make sure all my secret spots are covered. This should be perfect. I pull out my sheer, black cover-up wrap and tie it around my waist. My hair is still perfectly in place from when Mom fixed it earlier. I slip on my black, leather flip-flops with a matching gold metal piece that lies on top of my foot. I finish off with my clear gloss by applying it to my lips.

I exhale, hoping to get a reaction from Breyson. Shoving my things back into my bag, I make a mental note to pick up my dress and bra on the way out. I definitely don't want that left lying around. I open the door to him lying on his back across the bed with his feet planted on the floor.

As I walk out, he sits up and takes me in. His eyes widen as they sweep down my body. "Is that what you're wearing?"

Okay, so that wasn't exactly the reaction I was looking for. Maybe I don't look as good as I thought I did. Now unsure, I look down at the floor. "Yes, what's wrong with it? This is a designer swimsuit."

He places his hands together against each side of his nose, forming a line down the center of his face, as if he's frustrated. "Kinzleigh, will you please change? Don't take this the wrong way, because your body is sexy as hell, and I want nothing more than to undress you wearing that, but if we're going to hang out while I'm here, I don't want to have to break someone's jaw because they are ogling your body right in front of me. I guess it's a guy thing."

I smile. Ah, so he doesn't want someone else looking at me. Well, too bad. A little jealousy never hurt anyone. If he can rattle my thoughts all hours of the day, then he can deal with someone looking at my body. I'm not his property. I'll show him who the boss is. "This swimsuit is fine. Besides, it's the only one I brought. I only bought underwear in the mall today. Are you ready to go?"

"You're killing me. Maybe we should just stay here and I'll keep your body to myself." He raises his brows at me and I feel my face flush. Why does he embarrass me so easily?

I will not be weak.

I strut over to the door, my bag in tow, passing him in the direction of the couch when I hear a growl behind me. I smile brighter, knowing he can't see my face. It doesn't take long before I hear him walking behind me. I reach over the back of the couch to grab my dress and bra, quickly tossing it in my bag.

His hands take hold of my waist and he presses himself against my backside. Snaking his hands up my sides, under my arms and beside my breasts, he cups my shoulders, standing me upright in alignment with the front of his body. "Do you like torturing me, Kinzleigh?" His voice sounds husky and deep. My breathing picks up. At this rate we're never going to make it to the party.

I shake my head. "We need to get going. We're going to be late." The way my voice is coming out I'm not very convincing. Darn him. He runs his fingers lightly down my sternum, between my breasts, giving me chills.

He flattens his hand over my belly and pulls me closer, poking me from behind. "Now do you see what you're doing to me? A guy can only take so much. If you want to make it to that party, stop teasing me. And remember, two can play that game," he says and nips at my earlobe. "Now get your cute little butt in that truck. I'm giving you a five-second head start. If you aren't out that door, we're skipping the party."

He releases me and steps back, giving me room. One little tidbit of information about me—I don't have to be told twice. I turn and take off for the door. As I round the corner and cut through the gate, I can hear his laughter. I have to become immune to him and his flirtatious behavior. I need tips from Presley. I will not succumb to his seduction tactics.

Now sitting in the passenger seat of Ryland's Jeep, Breyson saunters through the gate in yellow swim trunks the same color as the Jeep and a t-shirt. He gets in and gives me that full on, breath-consuming grin. "You ready?"

I nod and bite my tongue, trying not to smile.

He will not win. He will not win.

The drive to Presley's was just casual small talk, thank goodness. I don't know why he gets under my skin so badly. It's driving me crazy and I feel like a weakling. Nothing ever affects me this way.

When we pull into the driveway, it's already packed full of cars. He has to park close to the road in the grass. As I look from side to side, people are consecutively piling in through the entryway gate. Opening the door, I grab my towel and step outside to walk to the front of the vehicle where I wait on Breyson.

He reaches for my hand. I'm not sure what to do. Holding hands is a little too intimate for what we are, and I don't want anyone to get the wrong idea. Instead of taking his hand, I wrap my arm around his and cup his large bicep in my hand. As our skin touches, he flexes beneath my hand. He must spend a lot of time in the gym with a trainer to have a body like this. Most guys our age don't have bodies this cut. Is it weird that I want to rub my hands down his torso, along the ridges of his stomach?

We come into the backyard, and it looks exactly as I expected. There are tents everywhere and tables full of food. The pool is packed with kids from school and the outer edge is lined with girls tanning. The first person I notice is Lexi with a scowl on her face. "Hey, Lex."

She narrows her eyes at Breyson before looking back at me. "Hey girl, what did you drag in?" Her voice feigns sarcasm.

What's up with her? Lexi is usually so bubbly and hyper. I don't think I've ever heard her sound this way, come to think of it. "Lexi, this is Breyson. He's Ryland's cousin."

She looks at him with a smirk on her face like she has an ulterior motive. "From the party right? At Logan's?"

Logan's? When did he go to Logan's? I look over at him, confused. He looks slightly nervous. "Yeah," he says, and looks at me. "You ready to go find Presley?"

What is up with these two? They act like there is something between them that they aren't telling me; like everyone is in on the same joke, but I missed the punch line. "I guess. I'll find you later, Lex."

We walk through the tents filled with people. I grab a bottle of water from one of the ice-filled tubs. In passing, I notice all of the single guys are staring at me. Some have their mouths hanging open and some look downright angry. What in the world is up with everyone at this party? I'm starting to get paranoid I have a boob showing or something and begin looking myself over.

I finally realize I am still holding onto Breyson's bicep. To make matters worse, his arm is wrapped around my waist and his hand is resting on my hip. Of course, everyone is staring. I've never been seen hanging on a guy, because I've never been with one.

Now that I look around a second time, every guy that looks angry is someone I've declined to go out with in the past. I drop my arm and Breyson tightens his hold.

How did I not even notice I was wrapped in his arm? I'm really weird about public displays of affection, which is why I'm always so awkward around Presley with her boy-toys. Feeling uncomfortable, I shimmy out of his arm and speed up my pace.

As I come to the end of the tent, I see Presley lying in a leaf shaped lounger inside the edge of the pool. Ryland is in the pool in front of her playing water volleyball. Madison and Amber—two of the cheerleaders from my squad—are on a lounger at each side of

Presley.

As I close in behind them, Madison is at Presley's ear whispering. I can't hear what she is saying, but the way Presley turns around, I know it had to do with me. Great, now I'm going to have the entire high school population of Laguna talking. This is so not what I need. "Hey, sweetie, it's about time you got here. Everyone has been asking about you." She scans my body and then Breyson's. She smiles, but bites her lip, trying to refrain. "Amber, sweetie, why don't you be a gem and scoot over to the next lounger. I need some Kinzleigh time."

If I ever thought I could hide anything from Presley, I was wrong. I swear the girl has some kind of weird sixth sense. "Don't be silly. Amber, you don't have to move. You were there first. I can sit in the next one."

Maybe I can dodge the conversation I know is coming. She won't say anything if I'm not beside her. She knows I'm a private person.

"Kinzleigh Berlyn Baker! Get your skinny little butt over here and sit down! Amber, scoot." She starts waving her hand at her as if she's shooing a fly, and then turns and points at Breyson. "Breyson. Pool. Now. I need girl time."

When Presley gets like this she is scary, and everyone knows she can be dangerous with her tantrums. She comes from money and her parents spoil her. I hate, with a special emphasis on the word hate, when she uses my middle name.

My parents have a strange sense of humor. Not only did they combine their first names to name me, but also, they chose to assign my middle name after the city in which I was conceived. Mom spelled it different, because she thought my spelling was more feminine than the spelling of the place.

Really, Mom, who is going to even get to the way it's spelled when they find out you're named after a city in Germany? The one in which you have to hear about your parents getting busy. That's gross. If I didn't know my parents have never tried a drug in their lives, I would think they were high the entire time my mom was pregnant.

Breyson shakes his head in laughter and turns to me, removing his shirt—slowly, might I add, each abdominal being revealed one at a time.

The guy has the best body I've ever seen, hands down. His shorts sit low on his waist, revealing the V of muscle. This view is better than the one at the beach. Why? Well, because he is standing before me doing his version of a male striptease. As his arms move up his body, each muscle flexes in front of me.

"Share the view with the rest of us!" I'm broken from the frozen state I didn't even know I was in by Amber's outburst. I turn to look at them and realize they are all staring, along with one angry Preston. The girls are looking between us as if something big is about to happen.

I turn to Breyson, smiling like a champion. He knew Preston was standing there and I'm gawking like an idiot. Kill me now. Could this get any worse? Why, oh why, do I feel like I'm unwillingly being tugged into a lo—lust triangle?

Breyson walks toward me, closing the space between us, and hands me his shirt. "Will you hold this for me?" His naked torso brushes against mine, goose bumps forming along my arms. I grab his shirt in my hand, but before he releases it, he whispers in my ear, "I told you things would happen if you wore that swimsuit and I caught another guy undressing you with his eyes. Don't say I didn't warn you."

With that, he turns and heads toward the pool where Ryland is watching, as if he's got front row seats to a big fight.

I turn, ignoring them, and Presley has a rather large smile on her face behind Preston. He is blocking my lounger with his exposed body. Preston isn't lacking in the muscle department; he just does nothing for me. No fireworks are shooting off and my girly bits are in check.

Whereas Breyson has more bulk of muscle and definition, Preston is more of a lean muscularity and tone. What am I supposed to do with him now? I am outside of my element here. It's not a good idea to go from no intimate contact with the male species to two in the matter of a day. Sighing, I walk toward my seat next to Presley in hopes that he will just move aside.

He watches me the entire time I walk toward him, not moving one. Not. One. Single. Inch. I stop, leaving distance between us. Everyone finally went back to what they were doing. I guess Preston having a thing for me is just as obvious as Presley always makes it seem. How was I the only one blind to this? Was I really that sucked into my own life? "Preston. Do you mind if I sit down in my seat?"

He's being annoying. I've never given him the impression there was something between us. He's just standing there with the vein in his neck still bulging. I can see the muscle in his jaw moving back and forth. "Preston! Did you not hear the girl? Are we going to have to have another heart-to-heart?" Presley is now standing to my right, facing the sides of us as we stare at each other.

He releases a deep breath and his face relaxes. I wonder what it was they talked about last night. "Hey, Kinz, you look gorgeous, as always."

Preston has always called me that. Hearing it calms me down. I need to figure out a way to deal with all this without getting angry with him. At one time, I was closer to him than Presley. Some nights when I stayed over at night, he would sit up with me until daylight watching funny movies when I was scared from Presley making me watch a horror film.

"Thanks, Preston. Look, can we talk later, just you and me? Right now is a bad time. I promise I'll give you my undivided attention." At this point, I don't know what else to do. How did I get myself into all this mess? I guess I was crazy to think I could totally avoid men forever.

Presley is still standing here, listening to everything we're saying. If they weren't brother and sister it would be awkward. "Okay, Kinzleigh, I can do that. I really need us to talk, though. Last night didn't go exactly as I planned, and then when I got up this morning you were gone."

His voice has a disappointed tone that usually isn't present where Preston is concerned. I've never seen Preston this way. He's usually arrogant face to face, with a different girl on his arm every time I see him.

I look at Presley, trying to hint for her to leave for a minute, so I can make sure he's okay. She, of course, doesn't get the memo, because she is the leader of all things related to drama and gossip. "Okay, Preston. I promise I'll come find you later."

He nods and walks off. I notice he looks at Breyson on the way to the house. To actually think boys call us impossible to figure out is just crazy. I've been close to Preston since I was a kid and still thought boys had cooties. In all those years, he's never once acted like we were anything more than friends. Now, suddenly, he's throwing things at me like dating and forever. The thought of settling down forever makes me physically ill, especially at my age. If more women would be worried about making themselves happy instead of being at every beck and call of a man, there would be less heartache in the world.

I have my life planned out. I want to travel the world and spend my younger days cheerleading in the NFL, maybe do some coaching on the side. I don't know in terms of a career yet when it comes to a college major. I have plenty of time to decide.

When I'm older and have lived a little, I want to start a cheerleading company and be known across the country for training the best cheerleaders around. No one got to the top with a baby on her hip, doting on a man.

I start toward my lounger and Presley is keeping pace. "You, missy, have some explaining to do," she says with a devious grin on her face.

I lay down the towel I've been carrying and sit down. Presley really does have the coolest pool around for pool parties. It's a full-sized pool, but the difference is, there is a platform completely surrounding the inner edge of the pool that rests a couple inches below the water. It is lined all the way around with leaf shaped loungers made for the water. I love it in the summer, because you can lie barely submerged in the water while you tan.

In one corner there is a rock formation wall, suspended in the air for a waterfall that harbors a small cave like opening behind it. Diagonally across the pool is a water slide formed into the same kind of rock. Between the pool and outdoor kitchen and fire pit, Presley's house is known for her backyard. Her parents had it built for this sole purpose—to entertain. In California, residents pay a lot for outdoor entertaining. We are always at Presley's, with and without parents present.

"What is it that you want me to explain to you? Did I leave my sunglasses here?" There is no way she knows I was slightly naughty earlier. That is my secret.

She dangles a pair of black Versace sunglasses in the air with an evil gleam in her eye. "Oh, you mean these sunglasses?" I reach for them and she pulls them back out of my reach. I hate that she is shaped like a model—tall and thin with arms and legs for days. "Tsk, tsk, tsk, you know what you have to do to get them back. I want information and I want it now."

My four hundred-dollar sunglasses are my favorite accessory and she knows this. I'm very particular about my things. My parents work hard to give me the things that I have. "There is nothing to tell you," I whine, reaching for my sunglasses again. She pulls them higher than before.

I huff and look out at the pool. The boys and some of the girls have a volleyball game set up in the middle of the pool. My eyes land on Breyson as he jumps in the air to spike the ball back over the net. Water beads trickle down his back as his muscles flex.

His tattoo waves as his shoulder muscles protrude with the rotation of his right shoulder as he smacks the ball with the palm of his hand. I bite my lip as I think of being wrapped in those strong arms. "Uh huh, someone got some action. It's written all over your face. You must really think I'm stupid. I know you better than you know yourself. I could see it when you got here and now you just confirmed it. Spill."

I look over to Presley, now that I've been caught gazing at his body. I can't help but to smile, thinking about earlier. "Why must you know everything? One of these days your brain is going to explode from all of the information that lies in there."

I look around to see who all is listening, not wanting anyone to overhear. When I turn back to Presley, Lexi is standing behind her. "Hey, girls. What have I missed?" She has a malicious look on her face. I wish I knew what was wrong with her.

"Hey, Lex. Are you okay? You don't seem like yourself today." She looks out at the pool. Her eyes glass over. When I turn to see what she is looking at, it's Breyson. They did act like they knew each other earlier. Maybe I'm missing something.

"So, he's trying to screw you now too, huh?"

I whip my head back toward her. I couldn't have heard her right. "Excuse me? What do you mean?"

"Awe, that's so sweet. You really thought he liked you," she says sarcastically sweet. "Poor thing, we really need to teach you a thing or two about boys. It's not your fault; you aren't used to the dating thing. They can be hellacious creatures. Always after one thing and not thinking of the destruction it causes in its path."

"Lexi, what are you talking about?" I'm starting to panic at this point. I hate being out of the loop on things.

"I met him the other night at Logan's. He was drunk and all over me. I was about to go upstairs with him until he accidentally mentioned he had a girlfriend. It's sad, really. She's probably sitting at home all alone, waiting on his return, and he's out here hooking up with other girls. I don't really care, but sloppy seconds aren't my style."

Presley has her eyes narrowed at Lexi. "You're lying. I know you, Lexi Callahan. What I can't figure out is why. Kinzleigh has never done anything to you. Why would you be such a conniving little bitch?"

She pulls her sunglasses down from their resting place on top of her head as a smirk forms on her lips. "Don't take my word for it, just ask him." She looks out at the pool one last time and prances off.

How could I be so stupid? I feel sick. I think I'm about to have a panic attack. There is one thing I will not tolerate and that is cheating. I may not be the relationship type, but I will not be the floozy either. My brother has been shattered over a cheating little harlot and I will not be the cause of someone else's pain.

"I need to go. Presley, I'm sorry." I am staring down at my feet, trying to breathe.

"Okay, sweetie. Do you need me to give you a ride? Don't let her get to you, Kinzleigh. She probably isn't telling the whole truth. You know she is a spoiled little brat and will do anything to get her way."

I look out in the pool and see Breyson. The color drains from his face. That was all the answer I needed. It said enough. It doesn't matter if some of what Lexi said was a lie, because he just answered the one part I'm interested in. "That's okay. Stay here with your party guests. I'll find Preston and get a ride. Call me later, 'kay?" Breyson is making his way across the pool. I've got to get out of here.

I stand quickly and step out of the pool. "Kinzleigh, hold up," he calls out. I run. I can feel a meltdown coming. I've been having panic attacks since the day Grams died but have had them under control for the last year. I don't even have to take medication anymore, and over the last few days they are starting up again.

I make it to the patio door when I feel a hand on mine. "Kinzleigh, stop. What's wrong? What did she say to you?"

I'm angry, and it all starts to set in. Turning around to face him, he steps back. "Why didn't you tell me you had a girlfriend? Do I look stupid to you? Did you think I wouldn't find out? I may be inexperienced, but I have boundaries. I am not a cheap whore you can just use and run back to your girlfriend in a week. I didn't care that you've been with several girls, but this crosses the line. I should have known. People like you are all the same. You should all stick together—cheaters and liars. I am not one to judge, usually, but my brother was destroyed over a girl just like you." I'm yelling at this point, but I can't help it. This is a very sensitive issue with me. I've watched what's left of my brother day in and day out, trying to piece himself back together.

Preston opens the sliding glass door. "Kinzleigh, are you all right?"

"I need a ride home. Can you take me?" My heart is pounding in my chest and I feel like I'm going to pass out.

"Of course, let me grab my keys." He turns and disappears out of sight.

Breyson is tightening his fists by his sides. "So that's it then? You're not even going to let me explain? You won't even hear the story from both sides before just believing someone else? I thought you were different than that, Kinzleigh."

"What is there to hear, Breyson? Lexi told me you were all over her at Logan's until she found out you had a girlfriend. Did you think you were just going to move on to me next since she wouldn't give you what you wanted?" My voice is starting to break. The stress is taking over my body and I can feel tears stinging my eyes, trying to break free.

I only cry when I'm severely angry. I guess it's my body's way of releasing the toxins roaming through my veins. "I broke rules for you, because I thought you were different. I was okay with a casual fling, but I will not be the cause of someone else's heartache and I will not be used against my will."

"I don't have a girlfriend, Kinzleigh. I did, but it's not what you think." He starts pulling at his hair. "Can we please talk and I'll explain?"

"Did you or did you not have a girlfriend any of the times you

accepted FATE

kissed me?" It's a simple question and the only one I'm interested in. He stares at me as Preston appears back in the doorway and the look on Breyson's face gives me my answer. "Goodbye, Breyson. Have a nice life."

I turn and walk inside, behind Preston, leaving him standing in the doorway. When Preston gets to the garage door, he turns toward me as he grabs the doorknob. "Are you sure you're okay? I can make him leave if you want to stay. This is just as much your house as it is mine."

Preston has always thought of me first, especially now that I stop and think about it. I feel kind of like the story I learned in church of Adam and Eve in the Garden of Eden. I've gone all this time blinded to everything around me and now that I've tasted the fruit, my eyes are open. I want to go back to being blissfully unaware and it's impossible. It's too bad that I am not one of those girls that want to be in a relationship, because Preston honestly would be perfect.

He's sexy and our families are really close. We've been friends since we were kids, so there are no surprises. Him and Konnor have always been and are still close friends when he's home from school, so he knows what he's going through and how I feel about it. I don't know, but it's not enough.

If I were going to give my virginity to anyone else, I might consider Preston since I'm moving, but with him bringing up some of that crazy talk I don't think he can handle it without wanting more. I can't risk messing up our tight knit family circle. Plus, I don't get the butterflies when I'm around him like I do with Breyson. He doesn't make me weak in the knees or short of breath. Maybe it's stupid to compare, but I don't know, I liked the way being around Breyson affected me.

"That's okay, Preston, just take me home. I don't really feel well, and I promised you we would talk anyway. We can knock out two things at once." He nods his head and walks out the door.

"Nice car," I say, taking a seat in the sleek white Porsche with black, leather interior. Even though it's a luxury car, Preston has made it his own with black star like rims and a spoiler on the back. He backs out of the garage with a smile on his face.

"You could have one, you know. All you have to do is say the word the day I graduate. I get a big bonus when I walk across that stage and receive my business degree." I roll my eyes. He is not helping calm me down by trying to buy me. It freaks me out more.

"Preston, you know this conversation is having the opposite of the desired effect, right? I'm not that kind of girl and I never will be. You know that if you know me. I don't want to live off someone else. I want to be my own person. If I wanted a new car I would buy it myself. Are you forgetting I'm only seventeen? I still have to graduate high school and go to college. You act like we're on the same page and we're reading two different books. Where is this coming from? I'm pretty sure there are plenty of girls that would love to be your trophy and spend your money."

He's deep in thought as we drive down the road, listening to the purr of the engine. It really is a beautiful car. He passes my house and I wonder where we are going, but I keep quiet. Obviously, he has things he wants to say, and I promised I'd listen. I owe him that much. He has always been there for me, no questions asked.

He pulls in the harbor and I know where we are. The yacht our parents bought together is anchored here. He kills the engine and looks at me, resting his left hand on the door handle. "I know you don't feel well, but I wanted to talk. This is one place we can do that."

We exit the car and walk down the dock, passing a string of boats in various shapes and sizes. We finally reach the end of the dock where ours sits at port. We haven't been on it in a while, since summer vacation just started. We pretty much live on this boat during the summer, because our parents use most of their vacation time then. It's been a tradition since we were kids.

Preston steps across the space between the dock and the vessel, planting both feet on the other side. He turns around and holds out his hand. This part always scares me a little, no matter how many times I've been thrown or suspended in the air with cheerleading. Something about the boat being so high and rocking as you're trying to get a good balance with the possibility of falling in freaks me out. I take his hand and cross the barrier, but he doesn't release my hand.

As we walk across the deck of the yacht and down the stairs, I take in its beauty. I love it here. It's decorated in reds and browns and is so homey. I should take advantage of my last month to come here. He sits down on the couch and pulls me down beside him. "What's on your mind, pretty girl?" He was always so much easier to talk to than Presley; maybe, because he's a lot like Konnor and me. He's laid back and can talk forever or just listen. He's probably the only person aside from my brother I really would go to if I had a problem.

"Just thinking of how much I'm going to miss this place." I guess I might as well let the cat out of the bag. Then he will realize anything he is about to say is probably a waste of breath. "Mom and Dad are moving us across the country. I don't want to go, but I have no choice. As much as I want to kick and scream in a tantrum, they are pretty set that it's a done deal." Just thinking about this all over again is depressing. "I have no idea what I'm supposed to do about cheerleading and my national all-star tryouts are the same week we move I think."

He sits there looking at me, waiting to be sure I'm finished before he talks. Typical Preston. He's a very patient person, which will make him a good businessman. Him following in his dad's footsteps is exactly where he should be. "Dad mentioned that the other night. They are freaking out about it too. He left telling Presley up to Mom, so I don't know if she knows yet. By her behavior, I would say probably not. She will most likely have a meltdown since you two are like twins separated at birth."

"So, you already knew? Then where is all this nonsense coming from about you and me? You've never once made any attempt at a relationship becoming more than friendship, and now you act like you're planning our wedding." We are sitting sideways on the couch, facing each other.

He has his right leg resting against the cushion and his left leg planted on the floor, mirroring my opposite. His right side is leaning against the back of the couch with his elbow propped on the top of the backrest. His hand is resting just below his nose, index finger against his lips, and knuckles facing the ceiling. He is smiling as if he is amused. "Are you done yet? You always were headstrong about everything. If you would give me the floor I will explain everything, but I need you to promise not to say anything until you've heard me out and keep an open mind."

I have to give him credit where credit is due. He seems to have this all planned out. "Okay, I promise; although, I'm not sure what I'm getting myself into."

He turns his body to the left, facing frontward, with both feet now pressed against the floor. He leans forward and rests his elbows right above his knees, looking at the floor. "Kinzleigh, you've known me a long time. You know I would never lie to you. I think I've had plenty of moments to prove myself worthy of your trust, wouldn't you agree?" He looks up at me for a response. I nod for him to continue.

"I know you're seventeen and I know you still have to finish high school and college. I know everything there is to know about you. I've spent a lot of time learning what makes you, you." He looks back down at the floor, as if he's nervous. "I've wanted you, Kinzleigh, since we were little. I want you to listen to what I have to say before you freak out or say anything in return. I've loved you since we were kids. I will always love you, Kinzleigh. You're it for me. I've waited around, silently, because of our age difference. I know you don't want to fall in love because you have dreams; I get it. I have been buying time by being with other girls, but they don't satisfy me anymore. You will be eighteen in the next several months. I know how you are and I know you won't be in a long distance relationship. That's not what I'm asking you; today, anyway."

He takes a deep breath. I cannot believe I'm hearing any of this correctly. I have to be mentally unstable. "All I'm doing is planting a seed. I want you to think about it this year, while you're gone—think about us. I know you're not the kind of girl to make a hasty decision. I know you have your certain views in regard to dating. I've seen many guys crash and burn in an attempt to capture your heart. And I can't say that it hasn't made me happy. But regardless, I want you to know how I feel. No regrets. It's always been you, Kinzleigh. You're the only girl that's ever stolen my heart. I'm not telling you this in hopes of getting a response today or anytime soon. You won't hear me tell you I love you after today unless you choose to be with me. I'm only telling you now, because you deserve to know. I don't want to lose my chance to someone else, because I was too scared to tell you how I felt."

He scans my face before he goes on. I know it's to make sure I'm not about to bolt out the door. "Before you jump to any conclusions, I know you don't want kids and that's why you don't want to get serious with someone, and one day married. I've been around you long enough to know that you don't want to be held back. I'm okay with not having kids if it means having you. Not much would even change. I will never make you give up cheerleading. I will never pressure you to marry me unless I know it's what you want. It's not a contract that takes away your freedom. It would just be a life together. We could go wherever you want, live wherever you want to live. We have businesses all over this country and Dad wants to expand globally. I have the means to make you happy. Everything is within reach. I just need you to trust me. To choose me."

I rub my forehead, trying to process all this information. I'm not used to someone knowing me like their favorite movie, reciting every line as I would say it. It's a little intimidating. I didn't know I was so obvious. "What exactly are you proposing?"

"Nothing as well as everything. I don't want you to take this for more than it is. When I come to your senior graduation, I would like an answer to a question I've wanted to ask you for years. Can we be more than friends? That's it. I know you want to be in California. If your answer is yes, then you will move back here with me and we will see how things go. I just want you for myself. I know you're not like many girls and that's one of the things I love about you. I learned a long time ago, if I wanted a chance, it had to be on terms you could handle. Don't overthink it. Live the way you would if I never mentioned it. I do want you to know, though, I won't touch another woman until then. I know I can't expect the same of you, but I can't pretend with other girls anymore when the one I want is right here."

I can't even begin to think about all this. At least I'm not completely freaked out. I guess when it's all laid out in front of you there isn't a whole lot to freak out about. Maybe it's that I can't fathom what next year will be like much less after. He does make some good points. The curiosity wins. "Why have I never noticed you felt this way?"

He smiles a genuine smile for the first time since we arrived. "You tend to only notice the things in the world of Kinzleigh."

"I don't really know what to say, but I'll think it over. I'm still a little shocked, to be honest."

He stands, reaching for my hand, and pulls me to my feet. He cups my face in his hands, like in the bathroom last night. "Don't be sorry, Kinzleigh. You're reacting better than I expected. I was prepared for a slap, screams, red cheeks."

He smiles, pretending he knows my little fits better than me. "I know I'm throwing a lot on you. You panic under pressure. I thought you would be in California senior year. That I would have more time to push you slowly. I've been thinking about all this since Dad mentioned you moving. It made me really think about my future and where I want it to go."

"Your future is bright, Preston, regardless of who is on your arm. She will be lucky to be loved by you, whoever she is."

He looks me in my eyes. "Can I kiss you? For real this time?"

What am I supposed to do? I'm not one for kissing multiple people in one day; it's rather trashy to me, and low class. But he's waiting for my response and I can see the hope in his eyes. One time wouldn't hurt. I won't be seeing Breyson anymore anyway. "Okay."

He pulls me in slowly, touching his lips to mine. He kisses my bottom lip and then my top. He sucks my lips between his. He kisses me as if he's trying to cherish this moment, memorize it. He lightly licks my bottom lip, asking for entry. If I'm going to do this I might as well make it count. I slip my tongue into the opening of his lips. He entwines his tongue with mine. It's warm and mingles with need.

He walks me backward until my back presses against something hard. He picks up pace, kissing me as if he's a dying man.

He runs his hands down my body and stops just below my butt, picking me up. I wrap my legs around his narrow waist, somewhat lost in what we're doing.

He continues to kiss and suck and nibble. I'm not sure how much time goes by, but he finally moans and releases me, setting me down onto the floor.

He cups my cheek in his right hand and brushes his thumb across my bottom lip. "You have no idea how long I've wanted to do that. And nothing could have prepared me for how it'd make me feel. This will be what gets me through my last year of school. I'll just have to make it last until I come back for you. I will come back for you, Kinzleigh."

The conviction in his voice both excites me and scares the crap out of me.

THIRTEEN

Breyson

I'm a pretty laidback guy in my opinion, but there is one thing I hate—to be judged. I'll be the first to admit when I've done wrong. In this case, I have. Even though I know the true situation with Natalie, I shouldn't have kissed Kinzleigh while I was technically dating her. I even understand her anger, because cheating is wrong to any degree. It hurts people. I have a dead cousin to prove it.

I attempted to fix the error of my ways by breaking up with Natalie and I even came clean that I had taken interest in someone else. What pisses me off is that she didn't even give me a chance to explain. We live in a country that prides itself on being innocent until proven guilty, so what was that exactly? If she doesn't want to speak to me once she's heard me out, fine, but I deserve a chance to explain what I'm being accused of. And that shit about Lexi? That's a damn lie. I'm the one that turned her down.

I'm so mad right now I want to hit someone. I want to hit someone hard and repetitively. I need to blow off some steam. I have been called a playboy, a jerk, and manwhore, along with everything else out there, but I will not be called a liar. I have always told the truth. We could both be termed being in the wrong. Not one time did she ask me if I was dating someone.

Some may say that omission is a form of lying, but I don't exactly think clearly when I'm around her. That has to count for something. I have been with my fair share of girls for a seventeen-year-old. Some my age, some older, and I'll own up to every accusation that is true, but I will not stand around while someone believes a lying, deceitful bitch over me.

I never once was all over that slut at the party. To lie on someone that way is low, even for a girl. Girls like her are what give guys a bad rep. I don't know if she's mad she got turned down, or jealous, but I will find out.

Right now, though, what bothers me more is that I just had to watch Kinzleigh leave with that little rich playboy just waiting to get his hands on her. I know his type. They sit around playing the best friend role until they can swoop in and take her when someone else takes an interest. What does it matter? She was pretty clear she didn't want to see me again. I sit down on the steps, trying to ponder my next move. What is it about this girl I can't let go?

Back home, I would just go find a random, willing, attractive girl, and take her somewhere private. The vast majority of the female high school population is so ready to be older, rebellion is high, and every chance they can act older, they do. Most of us *are* out partying and screwing around. Parents overlook it so they don't have to acknowledge and deal with it.

The problem is, I've now tasted something better than a hookup. Anything else would be like shooting cheap, student-budget whiskey after being offered a shot of Johnnie Walker, Black

Label—my dad's favorite drink.

I'm sitting here, lost in my own head, when red toenails come into view. I know it's not Kinzleigh, because there is no anklet surrounding the left ankle that is always there, it seems.

My eyes travel upward, along the seams of long, tan legs. She's wearing a black and red polka dot bikini, a flat stomach between fabric pieces, and a metal bar through her navel. Skinny with a nice sized rack. Maybe this is my answer to all this frustration, I think, until I reach her face.

Lexi.

Well, she does have some balls; I'll give her that. "What the fuck do you want?"

She smiles, but it has motive behind it. "What a shame. It's such a waste when a man chases after a girl that is better than him. We owe it to ourselves to stick with our own kind. By the looks of you, I'd guess you have plenty of experience in bed, and I bet you don't disappoint. I don't mind you being a man-slut; personally, it works in my favor, but Kinzleigh is different. Every guy wants her and every girl wants to be her. She's the closest thing to perfection any girl will ever be. Sweet, innocent, good, hot as hell. Ask any guy here at this party. Preston Dunagin has had his eyes set on her for years, and I'd say it appears he's pretty close to finally getting her."

She walks over and sits next to me. "If she were going to be with someone, it'll be him. Trust me. Those two were cultivated to be together by those parents of theirs. Everyone here knows it. Accepts it even. What makes you think you're different? I've watched so many guys like you attempt and fail; only to end up with a girl like me. I'm doing you a favor, you know. No other guy will lasso her heart. Isn't that a term you southern people use? I'm not saying he's innocent, because a boy like that is hard to turn down and he knows it. He has the looks, the personality, and the money, but he's done the one thing you haven't—put in the time with her. Been in the friend zone for years."

She laughs. "It's twisted, really. Every girl he hooks up with is a physical replica of Kinzleigh—blonde hair, nice body. One girl even mentioned he made her get on all fours and called out her name when he came. Once he gets her, he isn't letting her go. Just thought you should know. He'll get her when he gets out of school. That's always been the plan. He makes it obvious, so it's hard to miss."

I'm so mad I can't speak. I pop my knuckles in frustration, unable to look at her, because I'm afraid I'll hit her. "Awe, don't be upset, sweetie. You aren't the first and you won't be the last."

She runs her fingertip up my arm and down my front. "You want a girl with some experience anyway. All guys do. What fun is a girl that doesn't know what she's doing? Just lies there like a corpse. I know what a guy like you wants to hold your attention," she purrs in my ear, brushing her breasts against my upper arm.

She's not done. I can tell. "Come on, sexy. I'll even let you pretend I'm her, just like *Preston* likes to do. Would you like that? Makes a better lay, because then you can show me just how much you want her . . ."

God, she has issues. That's what this is about—jealousy. It's a poisonous emotion, and deadly in the wrong person. I guarantee she's used to getting her way. And she's little bit fucking crazy. She knows exactly what she's doing. Two can play that game. "You're probably right. I need a girl that can keep up with me," I seethe. She stands up and struts, thinking she's won.

"I'm glad you understand," she says, smiling. I trail after her in the direction of the side of the house. We enter through the mudroom door. As she walks through, she glances around, as if making sure she's unnoticed. I think Presley's parents were in the outdoor kitchen with a game on the television if that's who she's looking for.

We walk to a small set of service stairs. She ascends them quietly. When we reach the top, she walks to the end of the hallway and stops at the farthest room. Looking back at me, she smiles. "I can't wait for this. I've wanted you since I saw you at the beach. I can only imagine what's under those shorts," she says looking at my crotch.

We walk in what appears to be a guest room. In the center of the room sits a queen size bed. The walls are a light yellow and the bedding a bright print.

I walk to the center and stop not far from the bed. She circles around me like an animal circling its prey. "You sure you're ready for this, Lexi? I don't go slow. Slow is boring. I like it hard and rough is what I'll give. And you just took away the one thing I wanted. I have a lot of aggression to take out on you."

She licks her lips. "That's what I'm counting on," she says seductively. She closes the space between us. Wrapping her arms around my neck, she pulls in for a kiss.

I allow her to kiss me, but I will not touch her tongue. I don't want to taint my mouth with her bitterness after experiencing the sweetness that is Kinzleigh. I grab her thighs and pick her up roughly, hoping like hell it hurts.

She wraps her slender legs around my waist. I slip my hands underneath her bottoms, close to her sweet spot but not touching— only to tease.

She moans against my mouth. "I need more." She begins rubbing herself against me, clearly ready for me. I release her lips. I can't stand her touching my mouth any longer. I hate kissing—except with Kinzleigh. I kiss down her neck to distract her.

Walking her backward to the bed, I throw her down roughly on the mattress. She spreads her legs automatically. Girls like her require no effort at all. They are all the same. There is no chase and it's boring. All they are good for is a quick lay—an easy dick lubricant. No one ever takes this girl home to meet Mama. I pin her arms above her head and straddle her. She rubs her foot between my legs in search of what she wants. "You want it?"

"You know I do. Get a condom and hurry up already." Her eyes are hooded, and she is begging. I got her right where I want her. I lower my bottom half, resting between her legs, allowing her to get a feel of what she could have. I've always been well endowed. It's not showboating it's the truth. I don't have to brag about it. When I want someone to know about it, she will.

When she feels it against her, she arches off the bed and wraps her legs tightly around my waist. "Oh, damn. I need you inside me; fill every inch of me."

I lean closer to her, next to her ear so she can feel my body against hers. Whispering into her ear, I ram myself against her swimsuit; the hardness under my shorts prodding between her legs.

Guys aren't like girls. It doesn't take feelings to arouse a man. Guys are physical creatures of habit. The right stimulation and physical attraction and it's ready to go. She can get me hard, and if I wanted to, I could screw her without going soft, even if I practically hate her right now. The funny thing is—I don't want her. I'd rather get myself off than get off for her.

With all my anger backing it I say, "That's too bad, isn't it? You'll never get this. I've been with plenty of girls like you. It's not fun anymore. I'd rather spend the rest of my life chasing after a girl like Kinzleigh and never get her than to settle for second best. The truth is, guys that sleep with you really are imaging a girl like her. It's sad that you know it and don't care to change it."

I grind against her. "This is all you'll ever be to a guy. Cheap pussy. You may get other guys by conning them into sleeping with you, but I'm not one of them. Just a word of advice—if you ever want to be more than a nice piece of ass, I suggest you stop being such a bitch and stop when you're not wanted."

I distance myself from her. She is laying there with her eyes wide open in a daze. She goes limp. I'm not an asshole, but she had it coming when she lied about me and then pissed me off. Someone needs to snap her back into reality from the warped self-absorbed world she lives in. I've done what I came here to do. I stand up and turn for the door. Moving quickly, I slam it behind me.

I'm going after Kinzleigh.

FOURTEEN

Breyson

I will make her hear me out, because the truth is, I'm already in too deep. I need a few more days with her. Rushing down the stairs, I dash to the front door.

I'm in a full-fledged sprint out the door, headed to the Jeep. When I get to the driver door, I realize the keys are back at the party. Linking my hands on top of my head, I'm trying to decide what in the heck I'm going to do. I don't want to go back to that party. From the corner of my eye, I notice Ryland's truck. Maybe he left the keys in it since it's close to the house.

I make my way back to the truck and open the door. The keys are in it. One problem down, but one problem remains. It is among several other vehicles crowded together in the driveway. There is a path I could get it out, but it's going to be a tight squeeze. I get in the truck and start the ignition. Pulling out my phone, I notice a text from Ryland.

Ryland: Dude, where did you go?

Me: Taking the truck. I need to find Kinzleigh. I'll explain later.

Ryland: Presley is freaking out about you having a girlfriend. Care to explain what happened in the five fucking minutes I had my back turned?

Me: Lexi started a bunch of crap and lied. Kinzleigh ran off with that Preston guy and didn't let me explain. I broke up with Natalie Friday night right after I kissed Kinzleigh. I was honest with her about meeting someone. No one cared to hear my side. Just handle it. I have to go, man.

Ryland: Aight, bro. I got you covered. Next time keep me in the loop, so I know what's going on and don't look like a dick.

Me: K

Looking around, I back out. I have to back up and pull forward a few times, maneuvering the truck, but I manage to get out. As I'm pulling out of the entryway gate, I realize I'm still in swim trunks. If her parents are home, this isn't the best way to show up. Headed to her house, I spot a thrift store on the way. This is better than the alternative.

Pulling in, I kill the engine and exit the truck. It doesn't seem busy, but it is open according to the flashing neon sign over the door. I walk inside to racks upon racks of clothing. There is an older lady about mid to late sixties with fully grayed hair sitting at the front counter, to the left of the door, reading a magazine. She looks up as the bell dings above the door. "Can I help you, son?"

The darkness is taking over as the sun goes down. I'm not sure if Kinzleigh's parents are weird about houseguests at night. Since I'm in a shortage of time, maybe she can help. "Yes, ma'am. I left a pool party in a hurry, and where I'm going I need some clothes. I don't have time to run by the place I'm staying. Do you have anything for me?"

She lights up as if I've just made her day. She must not get very many customers in here. "Oh, wonderful! I think we can find you something, dear. Come on and follow me," she says, smiling a grandmotherly smile and walks out from behind the counter toward the back of the store.

Come to think of it, she kind of reminds me of my maternal grandmother. She's warm and welcoming with excitement every time I see her and she always has something baked, such as cookies or cake. She doesn't get many visitors. I should go see her when I get home. Mom keeps telling me she won't always be here, but I never seem to listen. I'm closer to my dad's parents.

I trail after the older woman in the direction of the rack in the back of the store. On it hangs several t-shirts in all colors and sizes. She shuffles through the hangers but stops to look at me. "Hmm, let's see," she says, rubbing her chin. "Are you trying to impress a young lady?"

I smile at her sweet personality as she inquiries about my personal life. "Yes, ma'am, actually I am. She is a little angry with me right now, so I'll have to do some groveling."

She stares off at me for a moment and I wonder what she's thinking. "Ah, yes, I think I may can help with that too. My Henry used to be the champion at groveling. That's one reason it was so hard to stay mad at him for long," she sighs, making it clear he's no longer around. "You remind me of him. That sandy blond hair and those beautiful blue eyes. You have quite the smile too. I think I can give you a few tips and you're sure to have her back in no time." She winks and goes back to strumming through the hangers.

Stopping briefly, she looks me over. This should be perfect. "Come here, son; let me see if this will fit. Looks like we have a lot of muscle to cover."

I walk over and stop before her. She holds out the shirt, close to my body. It's a vintage, clover-green Jimmy Hendrix t-shirt. "I think this will work." She releases the hanger to me, and heads toward the sidewall. "I think I got some shoes in the other day that look your size; brand new too. I tell you, things just aren't the same as when I was young. Generations now are spoiled and wasteful. Back when I was a kid, we didn't get a new pair of shoes until our current pair was no longer wearable."

Yep, she is just like my grandmother—always on her soapbox comparing then and now. I can't help but to smile. I come to a stop behind her as she pulls down a pair of black and neon-yellow Nike sneakers. "What size are you, honey?"

"Eleven."

"I may be old, but I still got it. I knew they would fit. Now, let's talk about this special girl. I'll tell you a little something about women, but it's our secret. Got it?"

I nod, curious where she is going with this. "We don't know what the hell we want. We like to pretend we do, and sometimes even convince ourselves we do, but we don't. There are two things you need to remember, and you'll get far with the lucky lady. One— she is always right. It doesn't matter if she really is or not, just let her think so regardless. Two— compliments are better than candy is what I always say. You can't buy a woman's heart, but you sure can sweet-talk your way there. Romance her, woo her, and sweep her off her feet. You do that, and she'll forever be yours."

I have discovered one thing about the elderly—they tend to be wise. It's best to listen, even if I don't have the heart to tell her I have no intention on falling in love. They don't really care about the ways of the up-and-coming generations. They just like to give advice and keep the old ways alive. "I'll definitely keep that in mind, thank you. I need to get going before I miss my chance. How much do I owe you?"

"You're a cute kid. I'll tell you what, since you listened to an old woman ramble, it's on the house. You go make up with that girl. I have a feeling she's special."

"No, ma'am, I'd like to pay for the stuff." She holds up her hand to stop me as I put on the shirt and shoes. My shorts are now dry.

"I insist. This is my store and I can do as I please," she says, grinning. "Go on now. Flash one of those smiles of yours and I'm sure all will be forgotten."

"Yes, ma'am. Thank you." I turn to head for the door.

"My pleasure," she says, beating me to it and opening the door for me.

I get in the truck and back into the street. The old woman is still standing in the door, waving goodbye. I return the gesture and begin on my way. I have no idea what I'm going to say when I get there. Why I never thought to get her number when she left it at the pool house, I have no idea. I wish I could just get her alone. The thought of her family being there freaks me out a little. Maybe because I don't have that much experience with parents and the ones I do are because they are my friends' parents.

It doesn't take long before Kinzleigh's house comes into view. I pull in and park off to the side. I'm not even sure if Kinzleigh is home. I'd like to hope she is, because the alternative drives me crazy to even consider. My hands are slightly sweaty. In attempt to dry them off, I wipe my hands on the sides of my shorts.

I walk up to the front porch. Well, I guess what I would compare to a front porch. It's more of a tall entryway in front of the door with tall columns and a covering. I knock on the door. After a few seconds I hear feet trekking on the hardwood floor.

When the door opens, standing in the doorway is her brother. He doesn't say anything. This should be fun. "Hey, is Kinzleigh here? I was hoping I could talk to her."

He looks behind him and steps outside, shutting the door. "What do you want with her? Preston brought her home a few minutes ago, meaning, she obviously doesn't want to talk to you. If she did, you would have been the one to drop her off."

I guess I had that one coming. "Look, man, I know you don't know me, but it's all a big misunderstanding. If I could talk to her, I could explain."

Her brother is beefy like me. We're about the same height and both full of lean muscle. "I don't think so. Look, I'm not saying you're a bad guy, but you're only here visiting. Kinzleigh is . . . she isn't like most girls. She's headstrong and beautiful and has these twisted views when it comes to relationships. Right now, she's really on it, because of all my shit. I wish that wasn't the case, but it is. We're close, so my issues affect her and vice versa. If you've already screwed up, unfortunately, you're wasting your time. Trust me."

If the guy weren't so damn nice, I'd punch him in the face. Why can't he just let her decide for herself? "Are you saying you won't even tell her I'm here?"

He nods. "If I thought it would change the outcome I would, but she's already messed up over moving. She doesn't need more confusion. If she's upset, I won't further upset her. I'm sorry, man, but I think you should go and enjoy the rest of your time here, then head back home and forget about her." He turns and opens the door, disappearing inside.

If I can't get anywhere with him, it's pointless trying. I'm not really feeling the California sun anymore. Knowing what I'd be missing by staying here without seeing her, I'd rather just go back home.

I pull up at Ryland's shortly after leaving her house and walk into the pool house. As I come into the back bedroom, I pull out my phone and call a number from the Google search I made to get it. A female answers after the first couple of rings. "Los Angeles International Airport, Dana speaking, how can I help you?"

"I need to know when the next flight out from LAX to New Orleans is please."

"I can help you with that. Please hold while I check the system." I hear clicking of the keyboard before she comes back on the line. "The next available flight is scheduled for nine tomorrow morning with United Airlines."

"I'll take it."

"Your name?"

"Breyson Abercrombie."

"Okay, I show you had a ticket for Friday morning, will you be exchanging?"

"Yes, please."

"Okay, I have you booked on flight UA 504. I'll email your flight confirmation."

"Thanks," I say ending the call.

I begin shoving all of my things into my suitcase, with the exception of a change of clothes and my shower bag. It's now completely dark outside. Since I have nothing else to do, I might as well go to bed. Before charging my phone, I send a text to Ryland to inform him of the change in my plans.

Me: Can you take me to the airport in the morning?

Ryland: What the hell for?

Me: I'm just not feeling it anymore. There hasn't been anything but drama since I've been here. I think I'm going to head back home.

Ryland: Things go bad with Kinzleigh?

Me: I never got past her brother.

Ryland: Shit, dude, that's what I was afraid of. I'm sure Preston didn't hesitate to fill him in on the details. He can be a little bitch when it comes to her. What time is your flight?

Me: 9 a.m. is take off. I need to leave early.

Ryland: I got you covered.

Me: Thanks. I'll see you then. I'm going to bed.

I plug the charger into my phone and place it on the bedside table. I didn't even bother to read the last text from Ryland. I'm not in the mood anymore. I know he will try to talk me out of it, but I don't really feel like hanging around the easy girls while he hangs out with Presley. Nothing is going the way it usually does when I stay here. It's always Ryland and me doing stuff, but we're older now, and right now he's occupied. I don't want to be a little whiny bitch that demands boy time. This is best for everyone, so I grab my shower bag and head for the shower. I still can feel the chlorine from the pool like a film over my skin.

Ten minutes later, I emerge from the steam-filled bathroom, showered and in a clean pair of boxers. Lying down in the bed, it doesn't take long before I drift off to sleep.

FIFTEEN

Kinzleigh

It's midnight and I just crawled into bed. Preston dropped me off around seven and insisted he needed to talk to Konnor. After a day like today, I didn't want to argue. I ate a ham and cheese sub leftover from dinner earlier and took a shower. After that, I walked into the den upstairs and found Dad watching old home movies. He does it from time to time, reminiscing in the memories. He said it ensures he never forgets the details. If I catch him watching them, I sit on the arm of his leather recliner and lay my head on his shoulder, watching them alongside him.

I get underneath my oversized fluffy comforter and turn out my bedside light. Just as I'm getting comfortable, my door bursts open, shining the light from the hallway into my dark room. I sit up, realizing it's Presley. She waltzes in wearing pajama shorts and a tank. "Presley, what are you doing here?"

She jumps on my bed beside me, landing on her knees and palms. "You know I need bestie time after what happened earlier today. Plus, I need to talk some sense into you. I got the scoop and

accepted FATE

I'm going to have Lexi's ass on a platter when I see her. We will see what she thinks when I forget to catch her sorry butt next time she goes up in the air."

Now I'm really confused. "Mind telling me what you're rambling about?"

She sighs and places her keys and phone on the table, before moving to the other side of me, farthest from the door. She slides under the covers and turns on her side, facing me. "You know come hell or high water I'm always on your side, but I will always be honest and tell you when you're being a royal pain in my ass." She has such a potty mouth sometimes, but that is one thing that makes Presley, Presley. She is so sassy.

I roll my eyes and turn toward her. "How exactly am I being a pain in your butt? I can't wait to hear this."

"For starters, I get that you jump to conclusions because of what happened to Konnor, but would it have killed you to hear the boy out before you stomped off in a rage?" Weird, I thought she'd be pulling for her brother on this one. Back when we were kids we used to plot ways to become sisters. Ninety percent of the time the solution was she would marry Konnor; imagine that.

"He kissed me with a girlfriend after hitting on Lexi the same night. What do you want me to do? Maybe it was doing me a favor. I will not do to someone else what was done to Konnor."

"You always were the stubborn one. Kinzleigh, I talked to Ryland. He didn't hit on Lexi. As a matter of fact, it was the opposite. I knew she was lying when she said it to begin with, that's why I called her out on it. I can smell a lie from a mile away, regardless of the fact that she's horrible at it. She's such an obvious liar. The little jealous tramp just wanted him for herself." She is right; she's always been good about calling bullcrap.

"It still doesn't change the fact that he kissed me with a girlfriend," I say, needing to reiterate how wrong that is.

She sighs, clearly annoyed, though I don't exactly know why she's taking up for him in the first place. "Kinzleigh, when are you going to take off those rose-colored glasses you wear? When are you going to see the world for the bullshit that it is? Things happen, and people make mistakes, but you know what? We shouldn't be defined for those mistakes. You go to church every Sunday, but when it comes time to practice what you preach, you fall short every time. We can't all be as perfect as you are."

"So, what are you saying? I should just forget that he purposely omitted having a girlfriend, or *had* a girlfriend, and just go along like that's okay? I can't do that, Presley. Not only is it wrong to do that to his girlfriend, but also to me. I deserve to know something like that before I kiss someone. It goes against everything I believe. You know how strongly I feel about that. If you don't want to be faithful to someone, you shouldn't date them."

She exhales impatiently. "This is the part I was referring to about being a pain in my ass. Did you ever ask him if he had or has a girlfriend when you were thinking about losing your virginity to him? Hmm? Or what about when you were kissing him back?"

"Well, Presley, excuse me, but I would think it's an unspoken rule that you should mention that before you try and kiss someone. When he kissed me, I assumed that meant he was single. I may not know much about dating, but why would you kiss someone if you have a girlfriend?"

"Kinzleigh, I'm not saying that it wasn't wrong of him to kiss you on Friday with a girlfriend. What I'm saying is you should have given him the chance to explain his actions. If you had, you would have learned that he was only dating her because they were friends with benefits and he didn't want her to be a termed a slut." She pauses, as if thinking. "That sounds so dumb repeating it. I don't know, maybe it's a southern thing. Personally, I don't know why it matters. Anyway, he broke it off with her that night on the phone, because he wanted to spend more time with you, but didn't feel right about doing that to her. He even explained to her that he met someone he was interested in getting to know. I'm not excusing his initial screw-up, but at least he tried to make it right. Would you cut the boy some slack? You can deny it all you want, but I know you like him and want to see more of him too."

I roll onto my back and look up at the ceiling. I don't know what I'm supposed to do. I know she's right, but at the same time, this is becoming very complicated already and he is supposed to leave in like four days. "I don't know. It just seems like too much of a headache already. Could you have not told me all of this tomorrow? I've had enough for one day. First Preston and now this—it's too much to absorb."

"Preston? Jeez. What now?"

"Nothing." I lie. "Continue."

"I could have waited until tomorrow, but then he wouldn't be here. He scheduled a flight out tomorrow morning, because he came over to talk to you and Konnor wouldn't let him through the door. He decided he would rather go back home than to stay here with you not speaking to him. Ryland is freaking out about it, because he only sees him twice a year."

All I can do is blink. He came here to talk to me? Konnor didn't even tell me? That's not like him at all. "What exactly are you proposing I do?"

"I could take you to the airport in the morning. I know which gate he's at. You could easily clear up all this miscommunication."

That sly grin comes over her face, but then it disappears. Sadness appears in her voice. "Mom told me about you moving."

"Why didn't you tell me you knew?"

"I don't know. I guess I was waiting around for you to tell me yourself, hoping it wasn't real when you didn't. I want you to do something for me and I'm completely serious. This isn't a joke to me. You have to promise, and you know me and you never break promises."

"Okay, what is it?"

A tear rolls down her nose. "I want you to live this year. Get out there and do something you wouldn't normally do. I know I won't be there to push you, but I want you to venture out and have fun. You're such a likable person when you let yourself go; free the inner spirit that I know you keep buried deep inside." I've never seen Presley cry; not since we were little, anyway. It's a little overwhelming.

Before I know it, tears are falling down my face too. "Hey, you know you'll always be my best friend, right? I know I can be difficult sometimes, but I love you. You're the only sister I've ever had. It's only for a year and I'm coming back. This won't change anything between us. We'll still go to the same college, right? Be dormies like we always planned? Pinky promise me."

I hold out my hand, extending my pinky. When we were kids we saw on a movie where two people made a blood promise and thought it would be neat, so we made a blood promise we would go to the same college. It's silly, I know, but she's always been my sister, blood or not, and we always do everything big together.

A smile breaks free in the midst of her tears. "You're damn right," she says, linking her pinky with mine. "I wish you didn't have to go. Senior year is going to suck without my partner in crime. What about cheerleading captain? What about cheerleading in general?"

"Come on, you know I'm usually just holding you back. You're the co-captain, so that automatically makes you captain and Madison had the third highest score at tryouts; she will become co-captain. As for cheerleading, well, I guess I'm hoping this school has a decent squad and an extra spot."

This is so much harder than I thought now that it's real. "Will you visit on Christmas break?"

She wipes her eyes. "Of course I will. You can show me around and introduce me to some southern boys. I've always wanted to meet a real cowboy, and if any are like Breyson, I can't wait. That boy is hot, Kinzleigh."

Leave it to Presley to turn this into something about guys. I push her shoulder lightly, laughing. "Count on it. Let's call it a night if I've got to be up at the butt crack of dawn to go to the airport."

Her face lights up like a kid on Christmas morning. "I knew you'd see it my way. Night, sweetness," she says and kisses my cheek, before turning over to go to sleep. Always the one to have a glutton for punishment . . .

SIXTEEN

Kinzleigh

We pull into LAX at 8AM sharp. "You owe me a white chocolate mocha after this," I say groggily. "Extra-large."

I am not a morning person. I like my sleep, unlike a certain perky brunette I know. I don't think the girl ever sleeps more than five hours a night. She was up, showered, and dressed in a pair of my clothes when I was just stirring from my slumber. It's a tragedy we weren't sisters, a universal mishap. We do everything together and can wear all the same clothes except for jeans, because I'm short and she's tall.

She reaches over and squeezes my hand in an endearing way. "You do this and I'll buy you as many mochas as your heart desires. I'm proud of you, because I know this is hard for you. Ryland said they are sitting outside the gate."

We step out of her white Mercedes in the parking garage. "Let's just get this over with." Heading for the main entrance of the airport, we catch a ride to the door. "What terminal is it, Presley?"

She looks down at her phone, scrolling through a text message. "Terminal seven, flight UA 504 to New Orleans. Departure is 9 AM." I head in the direction of the terminal before I remember they won't let you through without a security check and boarding pass. Crap!

I stop mid step and turn toward Presley. "I can't get back there without a ticket, and we're already pushing for time."

A smirk comes across her face as she holds up a printout. "I have the ticket confirmation. We just need to get the boarding pass, so come on."

My amusement shows. "You spent money on a flight ticket? Isn't that a little pricey for this?"

She waves me off. "Do you know how many air miles we have on the credit card? Flying to Dad is no different than driving a car. He does it multiple times a week. Sometimes daily."

This is true. If Mr. Dunagin gets wind of a deal that will make him money, he's gone within the hour. Buying property for cheap and building on it is something he does all over the place.

We get to the cashier window. Presley slaps the piece of paper down on the countertop. The attendant looks at the printout. "Good morning, Miss Baker. Do you have some identification?"

"Sure," I say, and dig through my purse for my wallet. Pulling it out, I remove my license and hand it to the woman in front of me.

She clicks away on the keyboard in front of her and then hands my license back to me. "I have your seats confirmed. Here is your boarding pass. You will be in terminal seven. Enjoy your flight."

She smiles and hands me my pass. "Thank you."

We hurry to airport security and wait impatiently until I've been checked. It's almost boarding time and I'm running full speed. I cannot believe I'm doing this over a guy. A guy I'm not even serious with! If I didn't feel so bad about jumping to conclusions I wouldn't be.

As I come into the seating area, I stop to catch my breath. I spot Ryland standing next to the terminal looking nervous. He's talking to Breyson, who has his back turned toward me. As Ryland catches sight of me, a smile spreads across his face. I don't think I've ever seen him smile so big.

I'm not sure what he said, but Breyson turns around, staring me down. I can't move. Maybe I should have planned what I was going to say. Which is what, exactly? I always seem to be at a disadvantage around him.

He looks a little surprised, but he smiles. I'm not sure I'll ever be immune to him. I've heard the term *panty-dropping smile* and it never made sense until now. It makes me slightly weak in the knees seeing him smile.

He drops his bag next to Ryland and begins walking toward me, never breaking eye contact. He stops inches away from me. When he looks me in the eyes like this, I can't look away, as if he's forcing me.

"Hi," I say nervously.

"Hi," he quips back, his smile brightening.

"Why are you leaving early?"

"I didn't have a reason to stay."

"What reason do you need? I thought you were here to visit your cousin."

"I just figured if I couldn't hang around with you, I didn't have a reason to be here. You've kind of grown on me," he says teasingly, but then he shrugs. "And besides, he's having fun with Presley right now."

I can't help but to smile. "I guess you've kind of grown on me too."

"Look, I'm sorry about Friday. I shouldn't have done that to you. I did end things as soon as it happened, though. I swear. I should have told you about her. And about what happened at the party..."

I place my hand over his mouth, stopping him. "It doesn't matter. The only thing that matters is that you're upfront with me from here on out. No more omitting the truth. Honesty is a make or break with me."

He nods and steps closer. I remove my hand from his mouth, but he grabs my wrist and kisses my palm. Releasing it moments later, he cups my neck in his hands, tilting my head back for me to look up at him. "You have my word."

He then tilts his head slightly to the side and leans in, pressing his soft lips to mine. Each time our lips touch, tingles spread all over my body. Our tongues meld together, his commencing the flicking and twisting with mine in a playful jousting match. Our mouths fit together perfectly and his breath tastes of fresh mint, barely numbing my tongue.

The world fades away, and for a moment it's just us—two people becoming lost in each other. I may be young, and I may be headstrong, but even I know saying goodbye in four days is going to be the hardest thing I'll ever do.

SEVENTEEN

Kinzleigh

As the sun beams in through the windows, my eyes pop open. Glancing at my phone, I notice it's still early. I have too much to do to sleep. It's my last day with Breyson and I'm determined to make it count. I still haven't figured out the best way to tell him goodbye.

Sitting up, I rub my hands over my eyes, trying to wake up.

Swinging my body to place my feet on the floor, I stand from the bed and walk toward my balcony door. The large, panel windows are covered in sheer curtains the same hot pink as my satin sheets.

I love my room.

It's decorated in a black, pink, and gray color palette with Eiffel towers scattered about and a few black and white photos framed on the wall of the city. My parents always take us on a family vacation every year and the year we went to Paris I completely fell in love. I must admit; it's weird that I don't want anything to do with love, but my favorite place is known for the very thing I want nothing to do with—the city of love.

accepted FATE

I open my balcony door and walk outside. From my balcony I can see the beach in the distance. I love sitting out here, people watching and staring at the palm trees and the ocean. If I wake up early enough, sometimes I can even hear the surf.

Leaning against the railing, I close my eyes and bask in the sunlight warming my face and shoulders. It's hard to believe four days have passed since that day in the airport. It's all been very surreal. There is only one word to describe the emotions I've experienced—magical.

Breyson and I have been together the entire four days with the exception of sleeping. We've done just about everything time would allow.

Monday, when we left the airport, I took him around Los Angeles. He said this is his third year in Laguna, but I wanted this year to be special. I wanted him to experience the beauty and the personality of California the way it's meant to be experienced. I wanted him to see what I love about this place. I didn't only do it for him. Since I'm about to be gone for a year, it was a little for myself too. To date, it was one of best days of my life.

Tuesday, we hung around Ryland's pool house. The four of us swam for most of the day, playing pool games, and his parents grilled lunch for us. They are really nice people and a lot like my parents. We even played board games inside. I felt like a kid again.

Last night, though, was the best night yet. Breyson picked me up from my house when the sun was going down. He had told me earlier that day to dress comfortable. I had no idea what he had planned, but I was full of excitement. Once we got in the truck, we headed over to the beach. I didn't think much of it until we got there and I saw he had a picnic planned. I didn't know people even did that anymore, other than in the movies.

I couldn't help but smile when he pulled out that big picnic basket from the backseat. He slipped up and said his Aunt Susan helped put it together. We walked down to the beach hand-in-hand. He spread out a blanket and we ate fruit and sandwiches. Then we laid underneath the stars, snuggled up next to each other, and talked for hours.

It's amazing how much alike we are. He is as devoted to football as I am with cheerleading. He gets it—to want something so bad you'd do anything to obtain it. And I think that's what makes setting aside my fears for a little fun easier.

He has been nothing but a gentleman; quite the contrary to what I thought mere days ago. We have had quite a few heated make out sessions, but nothing more. Those times were absolutely amazing. No words will ever be enough to explain the way kissing him makes me feel.

So, I've decided that tonight—the fifteenth of June—I will give myself to him. At least in every way I am willing. I may not give my heart away, but I will give him my body. I realized throughout the week there really isn't a reason to hang onto my virginity anymore. If I had any intention of getting married I might save it, but that isn't the case with me.

With that thought, I don't want to be a slut either. I love Presley and she is always really picky and safe with whom she hooks up with, but all that is a job in itself. The only reason I have made this decision is because come tomorrow morning, Breyson will be hundreds of miles away. It will be special, but not permanent.

Tonight, I even have the house to myself. The timing couldn't be more perfect. Mom and Dad left this morning for Turks and Caicos, to celebrate their twenty-fifth anniversary. They won't be back until Sunday night.

accepted FATE

Konnor is with Kyle in LA for the night at some event that has several bands playing. They decided to get a hotel to avoid a late drive, they said, but I know it's really to party.

I have all day to prepare for Breyson coming over. Today he promised Ryland they could do guy things since he's spent so much time with me. I told him we could just watch movies and hang out since he has to get up so early for his flight. He is supposed to come over this evening.

I need to put together a mental list of what all I need to do. Isabella, the housekeeper, has already cleaned the house for the week, so everything is tidy for tonight. I thought about making a trip to the mall to pick out some lingerie and candles, maybe even a new outfit. I get one chance to do this. I'm determined to get it right.

I told him not to eat dinner, because I was going to attempt cooking. I'm not really sure why, because there are only a few things I can cook from watching Mom in the kitchen. If I fail, there is always take-out.

Walking into my bedroom, I make up my bed and pick up what I messed up since Isabella cleaned. I'm a neat freak and well-organized person, but I haven't been home much over the past few days. Karate chopping the middle of the decorative pillows to make a homey crease just like they do on staging shows, my bed is finished. I remove my favorite Lavender and Vanilla spray from my bedside table and spray my bed, so it will smell nice later.

Since I showered last night, I am going to wait until right before he comes over to shower, so I'll be freshly cleaned and shaved. I am nervous about having sex, since obviously, I've never done it before. Opening my dresser drawer, I pull out a pair of white denim shorts and a t-shirt, pulling them on. I tousle my curly hair and pull it into a low side ponytail to stay cool, before putting on my sneakers.

I imagine it will probably be busy at the mall, so I need to get started if I'm going to get back in time and have everything ready by the time Breyson gets here. I put on a pair of simple hoop earrings for the finishing touch and reach for my purse.

Standing in my doorway, I turn and look at my room one last time before I go. Next time I see it everything will change. I may only get to stay in the house I love another couple of weeks, but I will always have something to remember it by.

I plan the menu on the descent down the stairs. I think I am going to put salmon steaks on the grill with asparagus wrapped in bacon. It's easy and I know it will be edible. Excitement bubbles under my skin. After seventeen years, I'm finally going to do this. I close my eyes. I just hope I can make it memorable for him too . . .

I pull into the mall parking lot in record time. I lock my doors and head for the entrance. First stop on my list is the bath and body store. I usually keep a stock of everything scent related, but I haven't done much shopping lately with my busy schedule for cheerleading.

Walking in the store, I immediately notice the signage advertising a big sale they run a few times a year. Perfect. I grab a mesh shopping bag and begin loading it down with a little bit of everything; from scented plug-in refills to candles and sprays and body products in all different scents.

It doesn't take me long to make my purchase and head toward the lingerie store. Every time I go in this store now, I will think of the day Breyson was in here with me. It's the funniest thing; all it takes to embarrass a guy is to bring him to a women's store.

As I walk into the store with my bags in tow, a store associate immediately greets me. "Hello, I'm Heather. Is there anything in particular you're looking for?"

"Maybe. I'm trying to buy something for someone, but I'm not sure what to buy." Personally, it embarrasses me to be in here buying this type of clothing—undergarment might be a better word, or swatch of fabric. I've never bought actual 'lingerie' before. My mother would kill me.

The associate looks to be in her mid-twenties and can obviously sense my discomfort. "I see. Is this someone a special guy in your life?" I nod, because really, I don't know what else to say. The truth of what we are is irrelevant to the purchase. "I think we can find something for you." She smiles, discretely moving to the other side of the store. "Follow me, sweetie."

She heads toward the back of the store with me on her heels, stopping in the center of all the frilly and sexy lingerie. I'm getting more nervous the more I see, taking in fabric hanging from hangers that become scantier as the store deepens.

She walks me into the dressing room area, unlocking a door for me. "Tell me what you're looking for. Do you want something you can wear under clothes or something to change into?"

She makes a valid point; one in which I have not thought of. Maybe I should have chosen the outfit before I came here. I shrug my shoulders. "I'm not sure. I never got that far in the thought process. I'm not even sure what I'm wearing. I'm sorry I'm not much help. I've never really bought anything like this before."

"You don't have to be sorry, hun. That's why I'm here. Luckily for you, I'm a pro," she says, winking at me with a grin spread across her face.

She stands there looking me over. "Let's see. We probably want to stay sexy, but simple, considering your age." She pauses, and then taps her index finger over her pursed lips. "You have a killer body and gorgeous hair. What if we go for something under the clothes, so you can knock his socks off and it be unexpected?"

Clearly, I am out of my league here. "Whatever you think. I'm your model, so you can do as you please." Her face takes on a mischievous look. Apparently, I just made her day.

She opens the dressing room door she previously unlocked and leads me inside. "Stay here and I'll be right back with some things for you to try." Disappearing into the store, she comes back about fifteen minutes later with an armful of items. Oh my . . .

As I'm leaving the store, much later than I'd hoped, I have concluded I never want to go through this experience ever again. I have tried on more lingerie than I care to see again in my lifetime. Some of which was flattering and others that even make a slim person feel overweight.

I have no idea what time it is, because I've been stuck in a dressing room for what seems like forever, with different items being shoved at me. Now I know why people just hire personal shoppers for this sort of thing, or even better, order online and hope it fits.

I ended up leaving with a matching set that consists of some really sexy black and pink underwear, a skimpy bra, a garter belt, and stockings to go under my clothing.

I'll admit, with my natural skin tone pink is one of my favorite colors to wear. I'm comfortable in what she chose. It's sexy yet simple, just like she said.

The push-up bra is a black undertone covered in a lace design of dark pink with a small bow between the breasts. The panties are the matching design, a thong, with the same bow in the center of the back, sitting right above the beginning of my bottom. I didn't try on the bottoms, but I know it will look really good all put together.

The last stop is a boutique close by and then home to get ready. Looking at the time on my cell phone, I realize it's going to have to be a quick stop. I only have another hour or so before I need to be back at home, and traffic will take up a good portion of that time allotment.

I've gotten a few texts from Presley asking if she could give Breyson my number and he has asked each time we're together, but my answer remains the same. I don't want any complications. As much as I would love to talk to him more, it's not plausible living in different states. And he's also leaving tomorrow. There is no reason to continue talking once he's gone. It will only make things worse. When he leaves here I want him to take away a fond memory and that be that.

There are a few popular boutiques in town. They all have really cute clothing. I pick the closest one to me and pull in. As I walk inside, I notice a few people, but it's mostly quiet. I can already tell I'm going to do some damage today just by the things in the window. Presley would have a fit if she found out I came in here without her. We rarely shop separately. If I weren't in such a cramp for time, I would have told her to meet me here.

I walk through the store grabbing everything that catches my eye in my size. One thing I've learned when trying to find *the outfit* is to grab a few contenders and choose later. An outfit always looks different the second time you put it on, sometimes better and sometimes worse. The first time your mind is always too overwhelmed to judge how you really feel about it.

Once I've filled my arms, I leave them at the counter and continue on my shopping escapade to the shoes and jewelry. Of course, I can't omit my most precious accessory—handbags.

I finally make it out of the store with just enough time to get home and get myself ready before Breyson is supposed to be at my door. My backseat is loaded down with bags from my shopping spree. Presley and I always end up buying way more than we intend. It's an addiction I never want to break. As long as I can cheer and shop I don't need anything else.

I pull into my garage with absolutely no time to spare. If I'm going to get everything ready, I need to get a move on it. I unload all the bags from my car, but it takes a few trips. I remove all the candles from the bag and begin lighting them sporadically throughout the first floor of the house, saving my favorite for my bedroom and bathroom. Next comes plugging in the oil scents and spritzing the linens and furniture with the matching room spray.

As I finish everything downstairs, I grab the rest of my bags and run up the stairs toward my room. I toss them onto the bed and finish setting out and lighting the candles around my room.

Breathing heavily from rushing, I turn on the string lights that hang from the canopy over my bed. Sheer charcoal gray curtains hang from the canopy rail to the floor on each of the four corners of my king-sized bed. By the time he gets here, it should be dark outside. The wall directly across from my bed has my dresser as well as a wall-mounted television we can stream movies on.

I look around the room. Everything should be set. I can already smell the fragrance filling the room. It's a light and soothing smell from the sleep line. I walk into the bathroom and start the shower.

One thing I love about this house is that I have my own connecting bathroom, as does Konnor.

Freshly showered thirty minutes later, I grab my new underwear and put them on. I'm now in the negative for time, because I had to shave everything, including places I don't normally shave. Tuesday night when Presley and I left Ryland's house, she insisted that we have a little talk. If I've never thought before that having a friend know everything about you is awkward, I do now.

In this little girl talk 101, she informed me that girls having sex no longer have hair down there. I have always groomed with a trimmer, but never totally rid the area, in mild terms. According to her, if I am going to go through with this, then I need to be up to speed with everyone else. I have never done it, because for obvious reasons, I have never had to.

And well, it took longer than I thought in my effort to not cut myself with the razor right before a guy has his business and eyes down there. I look down at myself, taking in the sudden bareness of my pelvis. Bald. It's a sight that makes me feel like a little girl waiting on puberty. Maybe it's something I'll quickly get used to.

I exhale, trying to rid the nerves that have decided to go haywire in my stomach. I look out over the bed at everything I bought today. I finally decide on a pair of bright palazzo pants in a paisley pattern. The top I bought with it is a solid aqua boat neck cotton shirt with three-quarter length sleeves. I move it to the side and grab up the remaining clothes in handfuls and toss them into my closet. I will have to put them up later.

Shutting the closet door, I walk back over to the bed. I have to put on the garter belt and stockings before I can put on my clothes. Staring down at the contraption in front of me, I'm a little intimidated. The store associate gave me instructions on how to put them on, but because you never try on panties or stockings, I don't have hands-on experience. Linking the garter belt around my waist, sadly, is the easiest part.

Removing the stockings from the pack, I sit on the bed, holding them out in front of me. They are a black sheer in color and look complicated. Mom has tried to get me to wear stockings to church, but I'm usually bare or covered with leggings. I pull one foot onto the bed and pull the stocking over my foot. I manage to maneuver it up my leg close to the clasp that hangs from the garter belt. Standing up, I try to figure out this whole mechanism.

After a few tries I get the front done, but now I have to get the back hooked. People put forth a lot of effort just to have it taken off. It takes longer to get the back one connected, but I manage. The second leg doesn't take as long as the first. I look myself over in the full-length mirror attached to my closet door. Turning around and seeing the finished product has me excited. Maybe it's worth it to feel this sexy.

I pull on my clothes and a pair of flats to cover up my stockings for later. After drying my hair, I decided to straighten it instead of wearing it in my usual curls. As I'm putting on my gloss—the last of my makeup—the doorbell rings.

Shoot! I was hoping to have a head start on dinner, but I guess I can cook while we talk. I pop a piece of gum in my mouth and start for the door.

When I get there, I open it to Breyson looking sexier than ever. He is wearing a pair of faded denim jeans, hanging low on his hips and a pair of brown leather shoes, as well as a fitted dark-pink polo that looks amazing against his tanned arms. His hair is gelled in the front and he's holding a bouquet of pink Gerber daisies. I smile at the gesture, because he remembered they are my favorite from our conversation last night. He holds them out for me to grab. "You remembered."

"Of course, I remembered," he replies. "I remember everything you say. I thought it might brighten your day." I go to grab the flowers and he pulls me in for a hug, sending my face directly into his broad chest.

He smells so good. I'm not sure what scent he wears, but if I ever find a bottle I'm buying it, though I'll never admit that to anyone. "What's this for?" I turn my head to the side, resting my cheek against the center of his chest.

"Me," he says. One little word and I'm already shaking. This boy is dangerous to me; like kryptonite. I love the feel of being wrapped in his strong arms. He walks me backward, inside the house, but never releases me. Once inside the door, he pushes it shut with the bottom of his foot. "I've missed you, beautiful girl. You're hell on my ego." His voice makes me close my eyes. The sound is hypnotic.

He grabs my chin and turns it up to face him. I know what's coming next. Will I ever be ready for the havoc it reaps on my body? Probably not. Do I still want it? Heck yes!

My heart starts palpitating in my chest the closer he gets to my lips. As his lips touch mine, my blood starts racing throughout my body. I can hear my pulse boom in my ears and I feel like I'm frozen in time.

His tongue lightly brushes mine, playing and teasing. He sucks my bottom lip into his mouth and his teeth graze the skin. My stomach starts clenching, and a need I've never had, until him, begins forming down below, making me want to be touched in response.

I wrap my arms around his waist and continue to kiss him. I could kiss him for hours. I get lost in an array of emotions that I can't stop. I hate what he's doing to me, but I love it all the same. He runs his fingers through my hair, cupping the back of my head with one hand and trails the other down to my waist. At this rate we won't make it to dinner, or to my room for that matter.

Reluctantly, I break the kiss. "It's good to see you too." I smile. Grabbing his hand, I tow him toward the kitchen. "Come on, I have plans for you."

As we make it into the kitchen, I stop next to the refrigerator, opening the door. "Can you cook?" He raises a brow as if he's really not sure.

I pretend to be offended. I may be well taken care of and my parents may have money, but they are still practical people. Mom has a housekeeper that comes once or twice a week and that is as dependent on someone else as she gets. My parents are very family-oriented people. Cooking and eating together is a big deal in our house. We always eat at the table with the exception of Super Bowl Sunday. Football is a big sport in this family and my parents always have a big party for Super Bowl.

"Are you scared I might poison you?" Reaching into the refrigerator, I pull out the wrapped Salmon and set it on the island behind me. From the corner of my eye, I can see him watching me, but purposely I don't acknowledge him. I carry on as If he isn't standing beside me. I remove the asparagus and bacon next and place them beside the Salmon.

"I didn't mean anything by it. I've just never known anyone my age that could cook. I guess you're a little more down-to-earth than I realized. I kind of took you for a high- maintenance girl." It's really cute that he thinks I'm upset. I think I may let him sweat a little more. It may be cruel, but it's amusing. A little fun never hurt anyone.

I make my way around the island to get out the dishes I need. "Can you start a grill?" I look into the cabinet as I speak, because if I look at him I am going to break. I grab a glass baking dish.

As I stand up, I place the baking dish down and grab the Salmon, opening the wrapper. "Of course, I can start a grill. I have been man-handling the grill since I was tall enough to reach it."

"Good. If you walk outside the patio door, you'll see the grill on the left. I should be done seasoning this by the time you get back." Turning around, I begin searching through the spice rack for the seasonings I need.

As I'm standing against the countertop, a hand takes residence on top of the counter to each side of me. His body becomes flush with my backside. My heart rate quickens and my breathing becomes uneven.

He brushes my hair over my right shoulder. I can feel his warm breath tickle the back of my neck. On reflex my eyes close. He makes me weak and I need to be strong.

He kisses the top of my bare left shoulder and trails kisses up the side of my neck. He stops just below my ear. "Are you mad at me?"

His voice is low and seductive. How am I supposed to compete with this? He is playing in the major leagues and I'm still on a high school team. It's unfair how good he is at this. Oh, gracious, like now. He lightly licks the outline of my ear with the tip of his tongue. That feels . . . euphoric.

I turn around, trying to get some distance before I come unglued. Wrong move. He has a huge grin on his face, which is maybe an inch from mine. "Why would I be mad?" My voice breaks as it comes out, barely above a whisper.

Great, Kinzleigh, you're doing a swell job of being convincing.

He runs the tip of his index finger along my jaw line. "You're going to be the death of me, Kinzleigh Baker."

He continues his exploration down my neck and body, stopping at the small of my back. Resting his forehead against mine, he looks me in the eyes. It doesn't take a genius to know what he is doing. He is asking my permission to continue with his hands. In response, I place my hands over his, gliding them downward until they are perfectly covering my bottom.

His breathing becomes ragged and he closes his eyes as he squeezes his hands. He closes in for a kiss. It's much different this time. He is needy and choppy with his movements, twirling his tongue with mine. It's bittersweet. He picks me up, rubbing me against his front on the way, before setting me on top of the counter.

I wrap my arms around his neck, running my fingers through his hair. This is my last night to see Breyson Abercrombie and I'm going to cherish it. I return his kiss at full force, giving him everything I have. I kiss him for everything that tonight is. It's an end to something beautiful; something I will remember every day for the rest of my life.

Wrapping my legs around his waist, I pull him closer. He is a good bit taller than me. With me sitting on the counter, he is at eye level with me. He pulls me to the edge of the countertop, pressing me against him, allowing me to feel the effect of our little tryst in the kitchen. "I can't control myself around you. We are never going to make it through dinner. Why don't we just do something quick and go watch a movie?"

I will not let him get out of it that easily. I have been planning this all day. "No way. Get your butt outside and man the grill," I tease authoritatively, releasing him from my hold and then push on his chest for emphasis.

He backs away, holding his hands up in surrender. "Okay, okay. I'll be right back." He adjusts himself and turns as he walks toward the patio, stepping outside. I hurry back to the food—now sitting idle on the counter—to begin seasoning and preparing it for the grill. Heaven help me, because my nerves are taking a turn for the worst.

EIGHTEEN

Kinzleigh

The rest of dinner passed by uneventful. Mostly just small talk and glances between the two of us. Standing from the table, I walk to the sink, placing my plate inside. Breyson follows close behind me, doing the same.

I turn to face him as he grabs me by the waist. From behind, he grabs me by the inside of my legs, lifting me. I wrap my legs around him, interlocking my feet behind his waist and grab a hold of him by the shoulders. "What are you doing?"

"I can't take it anymore. I want to cuddle and kiss you until I have to leave." He walks to the living room, carrying me. "Where to?"

He stops in the living area where he met my parents a few short days ago. If only there was a button to make time stand still in those frames of life worth repeating. If someone asked me what moment in time I would want to hold onto, I'd say this week.

"My room. We have to go up the stairs, though, so you can put me down." He looks at me as if he would rather die than put me down.

He moves toward the stairs, but never looks away. I'm not sure how he can even see where he is going, but he climbs the stairs one step at a time. Something about that look leaves me wanting more. If I were interested in giving my heart away, it would be for him. It would never work.

When he stops at the top of the staircase, I know he is waiting for further instructions. "It's the room at the end of the hall."

Nerves are starting to take their toll on me. It's getting closer to the time I've spent all day preparing for. He opens my door and stops in the doorway. For the first time since he picked me up, he breaks eye contact to look around the room. He smiles and looks back at me. "This room is fitting for you."

Walking me inside, he lays me down carefully on the bed. He is so gentle with me, like he could break me if too rough. "It smells good in here. I feel like I could go to sleep."

I smile, because sleeping is not on the agenda for tonight. I have the rest of my life to sleep. I don't have the rest of my life to spend in his arms. And the fact that he's acting like he's not getting in my pants tonight makes me want to do this all the more. He hasn't tried anything since the couch before the pool party. I have a feeling when this almost ended early he cut out the possibility that he was still getting my virginity. He definitely is.

I seductively scoot backward on the bed. He watches me in amusement before getting on the bed himself, knees first. "Just so you know, we won't be sleeping anytime soon."

He crawls on his hands and knees until he is straddling me at the head of the bed. "What did you have in mind?"

"A little of this and a little of that." I tease, grabbing a fistful of his shirt and pulling him toward me. "I guess you'll just have to wait and see." I kiss his lips, hungry for his taste. I don't know what has gotten into me. I have gone from never kissing a boy to craving it, or him, in a matter of days.

I'm not sure how long we have been kissing, but a low growl radiates from his throat as he rubs himself against me, picking up pace. I can feel his need pressing between my legs as he lowers himself closer to me. I had a movie planned, but it can wait. I don't care about the movie anymore. I just want to feel him in every way possible. I am ready to move forward— more so than I'll ever be.

I sit up, pushing him back slightly so he is holding his weight on his knees, resting his butt on his heels. He rubs his hands over his face. I can tell he thinks he's gone too far. "Kinzleigh, I'm sorry. I'm really trying not to maul you like a bear. You're too damn sexy. I can't help myself," he says in frustration.

I press my index finger over his lips to stop him from talking. I raise my arms above my head to get my point across. His eyes widen in response as he bites his lower lip. "Kinzleigh, don't feel pressured to do anything. I'm okay with just kissing or doing nothing at all."

"Would you shut up already? You can lay the good boy act to rest for a while. I need the sexy Breyson to come out and play. Are you going to undress me or continue talking?" That was all it took and he moans. That voice does things to me that should be illegal. I still am not used to all these emotions and feelings roaming free throughout my mind and body. It leaves me feeling frustrated each time we stop kissing.

He grabs the bottom of my shirt and slowly pulls it up my body and over my head. It's dark outside, and the only lighting in here is the soft flicker of candlelight around the room and the dim glow from my string lights above my bed. It accentuates him, making him sexier than in the full light, if that's even possible. Tossing my shirt onto the floor beside my bed, he leans in and kisses me. His taste is like an aphrodisiac, making me deepen the kiss.

I run my hands along the band of his jeans, unsure of what to do next. Do I tell him what I want or just unbutton his jeans? He has the slightest trail of hair starting from his navel and running downward where it disappears into his jeans, tickling the back of my hand. His body is so hard and defined against the knuckles of my fingers.

I lightly caress my fingertips around to his back and up the seam of his spine, underneath his shirt, dragging it with me. I can feel goose bumps form beneath my touch. Once I reach underneath his arms, he breaks free from my lips and grabs it by the back collar, pulling it over his head and throwing it aside. He is the most beautiful thing I have ever seen. I know it's not the most masculine way to describe a man, but other words fail me.

He looks down at my bra-covered breasts. "Damn," he says, bending down and kissing my cleavage. He runs his tongue over my perky breast and down the crevice between the two, leaving a thin film of saliva in its wake. Thank you, Heather, at the lingerie store!

He presses kisses in a line down my center, stopping at the band of my pants. Grabbing my ankle in his hand, he pulls off my shoe, dropping it, and does the same with the other foot.

Sliding his fingers beneath the waistband of my pants, he begins inching them down slowly. I slightly lift my butt, so he can work them over my hips and down my legs. His breath hitches when he notices the rest of my hidden underwear. He sits back on his heels and raises my legs removing the remainder of my pants.

Disposing of them, he releases my legs to the bed. His eyes travel up my body and stop once our eyes meet. "You're absolutely stunning and I haven't even gotten you naked yet."

He backs up to the foot of the bed and stands before me. He really makes those jeans look good. I cross my legs from the increased pressure and sensitivity going on. The damp feeling makes me uncomfortable.

I prop up on my elbows, taking him in. When he notices what I'm doing he smirks and unbuttons his pants, revealing the top band of his boxers. He removes his shoes and slides his pants down with his thumbs, stepping out of them. "Are you sure your parents won't come home?"

"Yes. They called me when they landed."

"Your brother?"

I bite my bottom lip, trying not to laugh at the nervous undertone in his voice where Konnor is concerned. "He's been posting photos on Instagram. He's exactly where he's supposed to be, and drinking, so he's not going anywhere."

He nods, instantly relaxing. After removing his socks, he bends over toward the floor. My brows come together. "What are you doing?"

He stands up, holding out a condom. Now I feel stupid, because that never crossed my mind. I just nod.

He comes across the bed at record speed. Grabbing my waist, he pulls me down so that I'm lying flat. "Hey, stop it. I know that look and there is no reason for you to feel embarrassed. I love your innocence. Stop thinking it's a bad thing. Okay?"

"Are you always this perceptive? I'm not sure if I like being read like a book."

He shakes his head. "Only with you."

He leans down and presses his lips to mine. In one swift move he turns, pulling me on top to straddle him. The feel of his body beneath mine only turns me on more. He makes me feel small, and the way he looks at me sends an electrical sensation through my body that reminds me of the way a battery feels against your tongue.

Reaching behind me, he unclasps my bra and slides it off without ever breaking the kiss. He sits up, holding me in his lap. The closer we get to full nudity, the more nervous I become. I don't know what to expect. He places his palm against my cheek, rubbing his thumb lightly across my bottom lip. "Are you sure you want to do this? It's not too late to back out. You know I'll be gone tomorrow, and we'll never see each other again."

I don't even have to think it over. I nod my head, looking him in the eyes so he can tell it's the truth. "I know the facts. I want you, and I want to give to you the only thing I have to offer. I don't need to worry about tomorrow, because all I need is tonight. You don't need to worry about me clinging to you; it's why I don't want to exchange numbers. All we need is right now. We're alike, you know. I will never let someone break me, so yes, this is what I want. I've thought about it all week."

He smiles, pressing his forehead to mine. "Where have you been all my life, Kinzleigh Baker? It figures I would meet a girl version of myself and then never see her again." When he kisses me again, the emotion behind that kiss is overwhelming.

Wrapping his arm around my back to hold me against him, he turns, laying me back down against the bed. He unhooks the stockings from the garter and rolls each one, individually, down my legs.

He throws them over his shoulder and hooks each index finger inside the belt and my thong, pulling them down my legs in unison, until they are completely removed. I feel like I'm about to pass out from the nervousness. I've never been naked like this in front of anyone.

I press my legs together, feeling vulnerable. He shakes his head at me, opening them at the knees. "I want to see you; all of you."

I'm shaking now, and it's not from being cold. I can barely breathe. I'm afraid of it turning into a panic attack. I look up at the ceiling in an attempt to calm down. He touches his hand under my breast where my heart is pounding excessively. My breaths are coming out in short bursts.

He comes to rest between my legs and kisses me softly. "Damn, baby, you're shaking. Look at me." I do as he asked. He is directly above me looking down, holding himself off of me. "I won't do anything you don't want to do, okay? Just say the word and we'll stop."

His voice is already calming me down. "I'm okay. I'm just nervous." He leans to the side, holding his body on his left forearm and removes his boxers with his right hand.

I look down at him as he searches for the condom on the bed. My eyes widen at the sight before me. Oh gosh. I start to panic all over again. I try to calm myself before he notices. I will not do this again. It's humiliating. I have never seen one before, except a few times when Presley showed me a photo of one to tease me. I'm not sure what would be classified as big or small, but I'm pretty sure what I just witnessed is every boy's dream size. The pain that Presley mentioned comes to the forefront of my mind.

He pulls the condom wrapper between his teeth, tearing it at the edge. The word *Magnum* across the wrapper answers my question. Maybe it works like a needle—out of sight out of mind. I try to concentrate on him instead.

He removes the condom from the wrapper and slightly unrolls it on the tip of his thumb. His hand disappears from my direct line of vision. Moments later, he spreads my legs with his knee and rubs his finger down below; touching me in my most private spot. I can't even describe the way it feels when he slips a finger inside. "Damn, you're tight. It's snug on my finger and I'm a lot bigger. Are you sure you want to do this, baby?"

I nod and grab him behind the head, pulling him down to kiss me. I never thought I would like to be called baby, but something about it being from him makes it okay. "I've come too far to chicken out. Just go slow. I don't know what I'm doing, so it may not be that great for you."

I always hear girl talks about guys favoring girls that know what they are doing in bed. "Are you really worried about it not being good for me?"

"Maybe, don't guys like the girl to be on top and all?"

He settles back directly above me, looking me straight in the eyes. Grabbing my chin in his fingers, he angles my face to look at him. "Anything you have heard from a girl about what guys like, forget it. Girls that get around are only used for one thing—convenience. A girl like you is what every guy dreams of."

He kisses me from my forehead to my nose and down to my lips. I will never get used to the way I feel around him. It's a powerful emotion and a scary one. He kisses me soft and slow, marking me his.

No other kiss will ever come close in comparison. He moves one hand down my neck and over my breast, leaving excitement visibly behind. Once his hand is no longer visible, I feel a round tip swirl in the area down below, being rubbed up and down against me. This is it. It's hard to enjoy the kissing with all these stupid nerves.

Just then he pushes in slightly and releases my lips. That wasn't so bad. "You ready, baby?"

Ready? Ready for what?

"What do you mean? What did you just do?" He smiles and places a chaste kiss on my lips.

"That was just the tip, baby. Do you want me to stop?" I shake my head for him to continue. He grabs my lips with his in a hurry, and before I have time to think he thrusts forward. I feel a tear. One word enters my mind: pain. A searing, burning pain. I want to cry and scream out, but I will not let myself. I've never been great about enduring physical pain; just blocking out the emotional.

Once he has filled me to capacity, he stops and looks down at me. A tear trickles down each side of my face. "I'm so sorry. Are you okay? Do you want me to pull out?"

He looks truly concerned, but I can't think of anything but the pain. Oh the pain. It throbs with my pulse. He begins rubbing my hair. "Baby, talk to me. Hell, I'll stop."

Before he moves I grab his face and look him in the eyes. "No, just give me a minute. Okay?" He nods and wipes a tear from my face.

"I don't like seeing you in pain, Kinzleigh. This is messing with my head. It's not worth it if you're in pain. I can pull out." My body must be over the initial shock, because the pain has worn down to a dull ache and has been replaced with desire to continue.

I grab his waist and hold him between my legs, spreading them wider to accommodate his size. "I'm fine. Breyson. I just wasn't prepared for that amount of pain. I was warned, but I didn't listen. It's not so bad now, but I need you to move. Sitting here isn't enough. I need friction." He scans my face, obviously trying to read my emotions. When he can tell that I'm serious, he starts to smile.

As he begins to thrust in and out, slowly, it starts to feel blissful. His eyes never stray from mine the entire time. "You feel so good. It's not going to take me long."

I begin kissing him, memorizing the way his lips feel against mine. I'll never forget this day as long as I live. The sight before me will be forever branded in the banks of my memory.

He places his hand between us as he continues; touching another private area with the tip of his thumb that I've heard of, but never felt. "You remember the pool house, baby?"

He picks up pace, causing me to close my eyes. So that's how he did that? I nod. "Baby, look at me. Please. I want to see your face when you come."

I open my eyes at the feel of his finger making circular motions alongside him penetrating me. The different types of feelings working together have me lost in a sense of euphoria. It's taking over my body and consuming my mind. "When you feel like that again, baby, relax."

His voice is mesmerizing, and just like that the feeling from the pool house returns. I arch off the bed as it takes over. It pulsates through my body, consuming every part of me.

I begin moaning uncontrollably. "Breyson." Everything is tightening and my body shudders. It's like everything is going in slow motion.

"That's it, baby. God, bless. I can't hold out any longer. You're too tight. Shit." His voice comes out raspy and low. He thrusts inside me once more and stills. "Fuck, you feel amazing."

I run my fingers through his hair. He's breathing hard. I'm not ready for it to be over. For once, I'm terrified I'll never be the same after this. Maybe I'm not as strong as I think I am. I just want to feel his lips on mine. I always hide my emotions or block them out completely, but this once I'm going to let him feel all of me.

This is it. This is the end of something beautiful. He expects me to come pick him up and drive him to the airport in the morning, but I can't do it. Call me a coward, but I can't tell him goodbye. I know I will break down and give him my number, but I can't. We don't live in the same place; making anything more virtually impossible. I'll have to write it in a letter and send it with Presley. I will remember this blond-haired blue-eyed boy for the rest of my life.

His breathing calms and he looks down at me. We just stare at each other for I don't know how long. He has a look on his face that I imagine mirrors mine. It's one of those bittersweet things. One where it's been more of a dream than reality, but all good things must come to an end.

I could never tell him how I feel, but I can show him. Pulling him in, I kiss him with everything in me. For the first time in my entire life and the last, I put myself out there for a guy. I put everything into this kiss, telling him that even though the universe isn't on our side, and distance isn't our friend, that I'll remember him forever.

And from his panicked return of his kiss, he knows this is goodbye.

NINETEEN

Breyson

I can't get last night out of my head, and I'm afraid getting it out is going to be harder than I imagine. What I wouldn't give to be right back with her in my arms or buried inside her. She was supposed to be taking me to the airport, but I knew from the look when we said goodbye, that was it.

She's not coming, but why? I wish I knew. I'm standing in the driveway of Ryland's house with all my bags, ready to head to the airport. I have already said my goodbyes to my aunt and uncle. Ryland is on standby to give me a ride, but I told him to give me a few minutes to see if Kinzleigh shows up.

After a night like last night, I know my head is going to be forever fucked-up. My mind continuously replays the entire scene—in great detail—in my head, as if it's stuck on repeat. It makes me want to pull out a bottle of Jack and blast rock music to manually override the thoughts running around up there, and I may do just that when my brothers pick me up at the airport.

How do I go back to sleeping with easy girls after a taste of perfection? The thought alone disgusts me. I knew better than to let myself have her. One taste and I'm hooked. Something about her has me on edge constantly.

I didn't sleep at all last night. I kept staring at my phone like it would make her text me. Before I left her house, I gave her my number. She insisted she didn't want it, but I left it in her hand—physically balling her hand into a fist around the torn piece of paper. The ball is in her court since she refuses to give me hers.

I'm about to go inside after Ryland when Presley's white Mercedes pulls in the driveway. She isn't who I expected to see, but I find myself searching the passenger seat in hopes to see one beautiful blonde. "She's not here," she sighs as she steps out of the vehicle. "I know that's who you're looking for."

"Where is she?" It's the first time I've noticed Presley looking bummed since I met her a week ago today. She bends over into her car, reaching in the center console. When she stands to face me, she has a folded piece of paper in her hand. She begins walking toward me, not giving anything away.

"She's not coming. Kinzleigh is not one to get emotionally involved with anyone. I don't know what you've done to her, but I got a call this morning from her in a panic that she needed a favor. I haven't seen her this strung out since her grandmother died. I was afraid this was going to happen, but I pushed it anyway. "She stops before me and grabs my suitcase by the handle. Handing me the piece of paper, she begins rolling my bag toward her car. "Come on. Let's go."

"I don't need a girl to get my bag. Ryland can drive me." I'm aggravated, because I'm not a damn charity case. If Kinzleigh wants to coward away instead of telling me she doesn't want to drive me, fine, but I don't need any favors. After all, she is the one that told me this was nothing but a fling, so why can't she just drive me to the airport and say goodbye.

"I know you don't, but from the looks of her this morning, I have a feeling when you read that letter you may have some questions. I'll be the one that knows the answers if anyone does, so let's go." One thing I've learned from my mom is to never argue with a woman. You're a fool if you do and you'll surrender in the end, so you may as well save the energy. She places my bag in the back seat and shuts the door.

She pulls out of the driveway in a hurry, obviously not worried about speed limits. With a car like this, I can't say I blame her. "She went through with it, didn't she? She slept with you." That's a way to rip off the Band-Aid.

"It's none of your business. I don't kiss and tell. I have more respect for girls than that. It's one reason Lexi was able to lie on me so easily." I look over at her and she raises a brow at me.

I should have known that wouldn't work with her. The two of them are too close. I nod silently and turn to look out the windshield as the images of touching her and filling her replay through my mind.

I've got to get a freakin' grip. What is wrong with me? She's just a girl—one that I'll never see again. This kind of thing happens all the time. That's part of the appeal to vacation when you're single. I need to release all this pent-up frustration when I get home.

"I thought so," she voices in a low tone. She says nothing more; just watches the road in front of her. I'm not sure what is going on in that head of hers. Girls are the most complicated creatures on the planet. They say they want one thing and mean another. I guess now is as good a time as any to read this letter. I unfold it carefully to avoid it tearing.

Breyson,

I know you must hate me for sending Presley in my place, and for that I'm sorry. I really did want to drive you to the airport. I tried to talk myself into it so many different times, which is why I didn't forewarn you of the change in plans, but the truth is—I can't do it.

I can't look you in the eyes and tell you goodbye. Please don't misunderstand; it's not because of last night, and yet it is. I really don't know how to explain, so I'll give it my best shot.

I knew you would be leaving today, which is one reason I let last night happen. What I didn't realize was the way I have come to feel about you. Last night made it clear for me. I can't explain these emotions and I don't want them in my life.

I cannot let something we knew was ending interfere with all my plans. I've worked too hard to block out any emotional contact to change now. This is just a setback I can overcome. With that said, I know seeing you will make it harder on me and I will cave by giving you my number.

I hope you can understand how hard that has been for me. I've thought it over so many times, but it will only make things worse. I will not be that girl, Breyson. The one that follows a guy around like a little lost puppy. You don't have to worry; I shred yours, so I won't be contacting you.

You are a weakness to me I can't explain. A lethal dose of poison injected straight into my heart. I will not allow myself to be vulnerable to that kind of pain. I am terrified of what might happen if I allowed myself more of you; like an addiction you can't fight or a drug you can't live without.

I am writing this to you so you will know you are the closest I've come to feeling something for someone and you will also be the last. Last night I wanted to show you what you do to me. How you make me feel. I wanted you to be able to hold onto that forever, knowing we had one spectacular week we can hold close.

This week has been beautiful and I will forever cherish every memory and moment. I will always remember your touch to my body and your lips on mine. My virginity was a gift to you. You have forever marked me and ruined me for anyone else's touch. You set the bar high on how sex should be when you could have been selfish. You will make one lucky girl happy someday. I wish you the best.

With love,
Kinzleigh

Without thought, I punch the dash. This is the last thing I need. Not because of what she said, because for the first time I actually feel the same way. Dropping the letter to the floor, I place the heels of my hands against my eyes. I'm so angry my eyes gloss over, burning my eyes begging for release. What the hell did I get myself into? The one time I have feelings for a girl other than sex, she has to be just as stubborn as me or worse. Long distance can work. People do it all the time.

"Are you done trying to break my car?" she asks sarcastically. I had forgotten for a second Presley was in here.

"Sorry. I wasn't prepared for that and it pisses me off." I have to find a way to forget her. I have no idea how, but she has left me no choice. "Why is she so damn hardheaded?"

She takes a deep breath, as if the answer to that question will take a while to explain. "How to explain Kinzleigh Baker is like trying to explain advanced algebra to a toddler. It's impossible. I've been trying to get her to take a chance on someone since we started high school. She somewhere down the line developed this warped view of love, or hell, even just dating. I've even talked to Konnor about it and we can't figure it out. She has parents that have been hopelessly in love since college and her grandparents since high school on both sides. She has it set in her head that if she allows herself to like a guy, she won't get to fulfill her dreams. It's like she's afraid if she loves someone, or even just likes someone, that has to be it. That she can't do anything else. I have to say, though, that you are the only person that's actually been given a shot. Whatever you're doing, you're doing right. I just wish you both weren't so far apart. You two would likely be together if you lived here."

I can tell from the look on her face it's genuine. "Did she tell you where she is moving? I have asked her over and over, but she refuses to tell me."

She shakes her head. "Well, she told me the state, but not exactly what city it will be. She's been so upset, I'm not even sure she knows. My mom told me, I think, but I doubt I was listening past the point of 'moving'. Because I don't remember. Come to think of it, I haven't even asked where you're from. That's rude of me."

She smiles. I can see why Ryland likes this girl. She doesn't take crap off anyone, but she is still cool to hang out with and she has a sweet side I don't think she shows much.

We pull in the airport and it's getting closer to time to go. This week has flown by. She parks the car and stares at me. "Where are you from, Breyson?"

I reach for the door handle about to get out. "Mississippi." Her eyes widen slightly, but then they retract. She clearly doesn't want to give anything away. When her lips part, she forces them back together, as if she's refusing what she wants to say. I have a weird feeling I know why.

"Where is she moving, Presley?" She looks out the window, and at this point, I'm getting aggravated. She knows something she isn't telling me. Something that could help me. I don't know why girls have this code amongst themselves. "Presley!" The boom of my voice surprises even me. "Is she moving to Mississippi?"

I glance at my phone, checking the time. I'm getting impatient, because I don't have much time before takeoff and I still have to go through security.

"Look, I can't say without her consent. She's made her decision about this. If she wouldn't tell you herself, then I can't tell you, no matter how much I want to." She starts to smile and then stops.

I narrow my eyes at her, clearly displeased. "I'll tell you what; give me your number and I'll feel her out after I talk to her. She was bordering on a panic attack this morning when I rode by and she shoved the letter in my hand. I think she even has to take her medicine for it again after this all coming at her at once, so I don't want to make it worse. If I can, I'll text the information to you. If you don't hear from me, you know how to find me."

As much as I want the information, the thought of Kinzleigh having anxiety issues stops me from saying anything further. Once I'm out of the car, I pick up the letter and fold it into a neat square and place it in my wallet. "Give me your hand."

I pull a pen from my pocket. It's habit to keep one from school. I write down my number on her hand and I remove my luggage from the back seat. This is probably the one and only time in my life I'm waiting and hoping I get a text or call from a girl.

As I walk through the tunnel of the New Orleans airport, I look around for my brothers. They are supposed to be picking me up. I texted them all the flight details in a group message, so they better be here.

I am one in a set of triplets. Braxton and I are identical twins—split from the same egg—and then there is Briar, who would be considered my fraternal twin if Braxton weren't part of the equation. Two eggs fertilized and one split in two. We are a rare freak of nature to say the least.

Briar looks and acts completely different than Braxton and me. If we hadn't all three been males, my parents probably wouldn't have tried for Brylee, but Mom was determined have a girl, fertility problems be damned. Brylee is the one that will be in misery her entire existence—three older brothers. Every male within five counties is considered an enemy.

As I come into the baggage area, I see Braxton, but not Briar. He spots me and smiles. As I get closer he slaps me on the back. "How was your trip, little bro? Score any hot California girls?"

"Why do you call me that? Being one minute younger than you does not make me your little brother. Besides, I am physically bigger than you and better looking. You look like you've been slacking in the weight room. I'm surprised Dad let you leave the house." I tease, punching him in the arm.

We are really about the same size, but it drives him crazy to be called small. He is the egotistical one of the three of us. I guess being a prized player does that to you. He is the starting quarterback and

I am the star running back, so we usually dominate the games at our school.

Briar plays baseball exclusively. He's definitely more laidback and toned down in comparison to Braxton and me; more content with less words. He's not into the hitting and violence that comes with the territory of football. Braxton and I thrive on it, and we're much more extroverted. If we weren't born at the same time you would never believe Briar was our triplet. "Where is Briar?"

He looks at me with an ugly scoff on his face. "Dude, you are not bigger than me. We are physically identical, so shut the hell up. Briar is tailing around after Londyn. It makes me sick. She finally gave him the time of day and he goes and gives the Abercrombie boys a bad rep with the way he acts love-struck around her. You need to help me knock some sense into him. Her girl parts can't be any better than the other hot girls at school. He must be spellbound by her exotic features."

Braxton and I are pretty much identical in everything down to personality; it's why we're so much closer to each other than to Briar. And by exotic features I know exactly what he means. Londyn is mixed—Asian American. Her Dad met her Mom when he was in the military stationed overseas. I've met her Mom a time or two. She's fluent in English, but when she starts talking fast it gets harder to understand her. Londyn, however—the girl is hot. She got just the right amount of each feature.

"Londyn? When did Londyn show an interest in Briar? Wasn't she just trying to hook up with you like the week before I left?"

"Yeah and I shut her down, because Briar is so damn obvious with his lusting over her or I would've taken some for myself. The girl is hot. I'd love to see some of those dance moves off the field, but it's bros before hoes. Last week at the creek she went for Briar.

You know no girl turns down an Abercrombie boy." He laughs and grabs my neck in the crook of his arm. "Let's go. I want some details about your trip. Don't hold out on me either."

I laugh back on the walk to baggage claim. I have missed my family. "It was boring. Ryland got more action than me."

He rubs his knuckles over the top of my head, roughly. "You're full of shit. I know your dick just as good as you do. You forget, we were wombies for nine months."

I can see baggage claim. I shove into him, trying to knock him off, my laughs becoming more frequent. "You're a damn idiot. Take me home."

New Orleans is about an hour and a half to two hours from our house, so I'm sure Braxton will grill me the entire way. The entire school probably knows by now that Natalie and I broke up. There is likely some ridiculous story floating around. That's the bad thing about living in towns where everybody stays in everybody's business. And generally, it's a twisted version of the truth.

We're headed down Interstate fifty-nine and not much has been said to this point as we've been stuck driving through New Orleans traffic. "Anything interesting happen since I've been gone?" It's easier to talk now since it's nothing but open road ahead.

He looks over at me from the driver's seat with the beginning of a grin on his face. "Well, aside from Briar's . . . whatever it is, I'm curious to know what you did to Natalie. Rumors are flying, my brother. It's about time, though. If you're just going to use someone for sex, why limit yourself to one chick? I'm glad you finally came to your senses. Plus, no one likes Natalie. She's a bitch."

This is what I was afraid of. Gossip ruins people's lives. If I had to name one good quality about myself, it would be that I never believe any bullshit that comes out of someone's mouth about another person. If I want to know something, I go straight to the source. "Well, if you must know, I met someone and didn't think it was right to pursue it with Natalie in the background."

"Sweet! Who is she? Did you hit it? Is she hot? Where is the picture? I know you have one, so don't even try to deny it." I did get a picture the night she was sleeping in my arms at Ryland's pool house, but that is mine to enjoy and no one else; not even my brother. I also got a picture before I left her house last night when we were goofing off in bed, after the most perfect night of my existence.

"Her name is Kinzleigh and she is gorgeous. What we did is none of your business. What's with the twenty questions? I don't like it." He rolls his eyes at me. I ignore him. It's the best way to get him to shut up. "What is going on back home tonight? I need to get my mind off some things."

He continues to look between the road and me. "There is a party tonight at Simon's house. I think his parents are out of town or something for the weekend. He is trying to keep it on the down low, but you know that's never going to happen. He always throws the best parties, because his brother can score the alcohol. I think he's home from Ole Miss for the summer anyway."

He smiles as he looks over at me. "You know you'll have your pick of any girl in school now that you ditched Natalie, but I'm sure she will have her claws out regardless. Who will be the lucky lady tonight?"

"Well it definitely won't be Natalie, because I'm not going down that road again. Several nights ago, I got a dose of her crazy side apparently, so that's over." I rub my hands over my face.

Hooking up with another girl is not appealing to me like it normally does, but I've got to get her out of my head. I voice my frustration out loud. "I don't know, dude, this girl is messing with my head. I'm in the dark here. I have never had this problem. I don't know how to get her out of my head. How do you downgrade when you've had the best there is?"

When I move my hands from my face and look at him, he has a knowing look on his face—one that I've never seen present before when referring to girls. "She's one of those? Shit, man. You better get ready, because she isn't going to just disappear. That type of girl is unforgettable."

"You know what I'm talking about? When did you ever feel that way about a girl? I didn't know you actually saw past a girl's physical appearance and the nearest place to strip her naked," I say jokingly.

He places his hand over his heart, pretending to be offended. "Ouch. Don't hate the game when you're one of the main players, Breyson. But for your information, yes, I know what you're talking about. Do you remember that girl that lived here for two years freshman and sophomore year? Her name was Madileigh Carlisle."

He raises his brow as if I should know this information without giving it much thought. Running my fingers through my hair, I try and remember who he's talking about. We do go to a pretty big school. "Wait, isn't that the girl you lost your virginity to? The army brat that moved when her dad got reassigned? Did y'all even date?"

His eyes zone out as he stares straight ahead at the road, lost in thought. "Yeah . . . we dated. We would have kept dating had she not moved. I had never seen a girl like her and haven't since. If this girl messes with your head like that, I'm sorry, man; it doesn't go away.

You can numb it, but never get rid of it. I haven't dated anyone since her. Hooking up with other girls is a temporary distraction and a lot of fun, but that's it. It's mental torture."

I just nod, because there isn't much else to say. We don't really ever have these deep conversations and it's a little overwhelming. We're usually emotionally incompetent. That's why our lives are generally easy.

The rest of the ride home is pretty quiet. We pull into the driveway of our house. Looks like Mom and Dad are both gone, as well as Briar by the lack of vehicles in the driveway, but overall, I'm glad to be home.

Mom and dad are probably at the clinic. I'm not sure what their call schedule is for the weekend since I've been gone all week. I am tired from having to change time zones, but I need to somehow find a way to get these images of her out of my head.

Leaving the cab of the truck, I make my way to the house robotically. After entering the front door, I continue to my room without stopping. Braxton stops by my bedroom door on his way to his. "Be ready at nine."

TWENTY

Kinzleigh

I walk into my room with my protein smoothie, my hair sweaty and up, pulling my earbuds from my ears. My entire body is damp from my midafternoon run. I barely got any sleep. I tossed and turned until lunch. Truth is, I've thought about last night so much I'm tired of thinking about it. The memory of every touch, every whisper, and every kiss is making me crazy.

The first thing that halts me is my unmade bed. I walk over to it and place my shaker bottle on my nightstand, and the second I sit down I can smell his cologne. I know I should wash my bedding, so my parents don't find out I had a boy in my room, but I still have some time to breathe it in before they'll be home. I'm not sure what I envisioned my first time being like, but that wasn't it. For something to be casual, he worshiped my body.

The condom wrapper on my nightstand draws my attention. I grab it up quickly. I can't believe I left that there. Konnor could have come home early. Not like him after a night of drinking, but anything is possible. I don't need him to find out about this. I know the condom is gone. Breyson told me he disposed of it in my bathroom garbage and I took that out this morning.

But it was . . .

Words fail me. I almost wish we had done it again. I mentally chastise myself for that very thought. He's gone. That would have made things harder. Which is the exact reason I asked Presley to take him to the airport. It's best to have cut our losses last night when both of us expected to see each other today before things could be awkward. I need to take last night with me and use it for what it was—an experience.

I sit on my bed, running my empty hand over the place we laid and watched a movie after it was done. Only we didn't just watch the movie. We kissed, touched, groped, and cuddled, but we didn't have sex again. I exhale the scent I've come to love.

I slide off and fall to my knees, lifting my bed skirt. The box immediately comes into view. I pull it toward me, grabbing the notebook off the top labeled 'Firsts'.

I pivot my body, placing my back flush against the side of my bed, and then run my hand over the sparkly design on the front I created with markers and glue and glitter several years ago. No one knows about this book, not even Presley. "You're worthy," I whisper, and then open the front.

I navigate through the pages, briefly scanning each one—first sip of alcohol, first time to try a cigarette, first crush, first kiss, first boy-girl party. Each page has an item from that time, and each page has a diary-like entry, so I'll always remember. Just because I didn't want to be like everyone else and continue to do those things, doesn't mean I didn't want to *try* those things.

I stop at a blank page and place the notebook on my lap to free my hands, and then pull the tape from the box. I place the condom wrapper on the page and secure it with two small strips of the clear tape.

I look at it, trading the roll of tape out with a marker I keep in the box. Then I uncap it and place the tip at the page, just below the wrapper, and I write everything I feel about the moment, letting myself keep it forever.

Summer of 2014
June . . .

I met this boy on the beach. <3 Breyson Abercrombie <3 He was unlike anything I've ever seen. Blue eyes that could make you tell the truth. Blond hair that makes his tan skin appear darker. And a smile that makes me question being single. When he speaks, I get lost in him. He has this accent that is like a time warp. I tried to avoid him. His ability to make me feel things I normally try to avoid scares me.

Mom and Dad told me we're moving at the end of the summer. In ways I feel like they're ruining my life. But then he found me, on the pier, and he just makes me feel . . . better. He kissed me, and I let him. It may not have been my first encounter with a kiss, but it was the first time I felt things before, during, and after it happened.

I tried to run from him on so many occasions. I tried. And I failed. So, I stopped fighting it, and I'm glad I did. I had one week with him. One blissful, perfect, memorable week this summer. We had some highs and lows, but I wouldn't change anything if given the chance.

He cared about me, and didn't push me, and so, I gave him my virginity. If anyone was worthy, it was him. I wanted it to be him. It was more than I ever imagined it to be. He looked at me as if he was scared to close his eyes. He touched me like I was a mirage. And he kissed me like I was a dream.

Then he pushed inside me, and everything in my world circled, and all I could see was him.

My eyes well up and I let it spill over.

I was a coward today. I couldn't say goodbye. A truth I will take to my grave—I miss him like I would miss breathing should someone take away the ability. I couldn't tell those eyes I'd never look in them again. I couldn't kiss him and know it's the last. I couldn't watch him leave without the smile on his face I love. I couldn't tell the boy goodbye that I know should he stay . . . I'd keep him. I couldn't let myself tell him—he's the boy that changed me, when no one else could.

So I didn't. And it'll probably be my only regret.

I cap the marker pen and close the book holding all of my secrets, placing it inside the box and returning it to its hiding place where it'll stay until I have another first that deserves to be a memory. I wipe my face and stand, returning to my bed. My phone sits in the middle. I grab it, pulling up Facebook instantly. The temptation is well on its way to killing me. One part of me screams to do it, but the other part of me says I'll regret it. I have today . . .

I touch the search bar and type in the words, letter by letter. Breyson Abercrombie. The profiles pull up in a list, the top hit stealing my breath. *One mutual friend.* I don't even have to look at the friend to know it's Ryland. Breyson's face is on the thumbnail. I know it's him. His hair is messy and all over his head, his face is layered with sweat, and he's wearing a football uniform. Black jersey with gold lettering. It must have been taken after a game. God, he's beautiful.

My pulse is racing as I go to his profile. I sigh a relief when his location isn't part of his 'about' section. And his profile is public, which is why his personal info is kept to a minimum I'm assuming. I can't help but smile, though, when I notice the relationship status: 'single'.

My thumb robotically flicks up on the screen, scrolling down his profile. He updated his profile ten minutes ago:

California. I want to come back to you.

I swallow hard. Is he talking about the state or . . . My thumb hovers over the like button, questioning if I should open that door, but my eyes are more interested in the comments that are steadily increasing in number. And not the comments from obvious male friends, but the other ones. The bigger percentage of the comments are from girls. One in particular makes my heart plummet to my stomach.

Natalie: *So glad you're home, babe! Celebrations are in order! Whoop-whoop.*

I force myself past it by going to his photos. I stop on one of three guys. One looks identical to Breyson while the other is totally different with his dark hair and darker skin. It's weird seeing two of him. Then there is one of a girl, younger, but looks more like the guy with brown hair than Breyson and his twin. That must be his sister.

Every photo and every status update makes me miss him more. It gives me a look into his life and I don't know if that's a good thing. Because I find myself wanting him more. One thing that puts me at ease—the only photos with him and that Natalie girl are the ones she posted and tagged him in. Looking at his uploads, it's like she doesn't even exist. Relief washes over me, and I'm not sure why. I should feel sorry for her, because it seems one-sided.

Something I don't understand overcomes me, and I go back to his status without thinking and hit the comment button. Before I can think, my fingers type.

Kinzleigh Baker: *California won't be the same without you.*

And like the adolescent I am, I post it and turn my phone off. I don't know why I did that. It opens us up for conversation. It's a jealous move. And I'm not entitled to make it. I refused him my phone number. I didn't show up this morning. He may very well hate me.

And he has every right to.

Breyson

I leave my luggage somewhere between the door and the bed, before falling face first across my mattress. I want to sleep, but my mind is processing about a million different thoughts all at once, making me restless.

I roll over and reach into my pocket, pulling out my phone. When I look at the lock screen, Facebook notifications cover most of it. I scroll through them and stop, doing a double take on one.

Kinzleigh Baker commented on your post.

Why *the fuck* didn't I think of Facebook? God, I'm a tool sometimes. I touch it and unlock my phone, waiting for it to go straight for the comments. My heart is pounding, and the gears in my mind are turning quickly. She sought me out. That has to mean something. I cringe seeing Natalie's comment. I'm going to have to deal with her at some point and I don't want to.

Kinzleigh Baker: *California won't be the same without you.*

I click on her name to go to her profile, immediately sending her a friend request. Her profile is private. Thank God mine isn't. I've never cared who sees my stuff. I don't post overly personal stuff anyway. I just keep my demographics to a minimum and usually don't post anything with a location.
I click on the message option and wait for the app to switch me to Messenger. I attempt the call option, but it's unsuccessful. I type a message.

Please call me here. Message back. Something. If Facebook is all I have with you I'll take it.

I stare at the screen, waiting for the 'delivered' notification to pop up, but it doesn't. I growl out. Then it occurs to me. If we aren't friends she may not even see the damn message. I go back to the comment to reply.

Check your messages please.

I turn my ringer on so I don't miss a notification. It never leaves vibrate, but she could call. She would call, right? I'm pathetic. What the hell is wrong with me? I growl out, frustrated.

But she looked me up. That has to be a sign.

TWENTY-ONE

Breyson

Still no response from Kinzleigh. I've checked it all damn evening. The fact that she did it and won't respond pisses me off. The friend request is still showing as sent, so she hasn't declined it. And the message isn't showing as delivered. I'm starting to think maybe her phone is off, but why I don't know.

We pull up at the party right as everything is getting rowdy. There is already a crowd of people here. As we walk through the door, I can smell the beer from the red plastic cups speckled throughout the room. Some people are sitting and some dancing or standing. It's packed to capacity.

As I walk toward the kitchen, I can see a beer pong table set up with the majority of the football team gathered around. "Breyson!" I look around as my name is screamed in a slurred unison around the table. "Get over here, son. I need actual competition. I'm getting bored," Jared says with more remaining cups than the other player."

"You sure you're ready to get beat, Jared? Looks like you're on a roll so far." Jared is one of the linebackers. He is a big grizzly looking guy with short, reddish-brown hair and a beard. When puberty hit him, it came all at once. He's got more hair than anyone I owe. He's also stocky and funny as hell, but one damn good linebacker.

"Dude, everyone is getting trashed but me. I need someone that can hold their own. It's about time you finally decided to come back home and quit running around with those California girls. Tell me, are they a good lay?"

"I don't know what you're talking about," I say, trying to smother the laugh.

"Shit, I ain't stupid. Fess up. We've already heard there is a special someone and based on that comment on your Facebook post that Natalie has been ranting about around here, I think we know who." He holds his hand up and whispers not so quietly. "She's fuckin' hot. How was it?"

"None of your business, asshole." I laugh.

"Okay, fine. I get it. You don't want to add drama where drama is due. You've been a hot topic of conversation among the ladies. Natalie is pissed, boy. Speaking of, you mind if I try to tap that since you're finished?"

"Have at it. You'd be doing me a favor. We're done." Gossip—something you can count on around here, and something I don't need.

Right now, I really wish I could turn back the hands of time and go back to last night. I want to be back in Kinzleigh's bed, holding her in my arms. I want to be able to look down at her as I enter her, making her mine. The look on her face when I kissed her goodbye will haunt me for the rest of my life.

She's beautiful and smart and knows what she wants. I'm well past pissed off. She is the one that chose not to have any more communication, and then she makes me aware of her, giving me an ounce of hope this isn't over, but won't answer any more, so why am I the one suffering from all these jumbled thoughts in my head?

I stood there and told her I wanted more; even gave her my number. I need to think about someone else. I need to forget her. I hope that Braxton was wrong earlier. I can't focus on anything like this. I grab the Ping-Pong ball from Adam, who's holding it beside me and drinking from his cups anyway, listening to the conversation. "Set me up. Let's play."

An hour in and the alcohol is taking effect, leaving me in a relaxed and peaceful state. I'm about to throw the ball into a cup when an arm snakes up my back, underneath my shirt, causing me to drop the ball into my own cup in surprise. "I'm really glad you're back, babe. Why don't we go somewhere and talk? I can give you the welcome home you deserve."

From the purr of her voice alone I can tell it's Natalie and she's drunk, which makes her difficult to deal with. As a matter of fact, I hate when she drinks. She's nothing but drama and I usually regret being around her.

All of the guys have smirks on their faces. You can never get away from the high school drama. Placing my hands around her wrists, I turn around and remove her hands from my body. "What do you want, Natalie?"

"Oh, come on, don't pretend you didn't miss me, Breyson. I know you did." I can smell the coconut rum and Diet Coke on her breath—her signature drinking choice. She's making a fool of herself. I'm starting to wonder if she's always been this way and I just looked over it because she is hot, or if she's grasping at straws because she's really in love with me. Either way, Kinzleigh or no Kinzleigh, I'm not into it.

"Natalie, you're drunk. I told you we're over. I meant it. Just because I'm home doesn't mean that's going to change. I think you should go home or go back to your friends before you embarrass yourself." She goes for my pants before I can stop her, trying to grab my dick. "Fucking quit. I'm not kidding, Natalie. We can do this here or you can take my advice and we hash out the details later privately."

"What happened to you? You used to be fun before you ran off to California and met that stupid little bitch. I saw her comment. It was all I could do not to message the slut that stole my boyfriend. News flash, Breyson, you're back now. You're not stupid enough to actually think that'll work. Are you going to let her ruin your life? She's not here. She's halfway across the country. I mean, what did you think was going to happen? That you were going to come back here and continue whatever it was you two had over there?" She laughs. "Right. I bet she's already moved on to someone else."

She's treading on thin ice with me. I can barely even look at her right now without wanting to hurt her. I don't believe in laying a hand on a woman and the thought runs through my mind as I'm listening to her call Kinzleigh name after name. She'll never be half of what Kinzleigh is. I need to get out of here. "Fuck you, Natalie. I was trying not to hurt your feelings, because we've been friends for a lot longer than fuck buddies, but you're getting brave with the way you talk to me. You need to remember your place. You don't even know her. Slut? Bitch?" I laugh. "Might wanna check yourself, sweetheart. You're just pissed I don't want you like that anymore."

I hold out my index finger and thumb for emphasis on how close she is coming. "See this? This is how close you are to me washing my hands with you. We can go back to being just friends or I can drop you all together. It's your choice. Don't follow me."

I notice her eyes widen as I storm off in a fury. I walk out the back door to the patio that is only a few feet from where the game is set up. Simon's house sits on Lake Serene. I walk out to the pier and connecting boathouse. Taking a seat at the end of the short pier, I clench the edge as anger consumes my body.

She may have some good points, but she has no right to voice her opinion; her and I are over. She needs to accept it and move on. It was bound to happen even if I had never met Kinzleigh. We weren't together for the right reasons.

"Breyson? Are you okay?" I turn around at the soft voice behind me. It's Adalynn, one of the cheerleaders. She's hot with her long red hair, green eyes, and tanned skin. She doesn't fit the typical description for a redhead. She is sweet instead of that fiery attitude you usually see. Instead of an orange shade, her hair is more of a dark red, and no freckles on her skin are present. She has a certain sex appeal about her.

"Hey, Adalynn, what's up?" She continues to walk toward me until she reaches the edge and sits beside me.

"Natalie being a pain?" She even has a sweet voice. She has legs for days and a nice rack. I'm not sure why I've never noticed how hot she is before.

"You could say that." She looks almost shy, but keeps looking at my lips as if she wants me to kiss her. I know that look all too well. Maybe this is the distraction from Kinzleigh I need. Grabbing her by the waist, I pull her closer to me. "What are you doing here, Adalynn?"

The rhythm of her breathing changes. "I just thought you could use a change of scenery, and maybe some company. Do you want me to leave?"

"You can stay, as long as you're good with it being nothing but a hook-up. I'm not in a talkative mood. I'm also not looking for a girlfriend. Dating Natalie was a disaster and a onetime deal. You should know up front what my intentions are."

"I'm okay with that. Friends with benefits, right?" She licks her lips.

Nodding, I say, "Something like that. Come on and let's go in the boathouse. I'm not one for groping you out in the open just to give everyone something to talk about."

Standing up, I hold out my hand to help her up. "I like that idea," she says.

As we enter the boathouse, I lock the door. It's pretty bare, with just a twin-size bed and supplies, such as life jackets, fishing gear, and skiing equipment. Turning around, I grab her by the fabric of her tiny dress and pull her toward me.

Grabbing the bottom hem of the tight material, I pull it up her body and over her head. I love hooking-up with cheerleaders. They have tight little bodies and they're limber. It makes for a better lay; one that I need desperately. I want her to ride me like I know she knows how. The perks of sleeping with someone that's already broken in.

She comes closer to kiss me and I dodge, causing her lips to press against the corner of my mouth. We can do this without kissing. It may be one of the easiest ways to get them ready, but not the only. I can find other ways to make them wet.

Kinzleigh is the only girl I have willingly kissed since the day I lost my virginity on a family vacation years ago. We had a cabin next to a family with all daughters. We had been hanging out with them a little since we arrived, and one night their parents left and so did ours for a few hours. We were all old enough to stay by ourselves for a while. The one I had taken an interest in was a couple years older than me, and more than willing to show me how.

I back her toward the bed, pulling her bra down and kissing down her neck along the way. She moans in response when I grab her breasts in my hands, clearly ready to go. When the backs of her knees touch the bed, I unclasp her bra to remove it all the way, letting it drop to the floor. Pushing her backward, she sits and reclines her back across the bed. Grabbing her panties in my hands, I pull them down her legs, baring her completely.

Coming down on top of her, she spreads her legs, wrapping them around my waist. "You're so sexy. Take off your clothes. I want to see your body."

Grabbing my collar, I pull my shirt over my head, tossing it aside. My jeans tighten around my groin as I take in her naked body. I look up at her and Kinzleigh's face flashes through my mind, blurring Adalynn's face.

Shaking my head in an attempt to clear my thoughts, I flip her over on her knees. "You like it like this, babe? I like where this is going."

Grabbing her breast in my hand, I squeeze, tugging at the hard nipple, trailing down the front side of her body with the other hand until I make it to between her legs. I push into her wetness, before pulling my middle finger back up, immediately circling the spot. She moans, and I swear I hear Kinzleigh's voice. What the hell?

Pushing her head into the pillow, trying to smother the sound, I increase movements to make her orgasm, so I can come quickly. Seconds in and she's backing against my hand, riding out her orgasm. When I know she's done, I speed things up before my thoughts get out of hand.

Unbuckling my belt, I grab a condom from my pocket, tearing it at the edge, and then push my jeans down my legs. When I look down as I roll the condom on, Kinzleigh's blonde curls and perfect body flashes through my mind, but I know it's Adalynn laying there.

Dammit! What is wrong with me? I pull my hair in frustration, trying to change the direction of my thoughts, but it only makes it worse. Every time I look at her it's Kinzleigh's face I see. Maybe I should just go with it instead of fighting it. I align the tip at her center and grab her hip, about to push in, but I stall.

I'm doing exactly what Lexi tried to get me to do. It's not fair to Adalynn. I'm not that guy. She deserves a guy that's thinking about her. "Breyson? Are you okay?"

Her breathing is heavy still from her orgasm. She's looking at me, concern clearly present. I swear she looks just like Kinzleigh, but I know that's not possible. Kinzleigh is in California. It makes no sense. Can my mind really be altering my eyesight?

"Kinzleigh," I whisper. Backing away from the bed I fall to the floor, landing on my knees. Covering my face, I voice my frustration out loud. I feel like I'm going crazy. "Adalynn, I'm sorry, but I can't do this. Trust me, I want to. You're hot . . . but I can't. I'm an asshole for this. It's not fair to you, though. Every time I look at you, I see someone else, and I'm not trying to. I don't know how to stop."

She moves off the bed and kneels in front of me. "Hey," she says, removing my hands from my face. "You don't have to be sorry. I can relate, believe it or not. She's a special girl to get your attention like this. She should feel lucky. She's the first, right?" I nod and look at how beautiful her body and face is. It's a damn shame my head is this messed up.

"I hate this. You're a cool girl, Adalynn. I'm sorry. You deserve so much better than this. When a guy looks at you he should see you for how sexy you are. He should see you for you." I hang my head in shame. I've never thought of a different girl while hooking-up with one. This is a new low for me. It seems I'm having a lot of those lately.

"Breyson, look at me. I swear I'm not mad or upset. Yes, it sucks we don't get to go further, because I think you're really hot and I needed the mental release too. It sounds like for the same reason as you, but I'm glad to see someone this torn over a girl still exists with guys. It says a lot that you can't go through with it. You're a good guy, Breyson. This can be our secret. Okay? Drama isn't my thing. I hope things work out for you with this girl."

She reaches for her clothes and begins dressing. I feel like the biggest douche right now. I fasten my pants and put my shirt back on, standing to my feet. "Where did you meet her? I hope you don't mind me asking."

"California, but she refuses to go any further than we have, so it's best to move on." I reach in and pull her to me, giving her a hug. "Thank you for understanding."

"No problem, babe. Don't stress over it. These things have a way of working out when it's meant to be." She kisses me on the cheek. "Come on, let's get out of here and you can take me home. You owe me that much." She winks at me, and for the first time in a while, I actually smile.

I pull in the drive from dropping Adalynn off and head straight for the pool

accepted FATE

house. Mom and Dad are both home, but I don't feel like talking. I told Braxton to get a ride with one of the guys from the team, so I could take the truck. There is only one thing I can do when I'm this stressed out and that is to beat it out of me.

Walking over to the punching bag that hangs in the corner, I pull my shirt off and grab the boxing gloves. Once I get them on, I swing my arms a few times to loosen up.

After a few seconds, I begin punching with everything I have, not letting up once. Each time her face scrolls through my mind, I hit the bag harder. I hit it until I can't feel my arms and then some. Once my arms give out completely, I begin kicking. Every sound, every tear, and every emotion on her face from that night is brought back full force.

I'm pouring wet with sweat when Dad walks in and grabs me by the shoulders. "Son, stop. You're exhausted. Don't overexert yourself. Want to tell me what's on your mind? I don't see you like this often. What's got you so worked up?"

Placing my back against the wall, I slide to the floor, barely able to catch my breath. Resting my limp arms over my folded knees, I rest my head against the wall. "Just a girl I met in California."

He doesn't say anything; just grabs a bottle of water from the refrigerator and sits next to me. "Here, drink this before you get dehydrated. I smell the alcohol in your sweat. What have I told you about driving when you've been drinking? I don't care if you're not drunk. You can still lack proper judgment and cause a wreck. Don't make me ground you when all you have to do is call. A DUI could ruin your chance of playing college football and I know that's not what you want. I'm disappointed you'd make such a poor decision."

"I'm sorry, Dad. I wasn't thinking clearly. It won't happen again."

We both sit silent for a moment, my chest still heaving. He breathes out, letting the tension roll off him. It's something he does often when he's mad at any of us. "Breyson, do you want to end up like Beau? I sure as hell don't want to get that call as a parent. I've always been honest with the three of you. You're about to be seniors. I know there will be drinking whether I let you or not. Teenagers always find a way. I'd rather teach you safety than you sneaking off and lying to me to do it. Call me next time. I'll come pick you up. It's not realistic to think you'll never drink, but I'll be damned if you're going to be stupid about it."

I drink the bottle of water in its entirety and throw it across the room, still frustrated. He's right. I should have called. I knew better. "Yes, Sir."

"Tell me about this girl." Even though my dad pushes me about being a doctor, he's still the coolest dad. I think he's seen too much bad in his medical profession to let us slide. I can talk to him about anything and he doesn't judge me. Even football he respects as far as college. It's professional he thinks is a waste of mind space.

A girl, though, is something I don't know how to talk to him about. I've never been this bent out of shape from a girl before. I don't know how to get her out of my head. I figured once we slept together that would take care of it, but it seems to have had the opposite effect. "How do you forget a girl that consumes your thoughts, but wants nothing from you; not even phone contact? I look at another girl and see her. I jump at every whim to talk to her. This is ruining everything. I tried to get her number, but she refuses to make things *complicated*."

"Did you sleep with her?"

"Uh . . ." I'm not having this conversation with my dad. It was awkward enough having 'the talk'. Living with two doctors—one being a gynecologist—you get STD photos, CDC statistics on shit like the percentage of teens walking around with HPV that carry no symptoms, and teen pregnancy stories. I don't want to know what he'd say hearing his seventeen-year-old son is sleeping around. I'd rather him just live in a state of ignorance when it comes to my sex life.

A laugh slips from his lips and he shakes his head. "What's so funny?"

"Son, you may think I'm old and my generation knows nothing, but I've known the three of you are sexually active for a while now. I'm not stupid. I'm a doctor for Christ's sakes. Plus, when I go to put up clothes for your mother and find boxes of condoms in each of your rooms, it blows my ignorance to shit and back, don't you think? But before you try to lie, I'll applaud you for using safe sex. That's all I can ask."

I cover my eyes. I cannot believe I'm about to tell my dad this. Maybe he'll call me a lunatic and help matters some. Or maybe he'll raise hell for doing that to a girl and make me feel better that she doesn't want anything to do with me. "She was a virgin."

He clears his throat. Yes, I feel the awkward elephant now in the room. "And by was I'm taking it you fixed that for her?"

"Call me an asshole. I can handle it. I'm ready for your wrath. It was stupid when I was going to be leaving. I can see how you'd think it was disrespectful."

"I'm not going to do any of those things."

I look at him like he's grown a second head. "What?"

"You're old enough to make those decisions. I presented you with the facts years ago. I explained safe sex. You know right from wrong. We've raised all of you in church. We give you limits on freedom with curfews and knowing where you are at all times. Your mother and I have done our part. I'm not going to keep you boys on a tight leash and you end up going crazy the second you get a little freedom. We are perfectly aware that high school kids drink and have sex and experiment. It happened when we were in school. I'm not going to pretend your mother and I didn't do some of those things."

"I feel a *but* coming on."

"And you're right. But, you shouldn't have taken that girl's virginity if you didn't really care about her. There are consequences for every action. You're dealing with your conscience. Respect isn't earned for the man that gives in to every desire, but for the man that can turn away. Have sex in a relationship if you're going to have sex."

"That's what I was doing with Natalie. It meant more to me that one time with that girl than a lot of times with her." I'm on a confession roll now, why quit . . .

"Because you realized she respected herself enough to hang on to something most don't. Am I right?"

I shrug. "Maybe. Maybe it was something else entirely. Maybe it was just her."

"Maybe your heart was telling you she's different for you. Love still exists regardless of what you think. I will never understand having a relationship that resembles polygamy. There is something to be said about monogamy and romancing your partner. You and the kids your age may think it's stupid, but it's so much better than whoring around. You're still young. Maybe it's love, maybe it's not, but you obviously feel something for this girl. Keep trying until you know it's time to move on. If it's meant to be, things tend to fall into place."

There is no way I love her. We've known each other a week. It has to be because she cut things off before I did, or maybe because I didn't get her out of my system. It has to be lust. Why is it that I feel like I'm having to convince myself?

I was a fool to think I could handle one night with her and nothing. I need more. I need to talk to her. Why is it that the thought of never seeing her again gives me chest pain? Dad stands and makes his way to the door. "Dad."

"Yeah, Son."

"How do you know when it's time to move on?"

"You meet someone else and suddenly you wonder why you spent so much time trying." He grabs the door handle as I stare straight ahead. "Oh, Breyson."

"Sir."

"Right now I'm going to tell you this as your doctor and not your dad. A condom is ninety-eight percent effective in a perfect situation. People aren't perfect. Cut that percentage down to eighty-five percent effective due to normal human error. Look out for you. Make sure she's on birth control if you're going to 'sleep around'. Even then, I've seen the situations where he 'thought' she was on birth control and she stopped taking it. Unfortunately, some girls will do crazy things to hang on to a guy. Be one hundred percent sure you love her before you take the risk of waking up one day with a child you didn't plan. Food for thought. Don't tell your mother."

He walks out the door, shutting it behind him. Fuck. Natalie was never on birth control. I just pulled out. With a condom.

TWENTY-TWO

Breyson

I walk out to the pool and sit on the lounger, staring out at the water. The pool lights are on, slowly changing colors. It's hypnotic to stare at. The red has always been my favorite. It adds a warm tone to an already cool hue.

A slight breeze is out, making the southern heat bearable. Humidity here is so much different than the west coast. Here, it's like constantly breathing in steam. It makes your lungs feel heavy and your heart is constantly working harder.

I look out across the yard at the lake that our house sits on, along with so many others. Most have their own boathouse and dock just like at Simon's; we do. The water is calm; all the boats from the day anchored or housed. I like it best like this—peaceful. I can hear a few kids from school yelling out not too far away—some guys with a few girls' laughs tossed in.

People may not admit it, but you're tagged socially by where you live here. I suppose it's that way everywhere. Everyone who's anyone chooses their residence by the name, and their kids reap the benefits. A vast percentage of Oak Grove is split between three major subdivisions; the kids that come from money anyway.

My phone vibrates in my pocket. I pull it out, my heart already pounding. I glance at the screen and freeze. *Kinzleigh Baker accepted your friend request.*

I close my eyes, trying to calm the hell down. That's not the reason for the vibration. It's the message. She responded. I open it.

I do want to be friends, but give me time. I need a little distance. Give me the summer. Then we'll go from there.

I blink, rereading it over and over. It's a start, right? It's better than nothing. Summer. That I can do. I usually work at Pops' ranch anyway, so that'll keep me busy. I quickly respond while she's at her phone.

Ok, Kinzleigh. I'll give you the summer, but then, I want to figure this out. I'll take what I can get.

Another message comes through.

If it means anything, I meant every word of my comment. Goodnight, Breyson.

So did I . . . Goodnight, Kinzleigh.

I stare at my phone again, but it never shows she's typing. That's probably all I'm going to get out of her. Before I can stop it, I smile. "Breyson, we need to talk."

I close my eyes, hoping I'm hearing things. I glance up at Natalie, standing maybe ten feet away. "What do you want?"

"I saw you with Adalynn earlier. I didn't want to do it this way, but . . ." She holds up some white stick. "I'm pregnant."

My phone slips from my hand and the corner of the rubber cover bounces off the cement and it hits the water, quickly sinking to the bottom. My mouth falls and bile rises to my throat. A wave of nausea hits. That fucking bitch. There's no way. Then everything Dad said hits me. And for the first time since I was a kid, my eyes sting with unshed tears.

No. Please, God. No.

CONTINUED IN CHANGING FATE . . .

ALSO BY CHARISSE SPIERS:

Accepted Fate (Fate, #1)
Changing Fate (Fate, #2)
Twisting Fate (Fate, #3)
Lasting Fate (Fate, #4)
Chasing Fate (Fate, #5)
Fated for You (Fate, #6)
Fated For Me (Fate, #7)
Fate By Forgiveness (Fate, #8)
Finding Fate (Fate, #9)

Fight For You (A Broken Soul Novel)

Marked (Shadows in the Dark, #1)
Love and War: Volume One (Shadows in the Dark, #2)
Love and War: Volume Two (Shadows in the Dark, #3)

Sex Sessions: Uncut (Camera Tales, #1)
Sex Sessions: After the Cut (Camera Tales, #2)
Sex Sessions: Passionate Consequences (Camera Tales, #3)

ACKNOWLEDGMENTS

There are so many people to thank, but that would take up pages. First and foremost I want to thank my amazing boyfriend, Patrick, for being my backbone and such a huge support, and also for understanding when I have to take time out of my schedule to write. I talk about my characters as if they are real people, and instead of getting annoyed you sit there and nod, letting me ramble. There are times that I get stressed or strap myself out because I can't say no, but you are always there to keep me going and to keep me sane. I love you more than you will ever know and I am so blessed to have you as a permanent fixture in my life. Your support and encouragement means more to me than you'll ever know.

Writing was never something I dreamed of like most writers, but a fellow writer and amazing friend, Victoria Ashley, took a leap of faith and told me to give writing a try. I did, and now I feel like it's where I belong. I still feel like I owe her the moon for introducing me to this amazing life. Victoria, you will always have a special place in my heart that no one can touch. I know you are getting busier with your own writing career and some days we barely say two words to each other, but know that I'm always thinking of you. It is amazing the feeling that I get seeing your writing career take off, knowing I found you with the beginning, Wake Up Call. You are one of my best friends and always will be. You are an amazing person. You really are. There are no words to explain how much of a friend you've been since the very beginning when being a writer was not even a thought. Thank you for being an amazing friend and advisor. I'm so glad that I found you. I love you, girlie.

Books have been important to me for two years now and storytelling for one. I get completely lost in the characters as I transfer the story from mind to manuscript. They have become my babies and I hope it shows in my writing. This has been the greatest journey I could have ever hoped for and I hope it continues for years to come.

Jessica Grover, my editor, thank you for branching out and contacting me as a reader. Not only did I find my editor, but also a very special friend. I will never be able to put into words the amount of gratitude I have for you. No matter how crazy and hectic your own schedule is you take the time to help me sift through countless words day in and day out to better the story for the readers. I absolutely love your crazy, sporadic personality. You have helped to bring me out of my shell more than you truly know. Never change, my dear. You have a beautiful heart and you will be in mine forever. You have a lot to bring to the table in contributing to the creation of what goes on in my mind. I think you know this based on the tears I've shed for book trailers. Thank you for crying right along with me at the close of Breyson and Kinzleigh's story. Not once did you judge or say they aren't real. Instead, you shared my heartbreak as if we both just lost an amazing friend, mourning their end. Thank you for purchasing Accepted and being a creeper on social media to find me. I assure you, I gained so much more than you. Know that I love you, my amazing friend.

Elizabeth Thiele, my personal assistant, you are also an amazing friend I found along the way. You keep me motivated by your reactions and responses as the story is being written. I know that you have a busy schedule and yet you continue to spend hours at a time promoting me and helping me in any way that I need. I appreciate everything you do and will do everything in my power to always show you. You are a twinkling star in my sky. Keep being the amazing person that you are. As an author and as a friend, I am very lucky to know you. You do a lot for me.

Heidi Sturgess, my lovely friend and beta reader, there are no words to place you in a category. You, my lady, are a truly amazing person inside and out. You have no idea how I look while reading those amazing Heidi emails regarding your thoughts for each chapter. You are that lucky penny that one stumbles upon somewhere in their life, not expecting what it will bring at all. Never ever change the person that you are. You are a valuable person. I hold you very close to my heart. Even though I've never met you, you are a treasured friend. I'm very thankful to have you in my corner. I love that we can get lost in a world of fiction with no judgments, no feeling crazy, but completely understanding one another. Thank you for giving my writing a chance.

Stephanie Phillips, my gem, I would never forget my first girl love. One comment thread about copyrighting is the irony to such an amazing friend. You have no idea how thankful I am for you my sweet, amazing person. Watching you grow as a writer has given me a sense of pride I never thought I could have. It's a beautiful thing. You mean so much to me, and even though you are thousands of miles away I feel like you are so close. One day we will get to see each other in person instead of our amazing FaceTime chats, but until then, know how important you are to me. You have been with me since I published book one and you will be with me 'til the end.

Hetty Whitmore Rasmussen, my promoter and friend, I haven't known you for long either, but you have been the sweetest person. I have no idea how Victoria found you, but that's just an addition to the list of things I will always be thankful to Victoria for. Thank you for everything you've done for me.

Clarise Tan, my cover designer, you are an amazing artist. You always take my vision for a cover and exceed my expectations, helping to bring my characters to life. I'm so glad Victoria sent me your way, because I can't imagine a better person to do my covers. You have also become a great friend.

To each and every one of you, I specifically tried to make each of you feel special as you have made me feel over the months, but as a whole know that I love EACH and EVERY one of you. You continue to give me an amazing amount of support. I could write page for page on what I love about you all, but it would take all day. All of you are important to me in ways you will never understand. I can only try to tell you over and over so you will have an increment of the way I feel when you make me feel special.

It doesn't matter if I become successful or stay a small time Indie just telling stories because they are screaming to be told, you all will be with me 'til the end. I will always make time for you, because you guys were with me from the beginning. Thank you for being amazing people and never ever change who you are. As a group you guys are my rare gems that cannot be assigned a price. That's how valuable you are. I'm not one for getting sappy, but know that I meant every word.

There are others as well that have recently become special to me, and if you're reading this you know who you are. Even though I didn't specify each and every person know you are no less important.

Love you guys!

Never let romance die, because it is something that should live in the hearts of everyone.

If you are a blogger, know that you are a tremendous help to authors. Every promotion helps to continue writing. We may not say it enough, but this would not be possible without y'all, so from my heart, thank you.

ABOUT THE AUTHOR

I found books when I was going through a hard time in life. They became my means of escape when things got bad. I realized quickly how much I loved to take a backseat to someone else's life and watch the journey unfold. That began my journey with books in November of 2012. I constantly had a book open on my Kindle app. Never in a million years would I have imagined myself as a writer, because I never thought I was creative enough. I'm living proof that things will fall into place when they're meant to be. People will make their way into our lives when we don't expect it, setting the path for what we are meant to do. Never give up on people. Never stop taking a chance on others. Someone took a chance on trusting me with her work when she didn't know me from a stranger on the street and gave me the opportunity of a lifetime as our relationship progressed, which led me to editing and writing as well. This is my dream I never knew I had. As soon as I sat down and gave writing a shot, it was like the floodgates opened. Now, I am lost in a world of fiction in my head, new characters constantly screaming for their stories to be told. Continue to dream and to go for them. No one ever found happiness by sitting on the sidelines. Sometimes we have to take risks and put ourselves out there. Thank you for all of your support, and may there be many books to come. XOXO- C

Stay up to date on release info
www.charissespiers.com
charissespiersbooks@gmail.com

Printed in Great Britain
by Amazon